"My dear, this story will be all over Town by morning.

And if you think being secluded with a well-known rake without the explanation of an engagement would not stop your sister's presentation before it ever started, then I think whoever sent you to London on your own ought to be horsewhipped. You are no more prepared to face it than a newborn babe."

He stopped, turned toward her and looked directly into those green orbs. "I am afraid, my dear, that I will not be a part of your ruination."

"Do all the women you know stand by and let you insult them to their face? Indeed, I understand the damage gossip could do to my sister. That is why I wish to see this situation resolved before that gossip can spread. Just tell me how we may fix this, and then we may go on our way."

He looked at her in a very peculiar way. "Madam, the only 'fix' is to continue with the engagement. We *are* betrothed, and my next step is to go see your father."

Books by Mary Moore

Love Inspired Historical

The Aristocrat's Lady
Beauty in Disguise
Accidental Fiancée

MARY MOORE

has been writing historical fiction for more than fifteen years. After battling and beating breast cancer, Mary is even more excited about her career, as she incorporates some of her struggles throughout her books, dedicated to encouraging others in the Lord and using her writing for God's glory.

Her debut novel, *The Aristocrat's Lady*, won several acclaimed awards, including the 2011 Reviewers' Choice Award by *RT Book Reviews* for Best Love Inspired Historical, and the 2011 Holt Medallion from Virginia Romance Writers for Best Book by a Virginia Author. She also received an Award of Merit for Best First Book and Best Long Inspirational by the VRW.

Mary is a native of the Washington, DC, area, but she and her husband, Craig, now live in the beautiful Blue Ridge Mountains in southwestern Virginia. When not writing, she loves to read, minister in her church and spend time with her husband, either at home or traveling.

Mary would love to hear from you! She can be reached by visiting her website at www.marymooreauthor.com, or you can email her at mmooreauthor@swva.net.

Accidental Fiancée

MARY MOORE

⟨H⟩ **HARLEQUIN**® LOVE INSPIRED® HISTORICAL

Recycling programs for this product may not exist in your area.

LOVE INSPIRED BOOKS

ISBN-13: 978-0-373-28297-5

Accidental Fiancée

www.Harlequin.com

Printed in U.S.A.

For by grace you have been saved through faith;
and that not of yourselves, it is the gift of God.
—*Ephesians* 2:8

This Book Is Dedicated To:

Jesus Christ,
My Savior and Lord

And To:

My Mom,
Jeanne Callaghan O'Leary.
Her life was such a tremendous
example of grace and love that it
touched everyone she met.
I love and miss you, Mom.

Special Thanks To:

Craig,
My husband and Best Friend

And To:

My Agent, Jenni Burke.
Without her help, encouragement
and passion, you would not be reading this today.

Chapter One

En Route to London, 1817

"Oh, Grace, it can be none of our concern!" Grace's younger sister, Lydia, warned softly. "I am persuaded it would be better if we did not get involved." But Grace was already walking toward their parlor door at the Blue Swan Inn.

Sitting quietly over a pot of tea in their private parlor, Lady Grace Endicott and her sister had been surprised to hear voices from the next room come clearly through the inn's thin walls.

"I tell you, Mama, it *was* Lord Weston pulling into the yard," said a faceless voice in a tone of loud frustration.

"But, dear, what does it matter?" asked a harried older woman in response.

The first voice, more menacing now, drawled, "Really, Mother, must I spell *everything* out for you?"

Grace now had the two women pictured in her mind

and she did not like the view. Would a daughter really speak so to her parent?

"My dear Charlotte," the mother complained, "Lord Weston is rich, to be sure, but should you like to be married to him? He has quite a reputation as a rake."

Charlotte snorted loudly. "What a singularly stupid question. Do I wish to be a marchioness with more pin money than you can even imagine? He *must* marry sometime. He has to beget an heir. Once I have provided one, I will be free to go my own way...with all the money I need to do so."

Charlotte's mother responded, "So you have a plan?" Then she asked eagerly, "You think you can catch him?"

"Mother, dear, I have a splendid plan," Charlotte replied, her tone oozing with evil intentions. "I will happen to encounter him when he enters the inn. I will insist he join us. He cannot refuse to pay his proper respects to my beloved mother. When I bring Lord Weston here, you must rush past us, claiming that you are ill, and leave the room. I will keep the marquess in here long enough to be fully compromised." She laughed wickedly. "He will be honor bound to marry me, and I will be very rich!"

That was the point at which Grace knew she must do something. She knew it was none of her affair, yet she would not wish such a thing forced upon an innocent person. She was appalled at the way Charlotte and her mother had spoken to one another. That they would contrive to trap a man into marriage went beyond her comprehension or experience. A husband at any price? Grace did not remember Society to be so avaricious in her own Season. She knew she and Lydia would never fit in with London's *ton* if deception and plotting was the way of life there.

Lydia was so looking forward to her Season, the purpose behind the girl's first trip to London, but Grace had visited the city many times and had always felt the people to be cold and calculating. She regretted having to leave her country home, even for a short while. She also worried that Lydia's innocent and kind heart would be hurt by the cruel *ton*.

The best way to protect her precious sister would be to lead by example, through helping others in need whenever possible.

Grace would start now.

"Darling Lydia, I cannot stand by and allow such a malevolent act." She walked out of their parlor, intent on saving this man from his conniving assailants. She knew she would appear forward to address a stranger, but that was a small price to pay if she could warn him of their intentions.

Grace need not have feared identifying the marquess; there was only one man and he was with the landlord. He was large, with the blackest hair, and he was obviously a Corinthian—as men of fashion were often called—based on the number of capes on his driving coat. With a short prayer, she walked up behind him.

"Sir?" she asked, summoning her most charming smile. "When you are finished making arrangements with Mr. Dobbins, may I speak to you a moment?"

As the most handsome man she had ever seen turned to her with a question in his dark eyes, she held out her hand, and indicated a small table centered in front of the benches beside the entryway.

The gentleman raised a brow and asked, "I beg your pardon?"

He began smiling lazily down at her, waiting for her to explain herself. But those eyes were awake upon every suit, despite his smile.

"Will you not sit, my lord?"

"I prefer to stand, I thank you." He looked at her askance. "But I *should* like to know how you know me." He leaned up against the wall and crossed his arms over his chest. "I admit I am quite at a loss as to know how I might be of help to you."

"No, sir," she said, almost in a whisper. "It is I who wish to help *you*." As he laughed out loud, Grace began to seriously regret not listening to Lydia's pleas.

Brandon Roth, Lord Weston, had no idea what was afoot, but he was enjoying himself immensely. When the tedium of the journey to London had initiated the stop at this inn, little had he known what awaited him. The woman before him was behaving in a peculiar fashion, to say the least, but he sensed no malice from her. He could not help but be intrigued by her plea for a private conference. They were in full public view, so he felt relatively safe from the traps normally set for him. Yet he remained wary.

"My lord," she said, "I have overheard a plot to compromise you into marriage, and I wished to put you on your guard."

He had not known what to expect, but he would have

never guessed this! She appeared to be telling the truth, and he wondered at such innocence in one certainly out of her girlhood. "You overheard?"

"Yes. You see, my sister and I were taking tea in that parlor there, and the women in the room next to ours were talking quite loudly."

"Ahh, an eavesdropper, are you?"

"Of course I am not…" She put her hands on her hips, frustrated. "You are making sport of me when I am trying very hard to be of help." Her voice had a low timbre. He would not go so far as to say sultry, but it was soothing, even in the exasperation he caused her.

Brandon did his best to avoid laughing. He wondered whether she was coming *from* or going *to* London. Already he hoped the latter and that their paths would cross again in Town; though he supposed even she would lose her charm eventually.

"Very well, madam. Why don't you finish your tale and we may proceed from there."

She tried to explain to him about the conversation she and her sister had overheard, and she finished with, "I thought if I could get word to you before she appeared, you would be able to handle the matter in whatever manner you wished."

He asked, "Did you by any chance catch the, ah… lady's name?"

She turned red at his insinuation. "Oh, dear, it was Charlotte, I think. Yes, I am sure it was Charlotte." She bowed her head, saying, "Godspeed, my lord," and turned to go.

He could not think of a Charlotte at the moment, but

truth be told he was not terribly concerned with her. It was obvious this woman was unaware of his reputation, but somehow, he thought she would have offered her help even if she had known of his well-earned title of rake. For the first time in a long time he was touched. Amused, but touched.

He grasped her hand as she turned away, and she looked askance at him over her shoulder. He pulled her back, to face him, and took hold of her other hand, as well. She smelled good—of lavender, he thought. He was still intrigued by her; he wasn't ready for their tête-à-tête to come to an end.

"As a man too often in the presence of grasping and manipulative women, I apologize for my behavior to one who is obviously not."

"Great guns! You are the strangest man I have ever met!"

"'Great guns'?" he repeated, and threw back his head in laughter once more, squeezing the hands he was still holding. "What a delight you are, my dear!"

"Shh! I beg your pardon," she said, eyes downcast. "I am not in the habit of having to watch my tongue."

He lifted her hands to his lips and kissed them. "On the contrary, you are the most delightful and—"

A gasp from across the room broke the spell, and his rescuer broke the hold he had on her hands. She nervously smoothed her gown. Looking over, Brandon felt his smile immediately give way to a frown. It had never occurred to him the Charlotte she had mentioned could be Lady Charlotte Marchmont, one of the most outrageous gossipmongers in all of London.

The lady's eyes were mere slits and her voice was insinuating. "Well, my lord, either you are being much less discreet, even for you, or it appears you have kept a budding romance secret from the *ton.* I wonder which it could be." Apparently if Lady Charlotte was kept from carrying out the seduction overheard through the walls, she would, at the least, be sure of retribution. Brandon feared it would be directed at the perceived interloper. So here he stood, free of Lady Charlotte, but bound now, in honor, to protect this woman. *Her* reputation could soon be in tatters, if Charlotte Marchmont had her way.

He could walk out that door as though nothing had happened; Charlotte could spread any tale she liked of his actions; Society would forgive him. And there would be no penalty to *Lady Charlotte* for spreading unsavory tales, from a society that loved juicy gossip more than reputations.

No, the consequences would rest solely on the woman in front of him, who had done nothing to deserve them.

He had not expected the backbone of the lady before him as she retorted, "I am not a secret *anything* to this gentleman. And I will thank you—" she said, just as Brandon announced:

"Lady Charlotte, may I introduce you to my betrothed?"

Both women turned to stare at him as if he had grown two heads.

"Mayhap, my love, we should take our discussion into your private parlor," he drawled. "Landlord, please have my horses stabled and a room prepared for me. I would appreciate dinner within the half hour." Bran-

don thought he did a very creditable job of not clenching his teeth.

He was now betrothed to this unknown woman. He
must keep up appearances. "Let me just give my coachman a word on the horses and I will join you, my dear."

As he passed by the first doorway, he bowed to the
flashy redhead and smiled. "Charmed, Lady Charlotte."

If the caterwauling coming from the room after the
door slammed shut was any indication, she was not
happy with the turn of events.

His coachman was still in the foyer, so giving him
his final instructions of the night took very little time.
Brandon leaned against the doorjamb outside of his new
betrothed's private room. Despite his attitude of non-
chalance, he knew he was in as much danger from the
unknown woman as he was from Charlotte Marchmont.

He would use the same tactics she had used: seeing
what he could glean through the thin walls.

"Oh, Grace, dearest, what kept you? I thought you
were just going to warn him and come right back. The
lady in the next room has been ranting. I had to cover
my ears, it was so loud." He listened, not recognizing
the voice that spoke. He would guess she was a younger
woman, likely the sister who had been mentioned. "Oh,
dear, are we in the suds this time?"

"Lydia, darling, we are not in the suds. But I must
clear up some confusion with the gentleman. We will be
on our way to London on the morrow as planned." From
the tone she used, it was clear that the second woman
was someone *"Grace"* loved very much. "I think if you

will just go up to bed, it will be easier to make the necessary explanations."

"Cor, my lady," interrupted the clear voice of a servant. "We can't be leavin' you alone with a gentleman, 'specially one you are unacquainted with." Hearing her called "my lady" by the maid made him more wary. It could complicate matters considerably.

"For pity's sake, I am six and twenty, not sixteen." So, this beauty had fire in her! "I apologize. Everything will be fine once I have spoken with the gentleman. The staff and guests here think I am betrothed to the man, so there is no reason for anyone to wonder at us being in here alone."

"Betrothed to him?" the one called Lydia asked.

"But I," Grace continued, as if she had not been interrupted, "cannot have the two of you watching us as we discuss what must be done. He did not seem in a particularly good humor at the end of our meeting, so I should like to get over this rough ground as smoothly as possible."

Hmm, she had been able to detect his shift in mood after the charade stopped being interesting. She was more than just a pretty face. He listened again. "I will join you upstairs directly." She resorted to pleading. "Please, Lydia."

He stepped back into the shadows as the door opened and two women left the room. From his vantage point, he could not see their faces, but one was definitely a servant and the other a very young lady.

When he entered the room, lowly lit by the fireplace, he found the mysterious woman leaning against the mantel, staring into the flames, and he had a few moments to study her as she remained lost in thought. She was not a conventional beauty, but standing in the glow of the embers, she almost took his breath away. She was a little taller than most and the colors of the fire turned her brown hair to a shining chestnut. Her tanned skin indicated she spent much time out-of-doors. It would not help her in the marriage mart, where porcelain skin was envied, but he thought it becoming to her.

She was an enigma to be sure, but until he knew her mind he would keep his guard up. Since he'd been nineteen years old women had been trying to entice him or entrap him into marriage. He knew every trick in the book, and if that was this woman's plan, he would put her in her place soon enough. For some reason, however, he believed her when she said her only thought had been to rescue him. If that proved true, he must act honorably now. He could not afford a scandal, at least not this Season. The stakes were too high.

"Well, madam," he growled, scowling from the doorway and making her jump. "Perhaps we should be properly introduced!"

My but his scowl was fierce! She hoped it was just to frighten her and not because he meant her physical harm. "Sir, you can glare at me from now until doomsday, but that is not going to accomplish anything. If you are trying to frighten me, you have succeeded. If you would like to sit down, we can discuss what we must do." She was frustrated, but still trying to speak calmly. "I owe you an explanation, and most likely an apology…."

"Definitely an apology."

"Is that not what I just said? I completely bungled what happened earlier, but if you think I am going to take *all* the blame for this fiasco, you are fair and far off the mark." She paced in front of the fire, then stopped and stared at him. "What could have possibly possessed you to announce we were betrothed? For all you know I may already be married with five children!"

She crossed her arms over her chest as he burst out in laughter.

"Perhaps, madam," he responded, "it was because we were holding hands and staring into each other's eyes in front of witnesses in a backwoods inn! I cannot entirely dismiss the fact that I have a certain, ah, reputation that does not help in this situation. But before we decide where to lay the blame, perhaps you would kindly recall that you were the one to first step forward and impose yourself on me."

"Oh, dear, it is all so complicated, and will you please stop calling me 'madam' in that odious way?" She stopped pacing and said, "Will you please sit down? I have already expressed that your intimidation tactics are working splendidly."

Lord Weston walked toward her, causing her a moment of fear. However, he moved past her and went to the chair in front of the fireplace, where he settled himself. "I realize it is very rude to sit while you stand, but as you will not sit first, I will obey your order. Only because I have been on the road a long time today. I am hungry, tired *and,* it seems, betrothed."

"Why, my lord, would you ever have said that? We

were in a public place. There was nothing clandestine about it."

He made himself comfortable and looked up at her. "It is precisely *because* we were in a public room, my dear. Anyone was free to see you approach me with no hesitation, and lead me immediately into a private conversation. Wicked minds need little encouragement to draw the worst and most damaging conclusions even from innocent behavior." He stopped and stared at her for a moment. "You know, when I came into this room and saw you against the backdrop of the fire, I certainly wondered *why* you were not married. No doubt I will discover the reason soon enough."

He was smiling at her! Was he teasing her? She could not tell.

"And since calling you madam seems to offend you, despite the politeness with which I have offered it, I will remind you that I actually have no idea *what* your name is. Should you grace me with that information, I will be able to address you as such."

She smiled at him. "Grace, my lord."

"I beg your pardon?"

"My name *is* Grace, Lady Grace." She spoke each word slowly.

He looked at her in the oddest fashion and then they both burst into laughter, letting go of the tension that surrounded them.

"My lord," she said, trying once again to look severe, "this is getting us nowhere. We must consider how to go on. And we must be quiet about it. As you now know, these walls are very thin and the entire inn could hear our conversation."

He had a wicked glint in his eyes as he asked, "Who are you?"

"I am Grace Endicott and I am taking my sister to London for her presentation this Season."

"Endicott?" he asked. "Where do I know that name? Who are your parents?"

"My mother passed away some time ago. My father is Robert Endicott, Lord Pennington." She was surprised when Lord Weston covered his eyes with his hands and began to shake his head.

She jumped when he growled, "Great guns! I have compromised the daughter of an *earl!*"

"Do not be absurd! You have compromised no one. Just tell me how we may extricate ourselves from this and we need never see each other again."

He looked at her in a peculiar way. She stood still as he rose and came to stand before her. "Never see each other again? I am afraid, Lady Grace, that far from never seeing me again, you will soon be my wife!"

Chapter Two

He lifted her chin with his finger and turned his most dazzling smile on her. "I believe we will take London by storm."

"My lord, are you never serious? Could you please speak sensibly for a few moments?" Her frustration was palpable, yet while they were far from being out of danger, he had to admit he was beginning to like her even though he had only known her this hour or more.

He was brought back to the subject at hand as she stood staring at him with her arms akimbo. "My apologies," he said, falsely contrite. "Lord Pennington... the family seat is in Essex, is it not? He studies rare tapestries and something else I cannot think of at the moment."

"Perhaps we will get to the problem at hand tomorrow!" she said nonchalantly. "You are the most frustrating man. Oh, what is the use? The estate is in Ware, more specifically, and my father *is* interested in artifacts, but his particular interest is suits of armor. My mother was the one who loved antique tapestries. They used to travel extensively, but he rarely leaves the estate anymore." She bit her lip and he could almost hear her mind at work. He waited for the inevitable. "Do you *know* my father, sir?"

There! She was finally beginning to understand there was more to this situation than playacting. Their positions in Society meant that any news of an engagement between them could not be brushed aside or ignored. If he did not unravel this mess as soon as possible, they were all doomed to serious repercussions.

"Your father and I have never met, but we are members of the same club. I have read several papers he has published. I believe his last was on the Elgin Marbles." He mumbled as an aside, "Will that debate never end?"

"Good," she said, relieved. "If you do not know him, there should be no problem in that regard."

He did not tell her that, on the contrary, it might complicate matters tremendously.

She began to pace and wring her hands again, a habit he now recognized as signaling her agitation. "I did not have time to formulate a particularly *good* plan."

"Ah, I see understatement is your forte," he said with a straight face.

"I only thought to keep an innocent man from being forced into marriage." He could not restrain his laughter at her description of him. She continued in spite of it. "I can see now that I…misjudged the victim."

"My dear woman, I wonder how you suppose I got to be the age of five and thirty and unwed without your help," he said in wonder. "I have been avoiding scheming chits for the last fifteen years, and now I am in the basket because I had help! You must allow me a *slight* vexation." His look dared her to deny him.

"Sir," she began quietly, "you are the most insufferable man I have ever met!"

"We shall start a list, shall we? Each time you think of a new description of me, we will write it down and keep it handy."

She put her head in her hands and groaned.

"I know! Stubborn might be the next one."

"My lord," she said through clenched teeth, with fists at her sides, "obviously, I misheard the part of the conversation that indicated you were such a catch! Indeed, that hordes of women are actually *trying* to marry you!"

He grinned. He believed he might have finally met a woman with whom he could match wits!

"My sole thought was to approach you before that woman could get you alone with her. I thought to explain what we had heard, and warn you to beware of her. How was I to know you go about kissing the hands of complete strangers?"

He sat back down and smiled.

She paced again. "Lydia warned me to leave well enough alone. Did I listen? No, and now I am talking to a madman." She put up her hand to stop him from speaking. "No! Do not talk about a list. Just tell me why you said we were betrothed." He noticed her blush as she remembered their very slight intimacy, and was again touched. She was a determined champion of chivalry one moment and a green girl the next. But he would be who he was…it was most entertaining.

He steepled his fingers and added, "I am afraid, my lady, that I did overstep my bounds with the kiss to your hands. I should have been more circumspect, especially with the knowledge that my actions were in plain view. And yet everything would be fine had Charlotte Marchmont not witnessed the scene. The Marchmonts have been on the Town for two or three Seasons. They are not only on the catch for a rich, titled husband for Lady Charlotte, they are also the biggest gossipmongers in all of London.

"The minute I realized she had witnessed our exchange in an out-of-the-way inn, I had no choice in the matter. I had compromised your reputation. So I indicated we were betrothed, for your protection."

He stopped and looked into the fire pensively. "Hard to believe, I know, but even the rake in me could not hurt such a green girl." He could not tell her the ramifications this day might cause. She'd thought she was helping him, but with one sentence, he may have jeopardized all he had worked for the previous two years.

Brandon's wild escapades had been curbed considerably over that time, as his mentor gave his life real purpose. Lord Langdon had become more like a father to him than his own, and his lordship might withdraw his support *and* his voice in high places should Brandon become involved in a scandal. More importantly, he might withdraw his friendship.

He came back to the present as she began to speak. "No one knows us in London. What if we delayed our arrival a week. Would any fervor not have died down?" She paused, possibly answering her own question in her

mind. "In any event, who would believe Lady Charlotte's insinuations about us when we arrived in London? I am long on the shelf and I am certainly too
managing by half to tempt you. Only witness our current situation!"

He was completely thrown off guard by her response.
She could not possibly believe that! Long on the shelf?
She was the beautiful daughter of an earl and the most
engaging woman he had met in a long time. He wished
he had by the neck the miscreant who made her feel
such an antidote.

"My dear, this story will be all over Town by morning. And if you think being secluded with a well-known
rake without the protection of an engagement would not
stop your sister's presentation before it ever started, then
I think whoever sent you to London on your own ought
to be horsewhipped. You are no more prepared to face
it than a newborn babe." He stopped, turned toward her
and looked directly into those green orbs. "I am afraid,
my dear, that I will not be a part of your ruination."

"Do all the women you know stand by and let you
insult them to their face? Indeed, I understand the damage gossip could do to my sister. That is why I wish to
see this situation resolved before that gossip can spread.
Just tell me how we might fix this, and then we may
go on our way."

He looked at her in amazement. "Madam, the only
'fix' is to continue with the engagement. We *are* betrothed and my next step is to go see your father."

He supposed it must happen at some point; but in his
mind's eye he had never envisioned this!

* * *

How had things to come to this?

She stood before a gentleman she had known for the space of an hour, who was telling her they had no choice but to wed. "My lord, I believe you may be overreacting. We cannot deny the engagement without risking my reputation—very well. But there is no reason to continue it. If the Marchmonts claim we are betrothed, all we have to do is decide we do not suit," she said, practically. "I believe engagements are broken all the time."

It was not a falsehood—engagements did not always last. But she was too practical not to realize that she couldn't end the engagement immediately without consequence to her reputation. If nothing else, she would be the talk of the Town for having an engagement announced and ended within the span of an evening. No, it could and should end at some point—but that was unlikely to happen right away.

No matter how little she liked the idea, she was veritably trapped in this arrangement…at least for now.

"Lady Grace, as relieved as I am that you wish this marriage as little as I," Lord Weston said casually, "I am afraid I know not the correct etiquette for breaking engagements these days. Do you have a plan as to how that might be done?"

She was saved from answering by the landlord knocking at the door. He entered with several footmen bearing trays of food and drink, which were laid on the large table in the center of the room. "Will there be anything else, yer lordship, sir?"

"Would you like more tea?" Lord Weston asked Grace. "I believe yours was interrupted quite a while ago."

"No, thank you."

"You know," he said, pouring himself a cup of hot coffee, "you have the most expressive eyes of any woman I have ever met. They are flashing emeralds one minute, and the next they are cool pools of sea green. You should know, in the event none of the clodpoles from Essex have told you, they tell of your thoughts, though you say not a word."

"No matter what my eyes *say,* my lord, I doubt very seriously you know what I am thinking at this moment." Sarcasm; he noticed she resorted to it often when she was embarrassed. His compliments seemed to discommode her, fitting though they were.

He laughed again and sat down at the table. "Lady Grace, I assure you I know exactly what you are thinking."

She held her hands out in anticipation.

After taking a bite of pigeon pie, he said, "First, you are wondering how on earth I can eat at a time like this. For some reason, women always seem to find it abnormal that men can eat in times of duress." He took a few more bites, laid down his fork and carried his coffee back to the chair before the fire. He continued in the same vein. "Secondly, you are wondering why I am being so blasé about this affair."

Her mouth opened in surprise and then she shut it and took up pacing again.

He chuckled.

"Very well, my lord, you excel at mind reading. Perhaps you also know sleight of hand and can make our circumstances disappear?" she quipped sarcastically.

"My dear, you are certainly not dull, which is fortunate. I abhor dull women." He crossed his legs before saying, "Shall we calmly talk this through?"

"Yes. We need to come to some kind of decision before we reach London tomorrow. This cannot tarnish Lydia in any way. If you think a temporary betrothal is the only way to accomplish that, then I will agree. But a broken engagement must be included in the plan."

"Lady Grace, much of my fear was dispelled when you indicated your wish to be rid of me. I am thankful that you do not want this marriage, either, though to be honest, I do fear that when you get to London and find out what a coup it is for you, you might well change your mind." He said it with a straight face, and watched as she stared at him, stunned. Then she laughed despite herself—just as he'd intended.

"Humble, too, I see. *You* may consider marriage to you a coup, but I do not."

"No, Grace, *I* do not consider myself a prize. I was speaking of the fortune hunters and title seekers. Oh, and their mothers, of course." He did not want her to see the bitterness he felt at that part of his life, so he finished with flair. "Now fathers, they are a different story altogether!"

This time she did not take the bait.

"Despite the prize," she went on, "I have no desire to be married to you or anyone else. I am perfectly content running my father's estate and household. This Season is for my sister. You need not fear I will back out of any agreement we come to on breaking our ties."

"The problem, my dear, is that we cannot go to London tomorrow and immediately cry off. With the Marchmont harpies spreading their tales, it would only add to the gossip surrounding you and your sister. I believe we shall have to play along for some period of time."

He smiled at her. "Believe it or not, if you think about it for a moment, our betrothal may even benefit both of us, for as long as it stands."

She looked at him with furrowed brows. "My lord, it will be a lie. Whether it benefits us or not, I cannot live a lie before all of London."

"Grace, it is not a lie. We *are* engaged." He wondered if he wished to convince himself as much as her.

Before she began an indignant reply, he put up his hand to stop her. "Hear me out. I *do* have entrées into some of the highest circles of the *haute ton,* despite my reputation, which could be of help to you and your sister. *And,* being already betrothed, I need have no fear of the matchmaking mamas. It may surprise you, I know, but there are more than enough people in Town who dislike me. When you do jilt me, you will be considered quite the heroine!" He looked at her with a decided twinkle in his eye. "I know it is hard to believe, but there it is."

"How absurd you are. Are you never serious?"

His whole manner changed. "I am being quite serious now. I will not mislead you, my dear—my reputation as a rake is well earned. Though my position carries with it some advantages, there will be many who will want to put you on your guard with stories about me, and a few who will give you the cut direct for your connection to me."

"I see. Hmm, a rake who becomes betrothed because he thinks—merely *thinks,* mind you—that he has compromised a lady, and then warns her about what she will face at his hands? You are a fearsome creature indeed. I am beginning to wonder if you simply enjoy making people *think* you are a rogue."

"You have discovered my secret, my lady."

"Very well, Lord Weston," she said. "Enough teasing. The engagement is settled, so the only thing left to do is to become acquainted with a few details of our lives. Perhaps we may do that on the journey to London, assuming you will join us in our coach?"

She paused, then looked him in the eyes. "My lord, I *am* truly sorry for the trouble I have caused you." The sincerity in her voice was heartfelt.

He turned away from her. He wished he did not have to share this part of his past, but he preferred that she hear it from him. He would ponder the reason for that another time. "You may tell me about your youth while we travel, but I would prefer it if your sister and your maid did *not* hear about a particular incident from mine. At least, not in my presence. They will hear it soon enough when we are in Town. Truth to tell, I would prefer *you* not hear it, but some gabster will be only too happy to repeat the story, so you might as well hear it from me."

Now he was angry, and he could feel the tic in his

jaw at the tension and self-chastisement the memory still evoked.

"My lord, it seems to me you have been completely honest with me. You have told me people will cut you, and perhaps me, and you have told me outright that you are a rake. Whatever tattle your enemies wish to share with me will only be part of your past. It was a time in which I played no part. I am in no position to judge you."

He looked up, astonished at her words and her candor. But they did not negate the responsibility to prepare her to meet with his past. He began his story quickly, wishing it over and done with. "You will hear from my sisters that my father and I never got along. My mother died when I was relatively young, and both of my sisters are older than I am. As his only son, he had high hopes for me. Too high, perhaps. I could never live up to his expectations, so I began to live down to them.

"I finished my education and assumed I would begin to help undertake the duties of my father's estate. But everything I did was wrong, and I realized he would never respect me. I asked him if he would buy me a commission in the army, something to allow me to feel myself useful. But I was the heir and he refused me even that. Idle and miserable, I left for London and began making the ever present name for myself. My actions tortured my father to distraction." He ran his hand through his hair. "Finally, I committed the cardinal sin."

"What happened?" she asked quietly.

"I was two and twenty and I fell in love." He began pacing the room. "Unfortunately, the lady was already married. She told me she was much younger than her husband and that he treated her cruelly. I decided to save her, and I ran off with her one night."

He went to the window, even though it was too dark to see out. "Perhaps you will not be surprised that her husband followed and caught us. When she had talked of his advanced age, she failed to mention it was all of four and thirty." His smile was cynical as he shook his head. "And her idea of cruel was that he had cut off her already excessive dress allowance for the rest of the quarter. But when he challenged me to a duel, I thought I was fighting for my lady's honor.

"I was the better shot, which it turns out she was counting on. But I did not kill him. When she realized he was not going to die, she told me I had ruined everything. It took me several minutes to understand what she was actually saying. You see, had I killed him, she would have been free *and* very wealthy." He turned back and walked to the fireplace. He was far from complacent and even the *retelling* of the story caused him more unease than becoming betrothed to a woman he'd just met.

"Perhaps you will now better understand my reluctance to be bowled over by marriage." He pulled himself away from the fire and faced her. "Once the husband healed, he took his wife abroad. To own the truth, I have no idea what became of her. But the scandal had sullied my family name, and I am sure you can imagine my father's disdain."

He could not tell her the rest. He could not say that his august parent had died only a few months later. His heart had given out, the doctor said. His sisters told him over and over that his heart had always been weak. They all knew he drank to excess; it was the reason Brandon did not imbibe. But as far as Brandon was concerned, he might as well have taken a gun to his sire's head.

He looked intently into her eyes as he asked, "Still think there is nothing to judge, Lady Grace?"

He was trying to shock her, and he expected some kind of horrified response, perhaps even a refusal to go through with their plan. Instead, she stood in front of him with a serene countenance. "I have already been told you abhor dull women, and I fear I shall fall off of that pedestal when I prove guilty of dreary repetition. But I still say I have no right to judge you or anyone."

"Somehow I find that hard to believe. Your goodness and innocence are clear to anyone with a brain, of which I am one."

"God's grace is greater than all of our weaknesses, my lord. I thank Him for that every day."

He stood dumbfounded.

"Do not worry, I am not trying to convert you. I am trying to say that we all have faults, myself included."

She waited, but he was stunned into silence. "Now that we have that out of the way, I think we have another few hurdles to overcome. I hope we may be able to solve them tonight and be on our way first thing in the morning."

He stared at her in astonishment. She was an amazing woman! He wondered if he'd ever be able to tell her how much her acceptance meant to him. Well, it would not be now. There was still much to do. But he vowed he would let her know one day, no matter the outcome of this coil.

Chapter Three

"Having known me such a short time, you would not know that the only reason I would even *consider* a duplicitous engagement is because of my sister, Lydia. Truth to tell, the only reason I would endure another London Season at all is for her. She is so loving and sweet and beautiful. I will not let her settle for less than she deserves."

"Very well, we have established that your sister is important in our plans. However, those plans still need to be ironed out."

She calmly replied, "It seems to me that breaking the engagement should be easy enough. We will go for a few drives, you will dance with me once or twice, we shall have a very public disagreement and I shall play the jilt. Where is the rub?"

"It is not the end of the engagement we must settle, but rather the way we shall say it began. I have two sisters who love good gossip and will want to know where we met and how long we have been engaged.

Why did we not announce it, or at a minimum, inform them? Why did I not escort you to London? When are we planning to marry…?"

"Oh, dear, please stop. I did not think of *any* of this." She sat in the flanking chair and put her head in her hands.

"As long as we are being completely honest, my dear, I must admit I gave a bit of attention to a widow in London last month during the Little Season, so our attachment will have to have been of a very recent nature."

"Oh, no," she cried. "You are in love and were ready to be married!"

Before he could even speak, she went on. "Well, there is a simple solution to that. We will tell her the truth from the beginning, and then when the engagement is broken, you will find it was she you loved all along. It is a perfect explanation." She sat back, entirely satisfied with the new plan. "We must tell her the truth as soon as we reach London, especially if the Marchmonts are before us spreading tales. Perhaps we should tell your sisters, as well."

"My dear Lady Grace, you have just said the only bird-witted remarks I have heard you utter all night."

Grace tried to hide her indignation. She was not bird-witted!

Lord Weston rose and went to lean on the mantel. "First of all, I am not in *love* with anyone," he exclaimed hotly. "I no longer believe in the silly emotion. Indeed, I am not the marrying sort at all. I have a perfectly capable cousin who will step into my shoes if anything befalls me. But my sisters are aghast at that prospect and continually nag me to marry and produce an heir. I decided to allow them to rest this Season by appearing as if I was trying to find a bride. This particular widow seemed as good a place to start as any."

She watched as he casually walked to the table and began to peel an apple with his knife.

"She would never expect too much from me, and would not be hurt when my interest faded."

How could he talk of courtship in such a cold, methodical way? She had never heard of anyone not believing in love! She knew some were not meant for it, or never found it, but to not *believe* in it? Her heart suddenly ached for him.

The moment of sympathy was quite short-lived.

"She will be mad as fire to learn I am engaged, but I had already discovered she has quite a temper. More, anyway, than I wish to take on. Are you certain you will not eat anything? The pacing back and forth you prefer would seem to require more sustenance than most."

When he saw she would not rise to the bait, he continued. "As to my sisters, I have not known either to keep a secret their entire lives, so we definitely will not tell *them*. Fortunately, I am not overly close to either one. But that will not stop them from descending upon you full of questions, so there will be much more we need to know about each other before we get to London. Our stories will have to match exactly."

"This gets worse and worse. My lord, I cannot look at your sisters and lie to them. It goes against all I believe in." She stared at him directly and tried to convey how important this was to her.

He scoffed. "If you are determined to believe it is a lie, then accept it as a little white one. What penance is required for that?"

"Lord Weston, please do not make fun of my faith. My relationship with God is an important part of my life. It now enters my mind that London will think it especially odd that their favorite rake would even marry a woman like me." She began to wring her hands.

The marquess put what was left of the apple on the table. He came to her and took her hands to pull her up before him. He opened his mouth to speak, but before he could, there was a knock on the door and Lydia stepped into the room.

"Grace, I cannot in good conscience stay away any longer. You have been closeted with this gentleman for more than an hour and it is not seemly." She turned her eyes to the man standing behind Grace. "I did not see you earlier. Are you Lord Weston?"

Grace looked back at him and started to laugh. His eyes were as wide as his open mouth! When he realized his reaction, he looked back at Grace with a decided gleam in his eyes and his dimple showing. She had been acquainted with the gentleman for a very short time, but she was already certain that was an ominous sign. Knowing there was nothing for it but to brazen through, she said, "Lord Weston, this is my sister, Lydia. Lydia, this is Lord Weston."

"Why, I am charmed, fair beauty. Surely the men in Essex have not let you go, as well as your sister?"

Grace watched in fascination as he addressed Lydia. It was impossible to see him rallying the full force of his charms and not realize his reputation was well earned. She *knew* this would happen once he saw Lydia, but she had not yet warned him of her beauty.

He took her hand, kissed it and put it in the crook of his arm as he walked her into the room. "May I call you Lydia, as we are to be brother and sister? It is my pleasure to make your acquaintance. Grace has been telling me all about you."

"Brother and sister?" She pulled her arm away and ran to Grace. "Are you really to marry him? Oh, dear!"

"Darling, you were right when you told me not to get involved in the machinations of the women in the next room. I shall mind you better next time." Grace heard a "harrumph" from the other side of the room, but ignored it. "My foolishness put me in a rather awkward position, and as a result, Lord Weston and I must be betrothed for a while. There is no doubt we will find we do not suit," she said. She shot him a glance that indicated he would be sorry should he interject once again. "But we must make our plans tonight so we may leave in the morning. I promise you I am quite safe with the gentleman. He has no interest in me beyond helping us out of this coil."

Grace turned as she felt him approaching.

"Lydia, Grace is correct—neither you nor she need ever fear me."

"Now, darling, Lord Weston and I have a few more items we need to work through, so you may go up to bed with a clear conscience. Do not worry, I will be up soon." She walked her to the door, kissed her cheek and wished her good-night. When her sister left the room,

Grace turned on him. "May I just jilt you now and that will be the tale we will respond with when asked?"

"My dear, you have made me laugh more tonight than I have in a twelvemonth!" When he came toward her and held out his hand, she had no fear of putting hers into it. "Own up, you looked so smug when your sister came into the room. You assumed I would immediately fall at her feet, and I wanted to show you that beauty is insufficient to sway me.

"She is beautiful, I grant you, Grace. But I am far more interested in you. We have been here this hour or more and I have not once been bored. You have a quick and intelligent answer ready for almost everything we have discussed."

"This is getting us nowhere," she stated, matter-of-fact, trying to hide the blush on her cheeks at his peculiar compliment. "We have much to decide tonight, so the sooner we start the sooner we finish, my lord."

When Lydia entered the parlor for breakfast the next morning, Grace and the marquess were still at loggerheads. A more complete explanation of the situation filled her with dismay. "Oh, dear! Must you go to all this trouble simply to avoid casting a shadow on my Season?" She paused only a moment and said clearly, "Grace, I do not need to be presented this year. I—"

"Lydia, we are definitely—"

Lord Weston cut them both off in a voice Grace had not heard from him. "Lydia, we *must* be concerned about your Season. There is no question about that. And," he said, shifting his gaze to her sister, "Grace's reputation is at stake here, as well. Her standing in London and Essex is no less precious than yours for this Season. I will hear no more about it."

Grace became aware of an overall feeling of security. Though Lydia's character was more important in her eyes—the dear girl deserved to make an excellent match, while she herself had no such concerns—Lord Weston wanted to protect her, as well. Grace had not wished to betray her own fears on that score, but he understood what this meant to her. She had always been responsible for taking care of herself. She was surprised at how happy she felt that someone was looking after *her!*

Breakfast turned into lunch as they struggled to concoct a narrative of their courtship that would satisfy Society and not violate Grace's innate honesty. She feared they would need to postpone their departure one more day.

Lord, please forgive me for putting all of us in such an awkward situation. Proverbs says, "A man's heart deviseth his way: but the Lord directeth his steps." I have erred by trying to direct the lives of others. Please lead us through this in Your way, protecting our path.

By luncheon, they had decided on a plausible way to explain how they had met. They would say Grace's father and Lord Weston had a mutual interest in the Elgin Marbles, which was true. When Lord Weston and Grace met, their speedy courtship had followed, which was also true.

It was then that Lydia, sitting on a bench watching travelers through the window, broke in on the discussion, "Grace, will you tell people that Lord Weston has fallen in love with you?"

"What?" The exclamation in response came from both Grace and Lord Weston at the same time.

In a much smaller voice Lydia answered, "I only meant... I did not know... Well, why else would you become betrothed?"

"I could have just as easily decided your sister would make me a proper marchioness after meeting her."

Grace became unusually quiet. She did not know how to answer that question, and to own the truth, the idea of it made her nervous somehow.

But Lydia suddenly overcame her fear of him. "Do you not see, my lord, it is that which will make the story work—the idea that Grace reformed the unreformable rake."

His lordship's only reply was to roll his eyes.

Grace finally spoke, but with such a blush she could barely look at him. "I am beginning to believe Lydia has the right of it." She saw the surge of anger starting to overtake him, and continued quickly. "You were on the verge of making a marriage of convenience in the Little Season. Why would you change your mind from a known individual to an unknown one in midstream?" She avoided his eyes. "I believe the only reason you would do such a thing must be a change in your...feelings."

He looked at her intently, then said quietly, "As usual, my practical and levelheaded delight, you are correct. And do not think I appreciate it!" He smiled at her, but he also ran his hand through his hair, still visibly uncomfortable with this scenario. Fortunately, he did not see her blanch at the endearment. He had called Lydia his fair beauty. *She* was practical and levelheaded. It was the first time those words coupled with her name had ever bothered her.

"Very well, I have developed a *tendre* for Grace. What would it be based on?"

This time she actually groaned. "I am persuaded if my ego survives this discussion, it will be no thanks to you."

He smiled at her, got down on one knee next to her chair and took her hand. "My dear Lady Grace, I did not mean that the way it sounded. What I meant was, despite your undeniable charms, we must find the *thing,* the one thing that would make me want to marry you, when I have always considered marriage a miserable prospect." He had been looking deep into her eyes and now kissed the hand he was holding. "My aversion to marriage, and marriage to an...innocent, is common knowledge."

"Oh, do stop flirting with me, you rogue, and make up something dazzling about me. You are the expert on women!" she said, pulling her hand from his clasp.

Was saving Lydia's Season worth this?

It was at that moment that Brandon realized, if he could not get out of this incredible fiasco, that she *would* be the perfect candidate for a marriage of convenience. The thought surprised him, but indeed, she had every attribute he would seek in a wife.

She was not an ethereal beauty as her sister was, but he had already decided she was the more handsome of the two.

She had wit and intelligence, and could hold her own in any conversation with him. She made him laugh.

He found, of a sudden, he would be interested in her views on many topics, and he could think of worse ways to spend an evening than in her company. He could also see her easily being included in the business endeavor he and Dennis had begun under the aegis of Lord Langdon.

"Perhaps it is not *one* thing that would make me choose you." He nodded his head as he walked around the room, thinking out loud. "Maybe it is what we have just been saying. You *are* quite different than my usual style, and that in itself could be enough. Most of those close to me know it is the sameness in women that bores me."

He stopped pacing and said with serious foreboding, "Very well, I will play the reformed rake. I know it will be hard, even awkward at times, but it will only be for a few weeks. I think it will serve."

"Oh, dear, I am losing my mind. We cannot *tell* people we are in love! The *ton* would laugh us out of Town." Then she said, less heated, "And it is a lie."

He began to realize that the faith she touted could cause some problems. It was more than a walk to a village church on Sundays. The thought of even telling a little white lie made her unhappy. He did not understand it, but he did not like to see her so troubled.

"Lydia?" he asked politely. "Will you leave us for a moment? I need to talk to your sister alone."

Lydia did as she was bade, and as he closed the door behind her, Grace walked over to the window and looked out. She felt chilled to the bone, but it was a beautiful March day, so she knew it was not from the weather. She spoke, still staring out, "How I wish I was at home and all of this was a terrible nightmare."

He walked up behind her and lightly took her by the shoulders to turn her to face him.

"Look at me, Grace," he said in a low voice. She glanced up at him in surprise. It was another tone of voice she had not heard him use before. "This is not meant to offend you, but I wish to show you something." He pulled her a little closer and continued to gaze into her eyes. "Do you know, Lady Grace, it is good that you do not lie, because you say the most amazing things with your eyes." She did not notice that his face moved infinitesimally closer to hers as their gazes remained locked.

He was speaking in a mesmerizing voice, low and subtle, and she was shocked when he very lightly touched his lips to hers. It was her first kiss. She did not even know it was coming, and her surprise turned to shock. He immediately drew back and her eyes widened at the realization of what had happened.

"What *can* you be about, my lord? How dare you take such liberties? I trusted you!" She was rambling, but she was angry and confused. She could still feel his lips, the sensation was odd but so tender. Yet tender was the last word she would ever use to describe him.

His eyes, only moments before so close to hers, changed, then he took a step back and straightened the cuffs of his coat. "I am sorry if I frightened you. I needed to show you that we shall have no problem proclaiming a relationship...without any words at all. Of course, most in London will never see such scenes, but it is obvious that we *can* be convincing as a couple for the amount of time you need to get Lydia married off." He turned, walked to the table and finished the cup of coffee he'd nursed earlier.

It had all been a game! The kiss was to show her that he *could* make her fall in love with him! Her fists balled in rage. "How dare you?" she growled in anger. "I have known you less than twenty-four hours!" She did not want her first kiss to be part of a game. It had come and gone, and meant nothing to him.

"I told you I meant no insult. I am sorry, but you have known me less than twenty-four hours and we are betrothed. You must come to terms with this, Grace."

"Very well, my lord," she said coldly. "You have made your point. I am going to go get my hat and pelisse, and have the horses put to. Perhaps, as we journey to London, you will tell me how we are to handle the widow you mentioned."

"You keep overstating that situation." Now *he* was angry! They were in her carriage and he knew she was still upset about the kiss. "During the Little Season I danced with her more than some others and took her up in my curricle once or twice. Since then, I have been at my estate and at Lord Southby's house party, and there has been no contact between us. As I told you before, she is *not* seventeen years of age, and has some experience of the world. She may have believed I was declaring my intent because of those few things, but I assure you I did not."

"As you wish," she said, turning to stare out the window. "The only thing left to settle is the termination of our betrothal. What causes that? Is it public or private? And what will that mean in terms of Lydia's prospects?"

"It could be a private decision between the two of us that we do not suit. One of us might wish to leave Town for a while."

"I will go, gladly. Home is where I wish to be," she said stoically.

He continued as if she had not interrupted him. "More than likely, however, with Lydia's beauty and her dowry, she will be spoken for even before we end the engagement. Then you can either leave or stay, as you please. Though I hope you will stay."

She folded her arms across her chest and cocked her head to the side.

"Assuming, however, that Lydia is not betrothed, you *must* stay. It will be the great *on dit* of the Season. And whatever cause Society assigns to the break, the sympathy will be with *you* in any event."

He wished they had the time for him to soothe her feelings and make her laugh. But they must work together now to save their reputations, and a sullen attitude would not help the situation. Seeking a way to make her smile, he said, "You really do have to get in the habit of calling me Brandon, or at the very least Weston, or no one is going to believe any of this. Why, even a significant sigh when you say my name would not come amiss a time or two." He winked at her as he said the last.

Chapter Four

After plans had been finalized, the trip to London passed uneventfully. Lord Weston sat languidly, listening to Grace and Lydia talk, speaking only when there was a specific question in his mind.

Even though Grace was still upset that he had kissed her to make a point, she could not forget his distress as he'd told her of his youthful indiscretion, reminding her that he had not always been so blasé where feelings were concerned. She wondered how many rakes were actually born to it and how many were driven to it by some horrible circumstance in their past. *Father, this man needs Your grace and Your forgiveness. You give it so freely. Help me to show him that.*

She told him as much as she felt he needed to know about growing up at the Abbey, without boring him to tears. She thought she saw surprise a few times when she talked about the estate matters she handled on her own now, her father trusting the training he had instilled.

"So tell me the truth, Grace. Why are you still un-married? Though estate managers have never been to my taste," he said, winking at her, "I cannot fathom why you remain unwed."

"My lord, that has little to do with our arrangement."

Lydia, always proud of her older sister, said softly, "She has had *three* offers, my lord."

"Lydia!" Grace exclaimed.

"Oh, dear, I am sorry. Did I say something wrong?"

Grace felt instant remorse for taking her mood out on her sister. "I am sorry, Lydia. I did not mean to bark at you. It is not…appropriate to speak of offers one has received, and it is of little consequence here."

"I am sorry, Grace, I did not know." Grace patted her hand, but Lydia apparently felt the need to fill the silence. "Perhaps you and his lordship should discuss your interest in father's armor, as that is one of the reasons we have established for his visit to the Abbey."

"I should not think that a matter of too much importance once we are discovered to be betrothed. According to *his lordship,* all of London will be lining the streets to see us when we arrive." Still ignoring him completely, she spoke directly to her sister. "That I have become attached to one or two of Father's collection will be of no specific use to him."

Lydia was so soft-spoken and shy, Grace didn't have it in her to staunch her conversation when she began again. "He will need to know about Max, the one in Town. To own the truth, I cannot wait to meet him myself."

Grace blushed at Lydia's mention of it. Max was her

particular favorite, a sixteenth century Maximillian suit of armor that adorned the foyer of their London town house. But she did not wish to discuss him with Lord Weston. Max was private, only for herself.

She had been in awe of him since she was a child, and called him Sir Maximillian when her father told her his proper name. He was the pinnacle of plate armor design, made of steel and iron with curved surfaces. Tall and imposing, he had stood guard at the bottom of their winding staircase for many years.

As a child, Grace had made up many stories about his adventures. She held back a smile, remembering the number of times rescuing her had been a part of those adventures. *Max* had become her sole knight in shining armor when she had given up hope of falling in love. One day, when her father was gone and Lydia was married, he would take up residence at Pennington Abbey with her.

She began to blush as she realized that even now she still thought of him as a real being rather than a fixture in their London home. She turned to find two sets of eyes searching her face. "I beg your pardon, I did not hear your question."

"Where did you go, Grace?"

"Nowhere important, I assure you, my lord." But she could feel his eyes watching her.

He had been listening to Lydia's prattle, but was watching Grace. She was blushing at the mention of a suit of armor in their home, which went by the name of Max. Why would she be so embarrassed by that?

Perhaps it was the mention of a trail of broken hearts she had left behind her that caused her blushes. He certainly was not surprised that she had been asked for her hand in marriage, and more than once, but he found himself wondering who these men were. Did they all spring from the surrounding countryside in Essex, or had it been during her own Season?

In fact, he did not know if she had even had a Season. She was nine years younger than him, and he likely would have given her no notice. But if the offers *had* come from someone in Town, he might actually know her suitors. Was she embarrassed at the thought of running into one of them while escorting Lydia?

"Perhaps, my dear, we should discuss those prior offers of yours. I might learn what you like and do not like in a suitor."

If a look could kill, he would definitely be a corpse! "There is nothing to tell, my lord. And, as I told Lydia, it is of no consequence and no business of yours."

"I am sorry, Grace, I should not have talked of it," said Lydia, contritely.

"I pray that we may now put an end to this ridiculous topic," she exclaimed.

"Methinks the lady doth protest too much." He stared at her from under his lazy lids. "Why," he asked, "did you turn them down?"

At Grace's angry silence, her sister spoke up. "She assumes she is too old for love, and will not settle for a marriage of convenience. She told me once that none of them made her laugh." Lydia pursed her lips. "I never knew that would be an object in accepting someone's suit. But Grace loves to laugh, so it is important to her."

"Oh, Lydia," Grace groaned.

Brandon never took his eyes off of Grace. Young Lydia might not understand such a sentiment, but he certainly did. Indeed, it was one of the things he liked most about Grace. However, he had no time to ruminate on it.

"One of them is from home. He never comes to town, so you would not know him."

"Lydia, say no more on this subject, please? I am thoroughly humiliated."

"Would you wish to tell this man the truth, Grace?" Brandon asked her quietly, with no hint of his usual sarcasm. He found himself holding his breath while waiting for her answer.

"I do not need to tell him anything at all. Besides, by the time he hears of it, the betrothal will have been broken and I will be back there. And you, sir, were the one who said the fewer the people who know the truth, the better."

He laughed at her. She continually amazed him with her innocence. "My dear, I do hate to disillusion you, but as the announcement will go in the papers as soon as we arrive in London, he will know of it." He turned his gaze to Lydia. "They do teach the young men of Essex to read, I presume?"

Lydia smiled, but seemed afraid to say any more. Grace appeared to be thinking of something else.

"An announcement in the papers?" she asked. "Is that necessary?"

"Not to make it known, as the Marchmonts have had a head start, but in terms of propriety, it is definitely necessary," he said, frustrated. "Grace, you must get it through your head that we are going to do this the proper way. I should have gone immediately to your father, however, I did not wish you to face the London tabbies alone. So, I must settle for sending him a letter as soon as I reach Town."

He watched as she physically blanched. Prepared for her next thought, he hurried to say, "Yes, yes, I know you are of age, but asking his consent is required for our betrothal to be valid. Your neighbors will know soon enough."

He knew her conscience was once again pricking her. She looked back and forth to her companions. "Father must know the truth. He certainly knows he never met you before."

"It is up to you, my dear," he stated categorically. He leaned forward, face-to-face with her. "You must think seriously before you make the decision to tell him. What will your father do if your Essex suitor goes to him, waving the announcement in the newspaper? Will *he* be able to convince your young man that we are in love? Will you want him to?" He noticed Grace beginning to twist her hands in agitation. He took them into his. He did not wish to upset her, but she must accept this.

"Listen to me. If you decide to tell your father the entire story, he has no choice but to truly make us marry. I insulted you in public, and his honor and mine require that we wed. If you decide we do not suit a month from now, and end our engagement, I would have to accept it. Your father would not. He would still demand that you marry me."

"This is a nightmare. My lord, I…I…cannot."

Lydia broke the tension with her question. "You insulted her? When? How?" He saw the righteous indignation take over her expression, and laughed.

Grace looked at him as if she would like to land him a facer. "Lydia, it makes no difference," she said. "Leave it be."

"I was caught gazing into her eyes and I kissed her hands tenderly. It was at the inn. Did Grace not tell you? Actually, I also kissed her lips, but no one saw that, so it cannot be part of the reason." He grinned, winking at her.

"Of course I did not tell her." Her color once again heightened.

Now *he* was surprised. "What in the world do you expect her to do when she sees us kiss in London? It would certainly not do to have her be surprised or shocked." He shook his head in exasperation. "No one will believe us to be in love at this rate."

Lydia was amazed. "He kissed you, Grace? Then there should be no farce, you must marry!"

Grace's ire rose. Taking matters into her practical hands, she said, "This has gone far enough. Lydia, I told you the Marchmonts saw us in a compromising position. The exact nature of the incident makes no difference." She turned fiery green eyes on him and said, "If you make one sound, say one more word, I will box your ears. I vow I will."

He held up both hands in mock surrender.

"As far as kissing in London, Lydia will see us together and will not be shocked by an occasional kiss on the hand, or you standing up with me for more than two dances, which is all Society would expect from an engaged couple."

He made a negligent gesture. "We are almost to Town—let us not arrive in fisticuffs. I think, however, we must come to a final decision." He turned serious once again. "Grace, are we to go ahead with our plans for a betrothal that will be broken once Lydia has made her match?"

"My lord, my father…"

"As I said before, I will write to your father posthaste. Did you not say that he rarely comes to London?" At her nod, he continued, "I will create an excuse for not calling on him before speaking to you, and I will promise him a visit to arrange all of the settlements."

He held up his hand to stop her from interrupting him. "I know you do not wish it to go so far, but as I told you from the beginning, *I* am honor bound to do so."

"Do you think I am happy about that? I may have ruined your life as well as mine. I do not take that as lightly as you do, my lord."

He must make her see it was in the best interest of all three of them. "We are doing everything in the proper way to protect us all. You *will* be betrothed to me, and either you will find reason to break it off later in the Season, or you and I will be married by the end of it. I assure you, I must take every precaution to be an honorable gentleman and to keep your reputation intact, as well as mine. If I did not write to your father or put a notice in the *Times,* no one would believe us."

He did not even wish to think about what might happen should Lord Langdon think the engagement anything other than honorable and appropriate.

He went on, "Grace, you cannot dismiss the signs of affections that will be required. With my reputation, if I am to have fallen in love, the only way Society will believe it is if they *see* it. There must be some such contact." He waited, trying to be prepared for whatever spirited reaction she would show him.

That she would be rational had never occurred to him!

"My lord, as we both know, to be thought in each other's pocket is very bad *ton,* and I suppose you would hate that even if you *were* in love." He was becoming quite reconciled to the fact that she would always surprise him. "Couples do not kiss each other in public. So we will show the required amount of affection, *when necessary,* and we will act like rational adults the remainder of the time." She turned to look out the window and began to hum to herself. Maybe it gave her some sort of peace in the middle of a brangle. Whatever the reason, it was a clear indication that the conversation was at an end.

As they were now on the outskirts of London, he let it drop, while Lydia pointed out some sights in excitement. Grace was naive, but beautiful and intelligent, and if she thought for one minute he was going to change his personality, she had a few surprises of her own in store!

Chapter Five

When they reached their town home in Berkeley Square, Grace asked that she and Lydia be allowed to greet their aunt alone.

"What? Ashamed of me already?" Brandon asked.

She turned and smiled when she saw the amusement in his eyes.

"I would like to explain our betrothal to my aunt without your presence complicating matters."

She thought he would understand, and she was right. As he handed her down after leading Lydia to the doorstep, he whispered into her ear, "Prepared to face the dragons, love?"

"To tell the truth, I do not think I am at all prepared, my lord. But I did think you might be a little more put out than you appear to be. I admit to being quite exhausted already, and the charade has only just begun."

"On the contrary, my dear, I believe this will be one of the least tedious Seasons I have attended in a long time!" He kissed her hand and then returned to the carriage, saying, "I will give you a day or two to gather yourselves, and use the excuse of your need to be properly outfitted, but I do not know how long I can keep my sisters tethered. I will put the announcement in the papers tomorrow and will write to your father first thing in the morning. If you need me in the meantime, just send a message to my house in Grosvenor Square."

He stepped away from the carriage once again and walked back to Grace. He leaned down close and whispered, "Try to keep from rescuing any other poor unsuspecting souls until you hear from me." He then entered the carriage, tapped the ceiling with his cane, and he was gone before she could say a word.

Upon entering her home, Grace found their ancient London butler waiting patiently for her to enter as the trunks were brought in by the footmen. "Welcome to London, my lady," Jamison said in his stateliest manner. "Lady Lydia has already joined your aunt in the drawing room. If you will permit me to take your cloak and hat, you may join them there while I send for the tea tray."

"Jamison, you always know just what the situation calls for. It is good to see you again, too."

Grace had not been to the town house in almost two years and realized she had forgotten how beautiful it was. Her mother had done the interior decor, and since her father rarely left Pennington Abbey now, everything remained much the same. Her mother had used several of the antique tapestries she so loved to adorn the entry hall. They struck awe and drew the eye upward for closer inspection.

Grace always thought it the most spectacular room

in the house, with the tapestries and the Baccarat crystal chandelier from the seventeenth century. But, of course, the best piece by far was Max. When she was very little, she'd been almost afraid of the intimidating full suit of armor. But as she got older, her love for him grew. Right now, he was a welcome sight. "How are you, Max?" she said aloud. "Have you missed me, my knight?" she whispered.

Grace looked around and wished she were here as Lydia's chaperone, as she'd planned, rather than as the betrothed of London's most notable rake. And she wished more than anything that she did not have to deceive her aunt and her father. Would that it were not so important for Lydia. But it was too late to repine now, so she turned to the drawing room to keep her aunt from having to search for her.

She crossed the threshold and stopped to take in the room and the two women seated on the divan. She had forgotten how beautiful this room was, as well, done in subtle shades of rose. With the fire and the candles, the atmosphere was warm and inviting. For a moment she was sad that her mother was not here.

Her aunt, still regal for her fifty-some years, was dabbing her eyes with her handkerchief and holding Lydia's hand. She rose quickly at Grace's entrance and hurried to embrace her.

"What a watering pot I have become, and you know I am usually no such thing. Stand back and let me look at you. I am afraid my tears started when I saw how much Lydia looks like your mother."

"I understand completely, Aunt Aggie. It is hard not

to miss her when we are here." Grace received and returned a loving embrace. Her aunt always smelled of rose water and lavender. It made her feel at home.

Grace knew why Aunt Aggie had insisted upon her help to chaperone Lydia. Just as Grace believed Lydia was wasted in Essex, so Agatha believed Grace herself was. She had no doubt Aunt Aggie planned some husband shopping for her, as well. At least this fantastic tale concerning Lord Weston would put a stop to that. She knew her aunt still had hopes for her. But Aunt Aggie would *not* understand. Grace wanted love. She wanted a marriage like her parents had; they had shared everything. But at six and twenty, she doubted she would meet such a man.

Her aunt placed her hand in the crook of Grace's arm and led her to the chair in front of the fireplace, across from Lydia.

"The thing we need to do in London, girls, is highlight your differences." Grace was brought back to the present at her aunt's words. "Lydia, in the country, men are as much interested in experience with estate matters as beauty, and if my letters from your father are any indication, Grace has both in abundance. There are just as many men, admittedly more in London, who want more ladylike accomplishments and a quiet demeanor, as well as beauty. When we go shopping this week, we will take all of these things into consideration, and you both will take the Town by storm!"

The time had come. She must tell her aunt about Lord Weston. She had secretly held the hope that Aunt Aggie had already heard the rumors and would berate her almost as soon as she walked in the door. Perhaps Lord Weston had exaggerated the Marchmonts' power.

"Aunt Aggie, we feared word would arrive ahead of us, but it seems you have not heard about the... betrothal?"

"The betrothal?" Aggie exclaimed. "Are you referring to the engagement of Lord Weston? I did not realize you had ever met him. The Marchmonts have been spreading the tale but I put no stock in it. He has yet to be caught..." Suddenly she looked at her blushing niece. "Never say...you do not mean you are the 'nobody?'"

Grace sighed. She remembered she was supposed to be in love with Lord Weston. "The announcement is to be in the papers tomorrow. I am so sorry we could not let you know before you heard it in Town. It all happened so quickly." She could not even feign happiness these first few hours in London. She and Lydia would *both* be ruined at this rate.

Her aunt turned her head toward Grace with eyes open wide. "Grace, my darling!" she gushed, as she jumped up and pulled her out of her chair, to embrace her again. "Why, this is all that is wonderful. Finally, you have met the man who will appreciate your character as well as your beauty."

Grace was stunned. "Pardon, Aunt, I thought you would be a little more concerned. I know he has somewhat of a reputation!"

"Nonsense! Lord Weston has had a hard life, and in my opinion, he has become so bored with the *ton* that many of the most outlandish exploits he devises are for his own amusement. All he needed was the right woman to straighten him up—you!"

She was smiling from ear to ear. "I cannot wait until all of London finds out tomorrow that it *is* true and it took my special niece to catch him!" She actually clapped her hands!

"And as for you, Lydia," Aunt Aggie continued, completely unaware of the nervous tension in the room, "with your sister settled so well, we will have every other man in London bowled over by you! We would have done just fine with my connections, you know, but with Lord Weston's sisters as sponsors, you will be invited everywhere!"

Grace felt awful. "Aunt, I have not even *met* Lord Weston's sisters. We cannot vouch for their cooperation when they find out he is marrying a country nobody."

"What is this all about, Grace?" asked her aunt. "You must not know Brandon Roth very well if you think he will allow his sisters to treat you with anything but respect."

Lydia said, "Aunt Aggie, that is just it, you see. Grace does not know him *very* well. They met, and before any of us knew what had happened, they were betrothed. It has been a whirlwind, and you know, dear aunt, Grace has never liked to be the center of attention."

Grace sent her sister a silent look of thanks for her gentle description of events, but still wrung her hands.

"Dinner!" Agatha proclaimed. "That is what we need. I will hear the story over dinner and we will decide how best to proceed. You both run upstairs to your rooms to freshen up and I will see you in half an hour."

As Grace walked past Max to go up to her room, she looked up at him and sighed. "Rescue me, my knight in shining armor," she said in a low voice. But Max stood steadfast and stoic. "I know, dear friend, I've gotten myself into hot water and there's no rescuing me this time!"

Lord Weston's temper flared as his sisters overtaxed his patience.

Upon arriving at his home and being welcomed by his butler, he had settled into his library in front of a roaring fire. His thoughts were on the past two days and a pair of marvelous green eyes. He was tired, but Hinson had informed him that his sisters had called several times already, so he knew he did not have long to wait for them. Face them he would, but he would give a great sum of money to be left alone with his thoughts for the rest of the day.

Within the half hour, Hinson again knocked on his library door and announced that Lady Wright and Mrs. Hale had been shown into the front drawing room. He rose and followed his butler out. He teased his starchy retainer by saying, "On the attack, are they, Hinson?"

"I am sure I could not say, my lord," he responded very properly. "They have been all that is polite each time they have come."

"They must be sickening for something," Brandon muttered as he turned the door handle to the drawing room. As he entered, a slightly older, female version of himself came to him, put her arms around his neck and kissed his cheek. "Brandon, I am so happy you are home. We heard of your betrothal. It is glad tidings, indeed!"

Brandon broke into an Irish brogue to tease her. "Maggie, me dear, I do believe you're lookin' prettier than the last time I saw ye! How is that Irish husband of yours? I hope ye'll tell me he's in Toon, too, so we can have a ride together for old time's sake."

"Oh, stop making fun," she said, smiling. "He is not with me this time. I came to refurbish my wardrobe and see my old friends this Season. But it was worth leaving Patrick and the boys to know I will be here for your wedding." She hugged him again and bade him sit with them.

His sister Maggie had always been his favorite. She was older than him by four years, but she adored her younger brother. He would never forget that whenever his father had belittled or berated him, Maggie always took Brandon's side, and came to his room afterward with a treat.

As he approached the fire and his oldest sister, he was expecting a very different welcome. "Good evening, Liza," he stated, bowing his head. "What a surprise to find my two siblings visiting me so soon upon my return." He smiled at her innocently.

"Brandon, do *not* call me that horrid nickname, and do not pretend you are at all surprised to see us. We want the truth about this betrothal so we may scotch the rumor mill. We will not be put off."

"I am fine, *Elizabeth*. How good of you to ask. I hope you, too, are well." He got too much enjoyment out of baiting her.

She sniffed. "I am in no mood for your nonsense. I do not appreciate the fact that Amelia Broadstone brought me the information that my brother is engaged."

"You should, perhaps, discuss that with Amelia Broadstone. I do not know the lady, but I do not doubt that she was only thinking of you as she spread the tale."

"Spare me your sarcasm and tell us what you have done this time."

At that moment there was a knock on the door and he was surprised for a moment that the tea tray was being brought in. Realization was not long in coming. "Elizabeth, feel free to order my servants around anytime you wish."

"Must you two always be at loggerheads? I have not seen either of you in over a year and I feel like I am in the exact same conversation as last time!" Maggie interrupted, very put out.

"A thousand apologies, Maggie, me love, though if we cannot argue, we will be left with nothing to say. You have just condemned us to being dead bores." He pinched her cheek and shuddered. "Anything but that. My reputation, Maggie, you must remember my reputation!" He went to lean against the mantel, one booted foot crossed over the other. "The rumors are true." He loved the gasps, even knowing they were for different reasons.

"Oh, Brandon, I am so happy for you. Who is she? The gossipmongers are calling her a nobody, but I assume that is because *they* do not know who she is." She stopped as something occurred to her. "Oh, dear, what have you told her about us?"

"Actually, I told her I would give her a few days to settle in and replenish her wardrobe before introducing you to her. You will not have long to wait."

Elizabeth drawled from the sofa, "Then your betrothed is *not* Lady Winslow?"

He was startled. "Of course not. Where would you get such an idea?"

"So you *have* caused another scandal. I cannot decide which is worse, that you might have married that awful widow, or that you have apparently jilted her for someone else."

"Well, when you decide, be sure to apprise me of it," he said sternly. His steely voice had put down the pretensions of many ladies over the years, and Elizabeth had just gotten her own dose of it.

Sadly, his sister had been raised with their father's scorn and was largely immune to even Brandon's harshest tones. "Come down off your high horse, Brandon. We have been waiting this age for you to do your duty and marry, and then we hear you are engaged to a woman no one has ever heard of." She sighed. "I think we may be allowed a little pique at your behavior."

"Of course, you are allowed all of the temper you wish."

"That is enough, both of you." Maggie stood and glared at them. "Elizabeth, Brandon told us ten minutes ago he was willing to tell us what we wanted to know about his betrothed, but your barbed remarks have kept us in the dark still."

"My noble defender!" Brandon bowed his head and kissed the tip of his fingers to her.

"Do not be flirting with me," she said. "You are just as bad as Liza—I mean Elizabeth."

He wanted to word his announcement carefully. Liza was determined to be unpleasant and Maggie already pictured him with six children. He decided to honor Grace's wishes against lying to them.

"Her name is Lady Grace Endicott and she is the Earl of Pennington's daughter."

Elizabeth could not hold back her exclamation. "I do not know the Earl of Pennington, but if you have been smart enough to choose an earl's daughter, then I owe you an apology!"

"I can die happy now, to be sure," he muttered.

"Go on, Brandon."

"I did decide during the Little Season that I might look around for a wife—doing my duty, isn't that what you call it, Elizabeth? You may think what you like about Patrice Winslow, but I have never offered for her or given her cause to believe that I would. You may ease your minds on that score.

"I recently attended a house party in Rivenhall. While in Essex, I was introduced to Lady Grace. Her father and I share an interest in the Elgin Marbles." Grace would have been proud of him, not a single un- truth. He smiled at the thought. "My admiration of Lady Grace grew rather quickly and I offered for her." Still the truth, although stretched to the breaking point.

"We wished to keep our betrothal a secret, as I had not yet been able to inform you. However, we both stopped at the same inn on our way to London. Grace is bringing her sister to Town for her come-out," he added in the way of explanation. "Unfortunately, the March-monts were staying at the same inn and quickly saw my attachment to Grace." He did not owe his starched-up sister any more details.

"I knew they would gossip, no matter what the circumstances, and we did not wish them to spread any malicious tale, so we informed them of our betrothal. They beat us to London. I apologize that you had to find out that way. It was certainly not our intention.

"The announcement will be in the papers tomorrow and I would ask that you both help us get over the rough ground as well as we can. What I care about most is that she and her sister are treated with every courtesy and respect." He said the last looking at Elizabeth.

"I see nothing distasteful in what you have told us. However, the Marchmonts are relating some intimacy between you and the girl. Really, Brandon, you must learn propriety."

"They saw no inappropriate intimacy, madam, except the kissing of her hand." He was angry now. He would hear nothing against Grace. "She is a lady in the truest sense of the word, and I will not have her slandered by you or anyone else. You may direct anyone who does straight to me."

"Yes, yes, this is all well and good. Having their father with them will scotch that type of thing quickly."

"The earl has not accompanied them to London. Their aunt is chaperoning them. But I believe his *name* will accomplish the same outcome."

"Who is this aunt? What is her name?"

"I cannot remember exactly," he said, stopping as

Elizabeth shook her head. "It is Grace's mother's sister, so I know her name is not Endicott. I think it begins with a *B,* but I cannot swear to it. I do know that they call her Aunt Aggie."

Elizabeth practically jumped out of her seat. "Could it be Agatha Burstow? She has almost as many connections as we do! This gets better and better, and I had not thought it of you. If, when we meet the girl, she is passable and well trained, all will be perfect. We can plan on a wedding at St. George's in July."

"Elizabeth, as much as your approval warms my heart," he said with irony, "I believe Grace is capable of making her own wedding plans. She is not a school room miss. And as to being passable, as long as *I* feel she is acceptable, I cannot see how that will affect you."

"Brandon," said Maggie, having remained silent during his exchange with Elizabeth, "tell me what she is like. Will I like her? Is she pretty? Will she like me?"

"Maggie, your husband's Irish curiosity is wearing off on you," he teased. "Is she pretty? Yes, I certainly think so, though I would say she is handsome—even beautiful. She has the most interesting eyes." Her face rose before him, her verdant eyes laughing at him. "Will you like each other? I hope so. Truth to tell, I have not known her long enough myself to have learned a great deal of her tastes. But she adores *her* sister, so I would like to think she will like mine. She has an excellent mind and has been helping run her father's estate for several years."

"Enough of that drivel, Margaret," Elizabeth interrupted. "Brandon, you must arrange a meeting between us as soon as possible so these nasty rumors may be put to rest. Do you think we could arrange tea with Mrs. Burstow two days hence? We may then decide the best plan of presentation and at which affairs you should start the Season."

He held back a sharp response. "I told you at the start that I would give them the time they needed before being available to you. Two days' time is barely enough. I will ask them when it is convenient for them, but if they agree to see you early, I will hear no complaints about their outmoded dress or the house being at sixes and sevens."

"Brandon, I don't care a jot how they are dressed. I want to meet the woman you love."

"There is nothing of use here," Aunt Aggie exclaimed as she threw gown after gown on the bed and over chairs, while rummaging through their wardrobes the next morning. "Girls, get your hats, we are going shopping!"

Lydia was very excited to see London fashions, but Grace knew this was all a waste of time and money on her behalf.

"I do not wish to hear one word from you, my dear," her aunt scolded when she tried to resist. "You are to be a marchioness and will dress accordingly." She knew no way to tell her aunt the new clothes would not be needed, so she accepted defeat as graciously as she could.

Day and walking dresses, evening and ball gowns were ordered for each of them! That was the *minimum*

Aunt Aggie would allow. She reminded her modiste of
the business she had referred her way over the years,
and graciously extracted a promise that at least two of
the day dresses would be ready the next morning. Reminding the woman that she was dressing a future marchioness sealed the bargain.

When they returned to Berkeley Square, the post
awaited them, and the girls jumped when Aunt Aggie
shrieked. "Dear Grace, Lord Weston is asking permission to bring his sisters here the day after tomorrow to
meet you." She returned the missive to the salver. "That
settles it. Tomorrow we will have to go to the milliners
for hats and the bootmakers for shoes. Oh, dear, and
we must go to Pantheon's Bazaar for your underclothes
and stockings. It seems the marquess is eager to present you to his sisters. That is as it should be, and we
will be ready!"

The day after tomorrow? Things were moving too
fast for Grace. This Season was supposed to be about
Lydia, and she would remind them of that. She would
also have to show Lord Weston that his high-handedness
would not be tolerated. He did not even have the courtesy to ask if it was convenient for them!

"Grace, there is a missive for you here, as well,"
Lydia said, exclaiming over the lovely vellum.

"I cannot image who would be writing to me," she
said, perplexed. Lord Weston would communicate
through her chaperone, as was proper. She glanced at
the frank on the envelope. It *was* from Lord Weston.
He did, indeed, flout Society without a care! As she
unfolded the page, a newspaper clipping drifted out of

the note. She bent to pick it up and noticed it was their betrothal announcement cut from the *London Gazette*. She turned her attention to his missive, and blushed at the first line.

Dear Grace,
I hope the day after tomorrow is not too inconvenient for you and your aunt. I fear our desire to take things slowly was a bit unrealistic. According to my sisters, rumors run rampant, and they are likely correct (as much as I hate to admit it). We must put a halt to the gossip.

However, if you are not comfortable about the day after tomorrow, please let me know and I will tie my sisters up somewhere until a better time presents itself.
Your Servant,
B.R.
P.S. I do hope the announcement meets with your approval. I left out the explanation of our falling head over heels in love to save space. I will be more effusive in the letter to your father.

Grace laughed out loud and supposed that must be the whole problem with rakes—their charm!

"Does his missive to you say anything different, Grace, dear?" Aunt Aggie asked, as she surreptitiously tried to read the letter over Grace's shoulder.

"No, Aunt, except that Lord Weston *does* say if the day after tomorrow is not convenient, we must let him know and he will set a later date."

"I suppose we may as well leave it as it is," her aunt said with a martyred expression. "I have never met the younger one, but I can tell you from experience that his eldest sister, Lady Wright, sets herself up as a leader in Society." She whispered to Grace so Lydia would not hear, "I believe she is a veritable dragon."

"If you truly believe so then you and her brother agree wholeheartedly, dear aunt!"

Chapter Six

The silence in the drawing room was deafening. Lady Wright and Mrs. Hale were seated on the striped sofa across from Grace's aunt, drinking tea. Lord Weston stood leaning against the mantel, arms crossed over his chest. He was enjoying himself immensely.

He had always been the focus of attention in drawing rooms such as this. Now he stood back and watched as these three women took each other's measure. He'd seen concentrated focus a thousand times over games of chance, when even the blink of an eye could determine which card was played. But this was as intense as any he'd seen, and he would wager the stakes were just as high to these ladies. It was only the first of many new pleasures he expected this Season, thanks to his lovely affianced.

As the strain rose and topics of conversation became fewer, he thought about returning to the great hall, a room he would love to explore. It was one of the most interesting entrance halls he had ever seen, one that had likely taken a woman's deft hand to make so beautiful. He wondered if that hand was Grace's.

He was brought back to the present by the strain in her aunt's voice as she attempted to converse with his overbearing sister. He was thankful for Maggie, or the uneasy silence would have driven him mad. "I pray you will forgive Grace and Lydia for not coming in immediately to greet you. As you know, they arrived in London two days ago and the modiste only delivered the first of their gowns moments ago."

Brandon knew what a coup that was to anyone who understood the fashion world, as did his sisters, so he gave the first round to Mrs. Burstow.

"Lord Weston had assured Grace you would understand if they presented themselves a little outdated, but I would not hear of it. I insisted they change immediately." Her tone was almost arrogant, Brandon noted. This was going to be most enjoyable. Even Gentleman Jackson himself, with his famous boxing club, might not have witnessed such a bout as was brewing between Grace's aunt and his sister.

At that moment, the door opened and Grace and Lydia came into the room. Both performed demure curtseys, but Lydia, in her nervousness, was the first to speak. "We are terribly sorry to be so late. Good morning, my lord," she finished, as if it had taken all her bravery. He smiled at her and winked.

Grace's aunt rose and brought the girls forward as she introduced them. "Lady Wright, Mrs. Hale, this is Grace and this is Lydia."

Before anyone else could speak, Elizabeth rose from

the sofa, strode over to Grace and held out her hand. "I am pleased to make your acquaintance, Lady Grace. I am Elizabeth, Lady Wright, and this is my sister, Margaret, Mrs. Hale."

Maggie could not be so stiff. "Lady Grace, Lady Lydia, I am so happy to meet you both. We have descended upon you far too soon, but we could not wait to visit our new sisters." Her smile was infectious.

Brandon stepped away from the mantel and gazed long and hard at Grace. He walked over to her, took her hand, kissed it and laid it on his arm. "It is good to see you again, my dear. The new gown was definitely worth the wait. You look beautiful."

Silence fell again in the room and Grace blushed. She raised her eyes to his and he hoped he saw his amusement reflected in hers.

She removed her hand from his and finally smiled at him. She turned back to his sisters. "Lady Wright, Mrs. Hale, we are happy to make your acquaintance, as well."

The tension in the room eased considerably and Lord Weston nodded his approval over Lydia's head. Grace's poise was phenomenal and he knew she would do well in London. He knew then, too, that he would not find it an onerous task to have her on his arm for the next few weeks.

Maggie joined in by walking to Grace and hugging her. "I am so happy you are to be part of our family." Her smile was genuine.

Grace's aunt began seating everyone again, and motioned for Grace to pour tea for herself and Lydia.

Brandon went back to the mantel, where he could

watch all the faces in the room. But his first notice was of Grace's new gown. It was dark blue with tiny white stripes. The sash at her waist was also white; he noted that she eschewed the Empire style, at least with this dress. A wide white stand-up collar completed the confection. At her age, she was able to wear colors, and in her new gown she looked somewhat regal. He liked it.

Lydia had not spoken a word since her opening remarks, but she had ended up next to Maggie, and Brandon knew his sister would do everything in her power to make the girl more comfortable. "This is a beautiful home. We were commenting on it earlier."

"Thank you," she murmured shyly.

Grace smiled at Maggie and winked at Lydia. "We must be perfectly honest with you, Mrs. Hale. Lydia had never been to the town house before two days ago. I have been in London several times and have come to love my mother's touch everywhere. The entry hall is my favorite. I hope you may soon see the way the chandelier lights up the tapestries in the evenings. And I must introduce you to Max before you leave. He is my knight in shining armor!" She smiled at each of them.

Brandon watched as she effortlessly protected Lydia *and* let her love for the house show in her words. That his favorite room was the same as hers did not surprise him.

"But my father rarely comes to Town, so it is almost as new to Lydia as it is to you. Our betrothal," she said, as she looked at Lord Weston and blushed, "happened rather unexpectedly. Our true purpose in coming to London is to bring Lydia out."

"Oh, I see," Maggie said, smiling at them both. "This shall be a most exciting Season. Lady Lydia will be the reigning belle, and with your wedding, Society may never be the same!"

Finally, his sister Elizabeth spoke again. "I see we have much more to do than I'd originally realized. I am very glad we pushed for this hasty introduction. We have much to discuss. I think the sooner we get some of the details settled, the sooner we can begin our planning."

His sister had directed her words to Grace's aunt, assuming, he supposed, that the two younger women had no notion how to go on. Brandon could see Grace's eyes beginning to flash emerald, and thought his sister might finally have met her match.

"Brandon," Elizabeth continued, "I am sure you must have somewhere else you would rather be. You may take yourself off while we discuss arrangements."

He did have an appointment with Lord Langdon in an hour; he wanted to be sure he saw him as soon as possible after the announcement in the paper. But he would stay where he was for as long as he could. He did not want to miss a moment! "Elizabeth, I resent the assertion that I would rather be anywhere but with my intended," he said in a wounded tone.

He leaned casually back against the mantel and waited for the fireworks.

Grace sat listening quietly for several minutes, her practical self screaming to get out.

"I do not see why we cannot combine the two events

to some extent, do you?" Lady Wright asked Grace's aunt. "I think, however, the first thing we need to decide is the date of the wedding. Lady Lydia will certainly be a big part of all the betrothal celebrations, and will be seen in the best Society."

"*Grace and I* will decide when the wedding will be," Lord Weston interjected decidedly.

"Well, of course you will, Brandon," Lady Wright admonished. "But since neither of you has planned a wedding before, we are only offering our advice."

"Of course you are, Elizabeth," he mocked her. "As of yet, however, we have not discussed a date. Therefore, we will need time to make our decision." Brandon looked at Grace and asked, "Does that meet with your approval, love?"

She would have to ignore the endearment, which she was positive he used with every woman he met. "May I make a suggestion?" she asked. Her teeth were beginning to clench and she had to force herself to keep a smile on her face. "Perhaps we should begin by planning Lydia's come-out, as we originally intended. Lord Weston and I may then share in *her* events. After all, our betrothal has already been announced."

The room turned into a cacophony of sound as everyone started to speak at once.

"We appreciate your concern for your sister," Lady Wright began, "but the engagement of a marquess certainly has priority over the come-out of a young lady."

"Oh, Lady Grace, you have hit on just the thing," Maggie said excitedly, getting into the spirit. "We can schedule Lady Lydia's come-out ball, introduce her to our friends, and your aunt's, of course, and then also officially celebrate your betrothal at that same ball!"

"Oh, Grace!" Lydia ran across the room and sat down beside her. "I do not mind if your wedding takes precedence. You know I do not."

"Enough!" Lord Weston demanded from the fireplace. All sound in the room stopped except for the teacups rattling in their saucers. He looked at each individual in turn, finally settling his glance on Grace. He walked to her and pulled her up gently by the hand to stand next to him.

"Grace, I will not have them ride roughshod over you. Do you feel capable and well able to handle this?" She nodded. "Good."

He then turned to the rest of the room at large. "I believe Lady Grace has as much experience socially, albeit not always in London, to adequately plan her sister's come-out. I agree with her suggestion that we keep the main focus on Lydia, and share our engagement celebrations with her." Grace could have kissed him! "Mrs. Burstow, Grace has not had a wedding, however, and I feel sure she will appreciate any *advice* you and my sisters may offer."

But Lady Wright had her back up. "I had planned on offering Wright House for your betrothal ball. It is just outside of town and would prevent the crush of carriages such a large ball usually entails. But clearly, you know better than I. Margaret, we can leave, and I am sure they will let us know the date of the wedding." She reached over to the table next to her and lifted her muff.

Grace's frustration grew. Brandon's deliberate set-down of his sister had to be smoothed over. "Please, my lady, do not wash your hands of us yet. Lord Weston seems quite used to getting his own way. But I *know* he could never mean to exclude any of you in the process of coordinating such a large event. You are more than kind to offer your home for our ball, and we will be delighted to accept. What I hoped was that we could begin with Lydia's introduction into Society *first,* so that she may meet people her own age, and do the pretty to all of Aunt Aggie's friends." She paused to see if there was any thaw at all in Lady Wright. There was not.

"Of course, I will need to be with her as Aunt Aggie chaperones her to a few of these preliminary entertainments, but I see no need for Lord Weston to be dragged, kicking and screaming, to such tame activities." She smiled at Mrs. Hale's choked laugh. "When Lydia goes to her first ball, or whichever function his lordship wishes to attend, I am sure we will receive our fair share of congratulations on our engagement."

Lord Weston summed it up. "If you are still so inclined, Elizabeth, we may share with Grace's sister the ball you wish to host. As Lydia will be your new sister-in-law, I do not think anyone would look askance if her ball were at your home. Would three weeks' time be adequate to prepare? Elizabeth, you and Grace may select the date that best suits you both."

Grace began to squirm as she realized that was very close to the time she intended to call *off* the engagement. They could not plan Lydia's come-out ball at Lady Wright's home if she and Lord Weston were no longer betrothed! She tried tugging her hand from his, but he only tightened his grip. "Indeed, it will be quite a coup for us all, and I would certainly be more than grateful."

"Tomorrow, Grace and I will begin making and receiving calls to introduce Lydia," Aunt Aggie said, tapping her finger against her chin. "Within a week, we may all be able to attend functions together, to share the two celebrations."

Lord Weston kept Grace's hand in his and she finally stopped struggling. Oh, but she would love to give him a piece of her mind. Why would he not let her go?

"Elizabeth, I will be removing the Weston emeralds from the vault to have them cleaned," he announced. "I will present the ring to Grace at the earliest possible moment. That should stop the tongues that may still be wagging."

Grace turned toward him in surprise and grabbed his hand with both of hers. She did not stop to think before she spoke. "My lord, that is not necessary. Please, do not feel obliged to pass your family heirlooms to me."

She realized from the thundercloud in his eyes and the gasp from his sisters that she had made a major faux pax. "Love," Lord Weston said, practically growling the word, "they are now *your* jewels, as my betrothed. Their major purpose is not to keep the gossipmongers in tow. I *want* you to have your betrothal ring."

Surprisingly, it was Lydia who recognized the possibility of another heated exchange between the two, and in her bravest voice yet, she said, "Perhaps Grace and Lord Weston would like a few minutes alone. Aunt Aggie, could we not show Lord Weston's sisters the rest of the house?"

The four women rose to leave the room. As Maggie walked past her brother, she whispered, "Behave yourself, Brandon." She followed the others, asking if they might not use their Christian names, as they were all to be family. The door closed behind them.

"Determined to botch this, my dear?" he drawled, finally letting Grace's hand go free.

She sat on the sofa and dropped her head in her hands. "I knew I would not be able to do this."

He came to her, knelt in front of her and raised her face to his. "I am sorry, love. Do not cry. Just think before you blurt out your feelings. I have complete trust in you. We shall come about, I promise."

"You do not understand," Grace moaned. "Even if I believed we were truly betrothed, I would have hesitated at taking your family's jewels. I still would have felt awkward discussing heirlooms as if they meant nothing to you to give them away."

"Zounds! We are in the suds. You must be the most *un*avaricious female alive!" He stood up and pulled her with him. "That may be the way I can explain it to my sisters when we leave. You quite adoringly thought I would feel sorrow at having family heirlooms passed on. They both know better, but they might think you do not."

He was not finished with her. "We are not safe yet. I am afraid your hesitation to accept my betrothal ring will cause other serious questions in the minds of my sisters. Maybe not Maggie, but in Elizabeth's, most definitely. I am afraid this calls for one of those drastic measures we discussed back at the inn."

She looked at him questioningly. What was he up to now? "I do not understand you, my lord. What drastic measures?"

"First, *Grace,* no one is going to believe we have fallen in love if you do not stop 'my lord'ing me at every turn. You must call me Weston at the very least. Even if you pretend embarrassment at odd moments, as you are starting the habit of calling me that, it will be easier to convince others. Next, when those women return to this room, they will need to see some kind of physical indication that our whirlwind romance is real."

She looked at him skeptically. "What kind of physical indication are you referring to, *Weston?*" She said the last quite sarcastically.

"I think you know, love, but if you want me to say it, I will. They will need to see the embrace the Marchmonts have been claiming that *they* encountered."

"The Marchmonts did not see us embracing."

"No, they did not, but that is their tale." He smiled at her impishly. She wished those dimples were not so distracting. "Let me see, how shall we best set the scene? You are overwrought, thinking you made me believe you did not want my betrothal ring. I think holding you in my arms would seem comforting, would it not?"

"You are teasing me!" she exclaimed in horror. "You wretched man! You are *trying* to drive me mad. Oh, I could box your ears for scaring me so."

He pulled her into the window embrasure. "I *was* teasing a bit, only because your eyes change so amazingly when you are angry with me. But what I said is true. Lydia saw you were upset, and we must take ad-

vantage of that. If my sister Maggie hears one dispar-
aging remark about our engagement after this, she will
know how to handle it."

"After what—?" she asked, but at that moment they
heard voices nearing the drawing room door, and events
happened so quickly after that she could almost swear
they were happening to someone else.

Lord Weston pulled her against him with one arm
around her waist, and with his other hand raised her
face to his.

As the ladies got closer to the drawing room, she
remained still, looking into his eyes, questions in her
own. He leaned down to say softly, "You see, it is not so
hard. Your beloved is whispering exceptionally charming sweet nothings into your ear." Her expression did
not change. "Oh, very well," he said, frustrated. "Perhaps the sweet nothings are only moderately charming.
But still, it would not come amiss if you took a deep
breath, then sighed."

Grace could not help it. She laid her forehead against
his chest, breaking contact with his wicked dark stare,
her shoulders shaking in silent laughter.

"Minx," he whispered, his head still bent over her as
the door opened to the returning women. He stepped
back from her slightly and she turned a flushed countenance to them, truly amazed how he had masterfully
created the look of a tender moment.

"Good gracious, Brandon, what *are* you about? Mrs.
Burstow, I must apologize for my brother. I think we
had best take our leave now and finalize details at a
later date."

Aunt Aggie was visibly stunned. "I do not believe he was taking advantage of her, Lady Elizabeth. Grace would never allow…"

"Yes, yes, of course. I was not insinuating your niece was indecorous. Margaret, we will await Brandon in the foyer."

Grace scowled at him and whispered, "You wretch! I will soon have a reputation as bad as yours." But he ushered her out of the drawing room with an arm still around her waist.

"I thank you for your hospitality, Mrs. Burstow," Lady Wright said to her aunt. "You will call on me for tea, say, Thursday of this week, so we may discuss things further?"

"I will check to see what we have planned for that day, certainly," Aunt Aggie told her. Grace smiled to herself as Aunt Aggie stood up to Lord Weston's sister. She imagined the two in a power struggle as the details were ironed out and she had no doubt as to who would be the victor. Aunt Aggie was indomitable!

Lord Weston was next to bid her aunt and Lydia goodbye. As he turned to kiss Grace's own hand, he made the mistake of looking directly into her eyes. She decided turnabout was fair play, and she sighed in a most lovelorn manner while saying, "Goodbye, *Weston*."

"Thought that girl was pretty sensible," Lady Elizabeth muttered. "Look what you have done to her."

Grace heard him try to repress his laughter by turning it into a cough. She spun back toward the drawing room, hiding the smug expression on her face.

Chapter Seven

Brandon was still smiling when he pulled up to 21 Cavendish Square. However, this meeting was very important, so he attempted to turn his thoughts from Grace as he was shown into the library of Lord Langdon. With its large leather chairs and book-lined walls, it had quickly become a sort of safe haven to him. He and his lordship had many business and personal conversations here and he had come to respect the man more than he could have imagined.

Only a few moments passed before the door opened and Lord Langdon came in. "Brandon, I am so glad you have come!" He clasped his guest's hand in both of his, real joy showing on his lined face.

"I am glad to be here, my lord," he said as his host motioned him to a chair before a large desk.

Knowing Brandon's self-imposed ban on alcohol, he asked, "As it is too early for coffee, would you like a glass of spring water?" At Brandon's nod he filled a glass and took it to him. Since Brandon's relationship with Lord Langdon began, he always made him comfortable by stocking it. "Shall we make this a toast? I have heard you are to be congratulated."

"Indeed, my lord. I *am* sorry I did not get to inform you of it myself. I can only hope that you heard it first in the *Gazette?*"

"Afraid not, lad," he said with a grin. "But I own to being quite happy to have it verified by the announcement in the paper."

"I can only imagine what you must have thought."

"I hope you know me better than that, Brandon. I admit to surprise, but I never doubted you would come to me when you were able."

"Thank you, sir." His response was heartfelt. Knowing how his father would have reacted, he truly appreciated the trust and respect of one wholly unrelated to him.

"I thought you might have brought her with you when you asked to come today."

"I had hoped to, my lord, but I am informed I must give the ladies time to update their wardrobes before they are ready to make calls. Truth to tell, I know Grace would not have minded, but she is here with her sister and aunt, and I find I am quite de trop for the nonce."

Lord Langdon laughed. "The newspaper said your affianced was Lord Pennington's daughter. I was not aware he had a daughter."

"Actually, he has two, but I am not surprised you were unaware of them. He has eschewed London for many years now. I was introduced to…" His words tapered off. Suddenly, Brandon's conscience was pricked by the lie. He felt an inordinate amount of remorse in lying to Lord Langdon. Was this what Grace felt? He had seen nothing in this world that proved an existence of God. Yet his reluctance remained.

"Yes, my boy?"

"I was introduced to the daughters very recently."

"I surmised *that* much or I suspect I would have heard of your interest in Lady Grace before this." Brandon almost flinched. His actions were so scrutinized by a society that lived to criticize one another. For so many years, he had not cared; indeed, he had actually tried shocking the *ton.* But he did care now that those same gabsters could seriously hurt his relationship with this man.

Could he tell him the truth? He wanted to, very badly. His respect for this gentleman was leaps and bounds above what he felt for any other of his acquaintances, and he would have gladly sought his advice.

But his fear of disapproval and condemnation, ingrained from a childhood with an overbearing parent, made him hold his peace. The relationship he and his friend Dennis had formed with Lord Langdon had certainly grown into mutual trust, probably even more on his part. But should his lordship find out how Brandon had gotten into this entanglement, would he lose that trust and thereby the voice this man had in Parliament? He was afraid to risk it. And, after all, he had denied Grace the option to tell her own father.

But he would no longer outright lie to him.

"You are correct, sir. Neither she nor her sister is

well known in London, though they are very well connected through the earl and their aunt, Mrs. Burstow."

"I believe I knew her husband in my younger days, but I do not recall his wife."

"I don't think they spent much time in Town. They traveled quite a bit, but Mr. Burstow has been dead for many years, I believe."

"You have convinced me she comes from an impeccable lineage, but I hope you know that would never be my primary interest in the lady you chose to wed."

"Of course not. I beg your pardon. Things happened so quickly once we knew of the Marchmonts' tales. I find I must temper my comments based upon whom I am speaking to."

Lord Langdon put his glass down on the table next to his chair. "I certainly hope that is not the case with me, Brandon. You may always be completely honest with me."

"I do know that, sir, and I do not take it for granted in any way."

Brandon had met Lord Landon a few years previously in quite unusual circumstances; being much younger in age, he had not run in his lordship's circles. Once Brandon began the path that labeled him trouble, he had never felt the need nor the inclination to take his seat in the House. As he grew older, he'd regretted that fact, especially since once the actual need for him to do so arose, he knew none would take him seriously.

When he and David, Lord Hendricks, his closest friend, discovered their passion to right one of Society's greatest wrongs, they'd assumed they would be doing it alone. Their progress had been slow. They'd wished to remain anonymous for many reasons, but that method garnered little support for their endeavors.

When David was killed in a carriage accident, Brandon had almost given up the fight. But David's younger brother, Dennis, would not let him. So Brandon and the new Lord Hendricks continued the work.

It was only a short time later that they were approached by Lord Langdon with his offer to help. The first reaction of both men had been shock. They had done everything they could to keep their efforts from becoming known. But his lordship was able to assure them that his discovery had come to him by small bits and pieces because of his desire to champion the same cause.

Lord Langdon had offered his support where they had no ear, in Parliament. None of them wanted an outcry of major proportions; it would only send the miscreants Brandon and Dennis wanted punished scurrying into hiding.

But there was much need for stricter guidelines *and* punishment for the offenses they had witnessed, and such action could only be done legislatively. Lord Langdon volunteered to be their mouthpiece. His only concern had been Brandon, for he had heard nothing good about him.

Langdon promised he would help them only if Lord Weston's scandals ceased. He would not risk his own reputation by aligning himself with one whose antics leaned more toward rake than those of a gentleman.

Brandon's first reaction had been to do the complete

opposite, just as he would have done with his father. But Dennis convinced him they needed an ally like Lord Langdon to make any serious inroads, and so began the unusual friendship.

Over the years, their relationship became one of mutual respect. Brandon sometimes wondered, if he had been more mature, whether he and his father might have come to the same understanding. But it always came back to him that he had been a disappointment to his parent from childhood. And it had made both their lives miserable.

Brandon became determined he would not disappoint Lord Langdon.

"You are very introspective today, my boy. Is something bothering you?"

"No, not bothered, just a little preoccupied."

"Too preoccupied to tell me about your affianced?"

"No, of course not. I do apologize. She is an exceptional woman, my lord."

"Of that I have no doubt."

Brandon chuckled. "You have many doubts, I daresay, but are too kind to say so." He settled back in his chair and pictured Grace in his mind. "She is very beautiful, but most unconscious of it. To own the truth, I have almost come to disregard her beauty, as she does. She has so many more important qualities that for the first time I find appearance quite low on my list of priorities!" He shook his head in disbelief at his own words.

"She is as intelligent as she is beautiful, and her sense of the ridiculous often catches me off guard. It is rare to find a female with a gift for sarcasm. She gives me no quarter, I assure you." He looked up from his glass. "I believe you will like her very much."

"Beautiful, intelligent and sarcastic? She sounds delightful." Langdon laughed, then paused. "I have sometimes been…afraid for you, Brandon. Afraid you would not wait for your perfect partner. That you might settle for mediocrity in order to beget an heir. You have oft times been most cynical when it comes to women and marriage. You will not credit it, but I have prayed about just this event for some time now. I am most happy to know you have found your equal, the person meant to go through life at your side."

Great guns! Was that how he sounded? Perhaps he had laid it on a bit thick. He had not meant to. But Lord Langdon had the right of it. Grace was his equal. He would enjoy this Season with her and be proud to introduce her as his betrothed. But when the time came for her to end their relationship, he would not repine. He stopped his thoughts there. He would need time to process Lord Langdon's reference to prayer.

"Brandon, how does she feel about the work we are doing?"

He hesitated. "Actually, I have not as yet discussed it with her."

"May I ask why?"

"It is twofold, I suppose. The first is that our courtship truly has happened quite quickly. We still have much to learn about each other. And I suppose I did not yet feel that I should share that information without first talking to you and Dennis."

"Do you have some reason to fear her response?"

"No, sir, not a bit of it. In a short time I have come to trust her implicitly. But I would not put her in the way of danger for anything."

He had not lied to Lord Langdon. He simply had neglected to mention that despite those feelings of trust, there was no need to involve her should this arrangement result in the separation they intended.

He was brought back to the present by Lord Langdon's question. "Do you expect physical danger to become a part of our work?"

"It is more a feeling than an expectation. The more changes we make, I think the opportunities for our detection increase. As we are dealing with the most unscrupulous sort of men, I never rule out the chance of trouble."

"That is wise, Brandon. Your instincts are well honed."

The two men shared a moment of easy silence.

"Shall I meet your paragon soon?"

"By all means, my lord—when it may be managed. As I mentioned, her aunt and my sisters have too much control over our actions for my liking. Add to that the come-out of Grace's sister, and you will see why I have been tossed aside to make way for the planning. I know Lady Grace is as unhappy about it as I, but for now we seem to be pawns in the overall strategy of this chess match. I do not take a backseat easily, but I have found Grace bears much of the brunt of my growling, so I have ceased for the moment."

"I have a hard time picturing that," Lord Langdon said with a laugh. "I should like to be a fly on the wall."

"Have no fear, I will give my sisters their heads for only a short time before I rein them back in. I have no patience for all of this posturing."

"Now *that* is the Brandon Roth I am accustomed to!"

Grace was having serious misgivings since meeting Lord Weston's sisters the day before. She actually *saw* the faces of two of the people who would be hurt when they ended the betrothal. She needed to think. So much had happened in the preceding week that she was overwhelmed.

She had let his sense of humor get the better of her when his sisters took their leave the day before, but she'd regretted it almost as soon as the door closed behind them.

How could she keep up this pretense? Her aunt was so very happy for her. She had all but said that she'd been afraid Grace would never meet anyone. Grace did not mind that; she had come to that conclusion years ago herself. But making her aunt unhappy by ending the engagement would break her own heart. And though she did not claim to know him well enough to read his thoughts, Lord Weston seemed to indicate that a broken betrothal would interfere in matters more important than his reputation.

Father, I am so torn. Either I will be yoked to a man who does not believe in You, or I will be a jilt, someone who does not keep her word. I know You never would have had me choose this path in the first place, and now the consequences seem so dire. Please show me how I can make it right.

She spent the rest of the day tied in knots. Tomorrow would begin Lydia's Season. They would join their aunt in morning calls and host a small, intimate card party in the evening. In the meantime, Grace needed to make a decision about whether to go further down this road or not. But she could not deny that the idea of Lord Weston's disappointment was paramount to her. She did not know why, but that alone carried the same weight as each of her other concerns.

In the end, it was Lydia who made the decision for her. She came to Grace after dinner, before their guests arrived for the evening.

"Grace?"

"Yes, darling?"

"I have been looking forward to a Season for so long, but now I am ever so scared I shall be shy and stupid."

"Lydia, you are never stupid." Grace's rejoinder was emphatic. "And you will no longer be shy once you have made a few friends. You are so sweet and selfless that you will have many friends very, very soon. You met some lovely young girls today, did you not?"

"Oh, Grace, I do not know how I would bear all of this without you. I know you did not wish to come to London, but as long as I can look around a room and see you, I know I will feel quite safe." She kissed Grace's flushed cheek. "Thank you for everything you have done for me."

For Lydia, Grace would continue what they had started.

Chapter Eight

As expected, Lydia captivated London. As soon as their new clothes were delivered, Aunt Aggie began accompanying them on morning calls, alfresco luncheons and some evening soirees and card parties. They attended many with Lord Weston's sisters.

Almack's had not been stormed, though vouchers had come. The decision was made that it would be best if Lord Weston was with them on that auspicious occasion. And as they had not been sanctioned to dance the waltz by the august patronesses of the prestigious institution, Aunt Aggie had decided that they would not attend any balls until they were able to do so. Grace was so happy to allow Lydia to ease into her Season. She could not wish for more.

Indeed, Lydia glowed, as Grace knew she would. Her sister was the perfect combination of beauty, humility and charity in one package, and she was so proud of her.

Grace had taken care of Lydia since the death of their mother ten years before. She'd felt called to console her father, tend to her eight-year-old sister *and* manage the running of the household. Seeing Lydia blossom so made all of that seem worth it.

Grace did not share the fact that she was not enjoying herself. When they had agreed that Lydia should be introduced to Society first, she had not known there would be *no* contact with Lord Weston. She had not seen him since the day she'd met his sisters. She missed him! Well, not *him,* of course, but a friendly face and someone to make her laugh.

Only yesterday, she'd been put in the most awkward situation. She was having tea with Aunt Aggie and one of her aunt's friends when Jamison interrupted with a note and a box for her.

She recognized the bold black scrawl of Lord Weston:

Dear Grace,
As I am apparently forbidden open contact with you during Lydia's introduction into polite Society, I am sending this to you by my secretary for safety.
I regret sincerely that I cannot put it on your finger myself. I truly do regret that, Grace. I will present you with the necklace and earrings when I hope to have that pleasure.
Yours,
Brandon

Almost immediately her hand had begun to tremble as she'd realized what was in the box.

Aunt Aggie had urged her to open her package. She had declined and said it would wait, but her aunt would not hear of it.

Grace had no choice. She'd opened the velvet box, and the awestruck sounds from Aunt Aggie and her friend confirmed her own thoughts as to the beauty of the ring. It was dazzling, a square-cut emerald surrounded by what seemed to be hundreds of tiny, shining white diamonds. It was more elegant than she could have imagined, yet not the least bit opulent. It was just what she would have chosen, given the option.

Suddenly, Aunt Aggie's friend went silent. Grace knew it was the natural progression of the woman's thoughts to wonder why Lord Weston had not wanted to put it on her finger himself. Grace had blushed, and her aunt had to swear her friend to secrecy and tell her of their decision to introduce Lydia first.

Yes, she would be better, Grace told herself, when the moratorium on seeing Lord Weston was over!

In White's, across Town, Brandon was sitting alone in the corner, thinking along the same lines. A voice behind him said, "The elusive rake finally succumbs to Cupid's arrow, yet sits here alone at his club. Has Rake Weston finally lost his touch?"

"Dennis, you rogue, stow it," Brandon said, slapping the tall man heartily on the shoulder while shaking his hand. "Sit down, sit down. Where have you been hiding yourself?"

"As much as I hate the tittle-tattle, old man, I am afraid that is what everyone has been asking about you." Lord Hendricks sat in the chair opposite from him and crossed his legs.

"What do the gossips want to know *this* time?"

"Why Lord Weston seems to be avoiding his betrothed of less than two weeks. Great guns, Brandon, they are placing bets at Brook's that it is all a practical joke you are playing on Society because you are bored with us." Dennis became still. "Or are you already bored with her?"

"Botheration! What a mess."

Looking at his friend, Brandon could not stop himself from thinking of the last time he'd been in a romantic tangle. Lord Hendricks's older brother, David, had helped him in his disastrous attempt at the elopement he could never forget. But when David was killed in that tragic carriage accident, Brandon took responsibility for helping Dennis get through the rough time, teaching him a little about managing an estate he had never planned to inherit.

Brandon debated for one moment telling his friend the truth behind his betrothal; he would trust Dennis with his life! But he had an obligation to Grace first. How odd that made him feel, when he had known her for little more than a s'ennight!

"Do give over, Brandon. If you do not wish to tell me, that is fine, but I would like to help if I can."

"It is not anything you can help with, my friend, but I appreciate the offer. It is a wretched coil that only I could get into, but as far as I know, it will be over on Friday."

"Is that all the explanation I am to receive?" Dennis asked with a laugh.

"No, I do not mind explaining. It is rather complicated and you will join me in wondering where my manhood has gone. Indeed, now that I think on it, I will give you the short version and you *can* do me a favor! What say you?"

"Until I know the favor, I believe I will withhold judgment."

They both laughed.

"Smart man. I assume you have heard of my whirl-wind romance with Lady Grace Endicott. Have you met her yet?" At the shake of Dennis's head, Brandon continued. "I think you will like her. In any event, she has this decidedly beautiful sister. If you have not heard *that,* you will, my friend, because all of London is agog with it. She is much younger than Grace who is over-seeing her sister's comeout.

"Her sister is very shy, however, and between Grace and her aunt, *and* my two sisters, they have decided to introduce Lydia into Society slowly. Apparently, I would be in the way in that endeavor. So instead of allowing me to dance the nights away in my betrothed's arms, those four silly women have determined that only on Friday at the theater may I begin to squire Grace through the rest of the Season. They did not, however, count on my in-convenient reputation and a society so given over to idle prattle when they decided upon their plan."

Dennis laughed out loud.

"Oh, pipe down, you young dog." Brandon said, scowling halfheartedly. "You are the tenth person to ask me why I bothered to get leg-shackled when I did not wish to be around my betrothed."

"So, then, what is the favor you need from me?" in-quired Dennis warily.

"We are one gentleman short for the theater party on

Friday. I told my sister Elizabeth I would come up with someone, which scared her to death, by the by, but I did not know you were in Town. The young beauty has no escort. Will you come?"

"I would even be *your sister's* escort to get a chance to be part of this! With all of London watching the famous marquess and the lady who caught him, I wouldn't miss it." Dennis chuckled. "I am sorry, but now that I know the truth, I find I am enjoying myself immensely!"

"I hope to be doing the same soon, my friend, very soon." Brandon signaled to a waiter. "Will you join me for dinner? I met with Lord Langdon the other day and we have several things to discuss."

"Of course."

They ordered dinner and Dennis became pensive for a moment. "I want to let you know that there is another rumor flying around Town that is not so funny." Brandon raised his eyebrow in question. "The widow Winslow is angry about the rattle."

He sat up straighter in his chair. "Patrice knew where she stood with me all along."

"It appears she did not. She is intimating there was an offer made, though the people that believe that are few and far between."

"I could certainly clarify that there was no offer made, if she so wishes," Brandon said, clenching his jaw. "But I will not waste my time."

"What if your betrothed hears of it?" Dennis asked.

"Grace knows all about Patrice. Well, not *all* about her. In truth, Grace knows about all of my past indiscretions. She loves me, anyway," Brandon said like a lovesick pup, with a hand over his heart.

Dennis only laughed.

Dinner was pleasant, as it always was in Dennis's company, but Brandon could not concentrate. His mind was greatly occupied with the upcoming Friday night and the thought of seeing Grace again—with his ring on her finger.

Grace was overjoyed that Friday had finally arrived. She thought about the shallow and selfish people she had met during her own Season, remembering one reason she had not accepted any of the offers for her hand. But somehow, the vanity and pettiness seemed multiplied during this Season.

No matter. Tonight she would see Lord Weston again and she was like a giddy girl. He might be a rake, but he was by far the most interesting man she had ever met. She realized she had missed him dreadfully.

She was also looking forward to the theater. She wanted to see one of the famous Shakespearean plays. But she was honest enough to admit that she wanted to see it in Lord Weston's company.

It had been arranged that he and Lord Hendricks would escort Grace and Lydia to the theater, where his sisters would meet them.

Grace took special care with her toilette this night. She had not seen him in more than a s'ennight and for the first time in her life wanted to compare favorably with Lydia. Lord Weston had sent her a dozen red roses that morning with a card telling her how much he was looking forward to seeing her. She'd placed them in her room, enjoying the delicious way their fragrance wafted in the air.

Grace's wardrobe was simple; her nature allowed nothing more. But tonight she had an idea! She would wear her ivory gown and make its only embellishment his roses.

The dress was satin, but below the Empire waist was an overskirt of ivory lace that caused the satin beneath to shimmer as she moved. The neckline was high in the back and came to a sweetheart bodice in the front, with more lace along the edging. The sleeves were short and belled, and the full-length ivory gloves Aunt Aggie had loaned her were perfect. There was no other ornamentation to the dress.

But she took lace and red ribbon and tied them around three rose blossoms, fastening them with a clasp in her hair. The ribbons streamed down through long curls falling from the top of her head, while the roses created a soft contrast to her dark auburn hair.

Next, she tied red ribbon around the short stems of three more roses, which she pinned to the V of her neckline, leaving the ribbons hanging down the front. They rested beautifully against the lace. She wore pearl drop earrings, praying the effect was elegant enough for an evening at the theater.

When Aunt Aggie and Lydia came to let Grace know the gentlemen were waiting downstairs, they both halted at the doorway and stared, transfixed.

"I hope that is a good reaction," she said in a teasing tone, "or you will never get me to leave this room!"

Lydia rushed forward and took her hands. "Grace, you look so *beautiful*."

Grace smiled at her. "I will settle for beautiful and allow that you are breathtaking, dearest."

Lydia smiled, but said seriously, "I have some outward beauty, Grace, and I seem to get all of the accolades for it, but wait and see. Tonight, every eye will be on you. And I pray that someday I will have your inner beauty, as well."

"That was the loveliest thing to say. But do not worry, only this last week I have seen my baby sister begin to blossom into a woman to be valued in every respect."

Aunt Aggie told them to hurry, as the gentlemen were waiting, and both girls suddenly became nervous. Grace put her arm around Lydia's waist and they walked down the stairs arm in arm. Lydia whispered, "I believe Lord Weston actually *will* fall in love with you when he sees you tonight, and we might just have that wedding!" They were both smiling as they neared the bottom of the steps.

As they reached the men, it seemed each sister had eyes only for one.

"My lady," Lord Weston said, so very seriously, "may I tell you how utterly beautiful you look tonight? And how I have missed you."

She thanked him shyly, believing him sincere by his tone.

He raised her gloved hands to his lips and kissed them. As he stared into her eyes, her heart fluttered like a butterfly and she felt herself to be truly, deeply admired. Was this what Lydia felt like each day of her life?

That brought Grace back to her duty. She turned toward her sister, to bring her forward, and her eyes widened as she saw the flush on Lydia's face and the shy curtsy she made before the tall, handsome stranger.

Grace had never before seen her glow like this. The gentleman was getting the full dose of Lydia's beauty.

"Grace, Lydia, may I introduce you to one of my closest friends, Dennis Henderson, Lord Hendricks." Grace curtsied to him, but then smiled as she realized he was completely unaware of it. She looked over her shoulder into Lord Weston's eyes and a knowing twinkle in his eyes met hers.

He appeared to be waiting for some comment from his friend, but after several seconds, realized none would be forthcoming. "I have never known him to go quite this long without *some* words, but I assure you he is usually quite garrulous. Hmm, his mind must be elsewhere."

Lord Hendricks scowled at him, but then regained his manners. "I am pleased to meet you, Lady Grace, and I congratulate you on your upcoming nuptials. Although I can see it is my friend here who should be congratulated."

He turned to Lydia and said softly, "I am also pleased to make your acquaintance, Lady Lydia, and appreciate the opportunity to escort you tonight. I know the line will be too long in the future to squeeze me in."

Lydia blushed and Grace watched her with love, as if Lydia were her daughter and not her sister.

"I confess I have heard of your beauty, but I have not been in Town long enough to hear you were so charming, as well," he added.

Lydia thanked him shyly. Lord Weston eyed his friend and leaned toward her. "And he has gleaned that after only three words at the most. He is not usually so perceptive. An excellent compliment, Dennis. Do you think I might be rubbing off on him?"

They all laughed, even Lord Hendricks.

"I don't know about you, Lydia," Grace teased, "but I have not heard that gentlemen are now trying to outshine the ladies they are escorting. I fear to leave the house with these two!" Though she was only slightly jesting, she was awed at how striking Lord Weston looked tonight. She had never seen him in evening attire and thought he was most handsome.

She was suddenly ashamed of the frivolity of her thoughts. Beauty and finery were not what life was about. She must remember to focus on what *was* important in this life—serving God and making herself useful wherever she was. Indeed, she would find a way to do so even in London. That would be the next order of business for her…as soon as this night at the theater was over.

Lord Weston brought her back to the present as he set her wrap around her shoulders. "Your hair smells like roses. I thank you, my lady, for so honoring my gift."

To cover her embarrassment at his compliment, she said softly, "I am very glad *I* will not be the one trying to remove the rake out of you."

"But, my dear, that is the part you definitely want to leave in!" He handed her into the coach, giving her no chance to reply, only her smile to show him he had been truly missed.

Chapter Nine

The crush of carriages seemed endless, though half the occupants of their own carriage did not seem to notice. Lord Hendricks and Lydia were in their own little world and Grace was surprised. It was what she had wanted for Lydia all along, someone to make her shine. But such an instant attraction! Grace never thought to see the like.

As they entered the foyer of the theater, the beautiful gowns, the glittering jewels and the handsome gentlemen were set off by what seemed to be thousands of candles. The opulent stairways, velvet drapes and gorgeous statues left her speechless. It all seemed so much more lavish than when she had come out as a girl of eighteen.

Lord Hendricks took Lydia's arm and Grace and Lord Weston followed them up the stairway to the box where his sisters waited. Grace noticed another couple coming down the stairs just as they were ascending. The very obvious age difference between the two, and the beauty of the woman, made them stand out.

The gentleman appeared to be in his seventies and very distinguished, while the woman on his arm wore a very low cut dress of red silk, which clung rather too closely to all her elegant curves. Almost instantaneously Grace berated herself for her judgment. For all she knew the woman could be the gentleman's daughter, and what gown she chose was none of Grace's business.

But just then she heard Lord Weston mutter under his breath. It was so unusual of him that she was startled. Before she could ask him what was wrong, the woman in red left her escort with a word in his ear and proceeded directly into their path. She had black shiny hair and the whitest skin Grace had ever seen. She was stunning in a way *Grace* could never be. But that did not bother her…then.

Lord Weston motioned to Lord Hendricks to go on ahead and take Grace and Lydia with him. "Dennis will take you to the box where Elizabeth and Maggie are probably waiting. I will be along in a moment." But before Grace could depart, the woman walked into her path and up to Lord Weston. She kissed him on the cheek while looking directly at Grace. He motioned for Lord Hendricks to take Lydia, and kept Grace's arm tightly in his, with his hand over hers.

"Brandon," the woman said, her voice low and raspy, "aren't you going to introduce me to your…lady?" Grace was puzzled by the strong emphasis on the last word. Did she doubt her parentage? "I have been dying to meet her ever since I saw the notice in the paper. I have seen you so often without her, I was beginning to believe she did not exist."

The woman looked at her for a moment with such hatred that Grace was taken aback. She must have been mistaken; she was sure they had not met before.

"Lady Grace, let me introduce you to Lady Patrice Winslow. Lady Winslow, this is my betrothed, Lady Grace Endicott." Grace closed her eyes momentarily. This was the widow who had been expecting an offer from him.

"How charming she is, Brandon," the woman said, in a manner that intimated she thought quite the opposite. "I can see, however, why some might have thought the other sister more to your liking. We all know how important beauty is to you."

Before Lord Weston had time for a rejoinder, she addressed Grace directly. "I am agog to hear how you met, my lady. Perhaps we might talk during the intermission."

Grace did the one thing she did not want to do, she lost her temper. "Oh, dear, are you addressing me? I thought I had become invisible!"

Lord Weston laughed out loud. "Touché, Patrice! If you will excuse us, we need to get to our box. It was a pleasure to see you again."

Lord Weston grasped Grace's hand, still on his arm, so she had to go with him up the stairs, but not before she saw Lady Winslow's fists clench in indignation.

"That was her, was it not, my lord? The widow you were thinking of proposing to before I interfered in your life at the Blue Swan Inn." Grace kept trying to pull her hand free. "I could box your ears for your 'beauty is not important to me' speech. The woman is stunning, if

you like them a trifle on the showy side. That was not
something you mentioned when you told me about her."

Grace was miserable. She was angry at being ignored
by the encroaching female, but was honest enough to
admit, at least to herself, that she felt dowdy and plain
standing next to her. She was jealous! Her normal self
would have very casually handled the woman's rude
remarks with a smile or a word that would diffuse the
situation. However, her emotions had completely taken
over when confronted with *this* woman.

She did not want that to be the kind of woman Lord
Weston wanted.

With that realization came the knowledge that *she*
wanted to be the type he preferred. And it scared her.
They were to part in only a few weeks time and she had
begun to care what he thought of her much more than
their plan called for. She could still feel the sting and
her eyes were filling with angry tears.

She finally escaped his grasp, and turned her anger
onto him. "You could have warned me, you know," she
exclaimed, forcing herself to speak softly. "You could
have prepared me for a piranha. And you could have
told me we might meet tonight, so I would not have
been taken off guard by it. I am ashamed of myself and
I could...plant you a facer!"

He laughed again and returned her arm into the
crook of his. "My love, I would not have missed that
for the world!" Astonished, she again tried to stop walking, but he kept her with him as he continued up the
stairway. "You are right, I owe you an apology, though
I did not realize she was back in Town and had no no-

tion that we would encounter her tonight. But I cannot understand why no one will listen to me when I tell them I never had any intention of proposing to her."

He pulled Grace closer and leaned his head very near to hers. "Look at me, Grace. Truly, she means nothing to me." And with that he kissed her lips quickly.

He continued almost proudly. "Do not worry, you were magnificent, my dear. I was prepared to make a few cutting remarks when your eyes flashed that dark emerald color and you showed her she was not dealing with a silly, simpering miss. Now stop fretting and calm down before we enter the box."

"People could not possibly believe you would choose me when they know that is the kind of woman you like. And why did you kiss me there on the stairs? I do not understand this anymore, my lord," she said, deflated. He must have thought the roses on her dress ridiculous compared to the gown Lady Winslow wore. She muttered under her breath, "I now know that subtlety is certainly not a requirement in your choice of brides."

He looked at her and burst into laughter, which bothered her no end. Yet it troubled her more that his smile and laugh could so easily take the wind out of her sails.

"You are one in a million, my lady. And, no, subtlety is not one of Patrice's strong suits." He let go of Grace's hand and put his own on the small of her back. He gently pressed her up the stairs as the halls began to empty and people took to their boxes. "If you think I prefer that gown over yours, then you do not know me."

"I do *not* know you."

"And," he continued, as if she had not spoken, "I

kissed you because I saw her gloating at the bottom of the steps while you were fighting me all the way up. That is no way to convince the *ton* that we are in love." Once again he soothed her with his soft words. "I did not want her to think she could cause contretemps between us."

All Grace could think of as they entered the box was that she must plan their parting before her feelings could take further root.

Brandon ushered Grace into their box to take her mind off of Patrice's sad want of character. However, he needed to get *his* mind off the kiss he had taken for selfish reasons that had nothing to do with the widow. Lady Grace was turning out to be one of the most interesting women he had ever met.

When Patrice was too rude to tolerate any longer, Brandon had been ready to step in and defend Grace. He was pleased that she could defend herself, but he did wish, for a moment, that *he* had been the one to do it. He wanted the *ton* to know she was under his full protection.

When he thought about her wearing his roses as ornaments on her dress, he was inordinately pleased. He found her simplicity and innocence in doing him that honor a touching thing.

He must stop this. It was touching, yes, but she was not trying to please him and he had certainly not had a change of heart where marriage was concerned. He would enjoy this farce while it lasted, but no more than that. He had her promise on that.

He came back to the present when the applause after the first act began. He joined in the clapping as if he had watched the play with interest, but kept his attention fixed on his affianced to be sure the encounter with Patrice was defused. This was only the first night with Grace on his arm; he decided it would definitely be the most interesting Season he had had in a long while. And he looked forward to spending the next few weeks at her side.

Grace could not wait the necessary weeks to get out of this betrothal. She felt the need *now.* Lord Weston's make-believe intimacies were beginning to wear on her.

Since the theater a week ago, she had spent some part of each day with him, and the longer they were betrothed, the more it all seemed natural. Too natural! She had been praying for God's grace to help her out of a situation she knew was totally of her making.

She had not forgotten the seriousness of every reputation involved. But the major reason for coming to London seemed assured, as Lydia and Lord Hendricks spent as much time together as decorum allowed. If the relationship between her sister and Lord Hendricks proceeded as Grace thought it would, that would negate the most important reason for continuing the facade of an engagement.

Her own reputation would have one blot on it, for no matter when she ended it, in a week or a month, she would be labeled a jilt. It was not a horrific stigma, particularly once she returned home. And home was where she wanted…needed to be respected.

Then there was Brandon, as she now thought of him. He had mentioned that it was very bad timing for him to cause a scandal, speaking of some interest that he and Lord Hendricks were a part of. Grace must make sure he came out of *this* relationship unscathed. There should be no consequence to the business he was involved in.

She had gotten them all into this by stepping in where she did not belong, and had agreed to the engagement to help lessen the potential damage to Lydia and Brandon. But now? It was no longer necessary, yet his family and hers were deeply invested in this relationship. And she was too attracted to a man she would certainly never marry, for he did not want it and she would never ask it of him. She must get them out of this before it got any worse, especially for her heart.

And beyond the worry that she would say or do the wrong thing, she had begun to hate London. Unfortunately, it was only Brandon that made life here bearable. The sameness of each day baffled her. Society had no desire other than going out day after day, night after night, seeing all the same people, gossiping about all the same tattle, over and over.

Of course, in her small community at home, everyone knew everyone else and people gossiped, but there was also work to be done each day. And because social events were few and far between, they were special.

For the most part, there was no giving back of any of what fortune had bestowed upon them. Grace had asked several people about charities or ladies' societies that she could join, and she was looked at as if she had two heads. It seemed these idle, rich Londoners had no time for such things.

For her part, that was going to change today. If she could not immediately remedy the situation with Brandon, which was heavy on her heart, she could be a pair of hands to help someone else and to serve God in some capacity.

After a little investigating, Grace had discovered the name of an orphanage. She hoped to go and volunteer some of her time there while she remained in London. Lydia was with Lord Hendricks and his mother, Aunt Aggie at a balloon ascension and Brandon was not scheduled to pick her up until five for a drive in the park. She truly wished to go by herself first, in any event. Should it be a place where she could be of help, she knew Lydia would wish to take part, as well, but first Grace must be certain it would be safe for her.

She came down the steps, pulling on her gloves as she greeted old Jamison. She wore a serviceable dark gray gown that was not in the latest fashion. She did not wish to go to an orphanage in opulence!

Jamison shuffled over to her as she stood next to Max. "May I ask where you are off to, my lady? Shall I call for the carriage?"

Grace sat down on the steps. "What do you think, Max? Do we tie up the carriage all afternoon at the orphanage? No, I do not think so, either. What if Lydia or Aunt Aggie need it when they get home?"

Turning to the butler, she said, "Jamison, Max and I agree, we will do the honorable thing and take a hackney. If you would call a footman to accompany me, that will do nicely."

Jamison tugged on the bellpull, mumbling about talking to old scraps of metal as if they were alive.

"It is too bad of you, Max. Why could you not be real?" Grace pouted, looking at her medieval knight. "You would rescue me from this predicament, wouldn't you?" While she waited for the footman and the hackney, she continued her imagined conversation. "You would be a hero and ride to this orphanage on Baxter Street and save all of the children, would you not, my Max? Maybe we would adopt them and give them full run of the estate, what do you think?"

Her thoughts suddenly turned inward and she was no longer in a frivolous state of mind. "Do you think God is punishing me, Max? I am about to fall in love with a man I never should have met, much less interfered with." It was the first time she'd admitted to herself that she could love a renowned rake.

Max stood tall and straight.

"Right you are, Max. God is not punishing me. But I am bearing the consequences of my choices. I interfered, I compounded the problem with a solution God would never countenance, and I let my enchanting rake...enchant me.

"I will fix it, have no fear. I know God's grace will sustain me. And I will go today and try to do His work instead of filling my remaining days here in mindless gaiety.

"But, Max, I fear I will miss my rake when all is done. I must prepare my heart for that."

The hackney finally arrived, and her footman handed her in and climbed on the box with the driver. When he gave him the address, the driver leaned over and said, "Don't think ye want yer lady goin' to that part of town, bloke. Ain't 'er type of Society if you get my meanin'."

The footman passed that information along to Lady Grace, but she would not be dissuaded.

As she looked out the window she began to notice real changes in the area the hackney was now passing through. How could such squalor exist only a few miles away from the pristine houses of the rich?

Adults and children seemed to be wandering aimlessly, not paying any attention to the muck and filth they walked in. Some men were drinking out of bottles on their doorsteps, shooing away little ones that asked for some. Grace shuddered. All her life she had dealt with the poor and sick. But they had been part of her "family"—her family's responsibility to the tenants on their estate. She had seen nothing like this. She finally had to put her handkerchief to her nose.

When the hackney stopped in front of the building that was supposed to be the orphanage, her thoughts of the area around it flew from her head. The building was nothing but a ruin, unpainted and in bad repair. It appeared that it stayed standing only because the buildings on either side were falling against it. Could someone actually house children here?

As the footman helped her from the hackney, she instructed him to return by four o'clock.

"If I might say so, miss, I don't think I should let you

go in there alone. The driver can wait a bit to be sure it's safe. I can pay him well enough."

"No, Ned, Jamison may have need of you. What harm could there be to me if a group of children live here? Besides, I sent a note ahead informing them I was coming, so they should be expecting me. Just be sure and be back by four, as I have an appointment with Lord Weston at five." She could see that he was torn, and smiled at him. "Go, go, all will be well."

As Grace walked up to the doorway, she tripped over broken bricks in the sidewalk. *I should have brought some paper with me to make a list of what is needed.* This place could use a complete transformation. She supposed a mental list would have to do.

When she knocked on the door she was met by a heavyset woman wearing a dirty apron and trying to put her unkempt hair into her cap. She smelled of onions and perspiration.

"Ye be Lady Endicott?" she asked. "How fine to 'ave ye visitin' our wee ones. They don't get many and they'll be mighty pleased, they will. I'm Mrs. Thatcher, the 'ousekeeper and cook, so I can be tellin' ye anythin' ye want to know."

Grace was led to a parlor of sorts, where she would have been afraid to sit on anything, as dirty as it was. "Ye just wait 'ere, my lady. I'll 'ave a few of the mites brought to ye over the tea tray."

The woman seemed affable, though coarse in appearance and manner, so Grace was determined to be friendly and personable. "That will not be necessary, Mrs. Thatcher. I thank you, though. I would rather go to where the children are. I wish to meet them and see in what manner I might be of help."

Mrs. Thatcher's expansive bosom visibly shook as she got more nervous. "I don't know yer ladyship. Mr. Brownlow, the caretaker, 'e ain't in until Thursday next, and 'e usually does that sort of thing. Maybe ye should come back then."

"My hackney is gone now," Grace stated. She could see that the woman was scared, and became worried about what she might see that would upset the house-keeper so much. Grace tried to calm her. "You will do fine, Mrs. Thatcher. I would just like to see the children."

"Well, they be in work period now, so's they're in the big room. Come this way."

Grace audibly gasped at the sight that greeted her. She guessed there were fifty children crammed into Mrs. Thatcher's "big" room. And there was no noise except what came from their work. They were mostly little girls, and the few that turned at the sound of the door opening were hollow-eyed and thin. So very thin. She swiped at the tears on her cheeks and walked down a row, lightly touching one on the head or one on the shoulder. On the whole, if they noticed, they gave no indication. Their vacant eyes remained on their work.

Oh, God, show me how to go on as I see Your children, the ones You loved having around You, suffer in this way. Where would You have me begin in a task this onerous?

Grace bent to speak to one tiny girl, embarrassed that she sniffled as she did so. These children should be the ones crying. "Hello, sweetheart, my name is Grace. What is yours?"

"Jane, miss," the child whispered simply.

"Speak up to the grand lady. Say 'yes ma'am.'" The housekeeper tsked. "I told ye they don't get many visitors, my lady."

Grace ignored the woman, who could watch and treat children this way. "Jane is a very pretty name," she said, smiling down at the little girl. "What is it that you are working on so very hard?"

The child did not answer, but Mrs. Thatcher did. "The little 'uns don't know, my lady, they—"

"Mrs. Thatcher, pray let the children speak to me as they will. I would know what they have to say."

The heavyset woman moved back a step, mumbling under her breath. Grace did not care one iota. She would continue to seek answers until she knew what to do. As she walked past a few of the children, she noticed that some were swimming in their clothes, while others had collars too tight and pant legs too short. And none of the clothes looked as if they had been washed recently, or maybe ever.

She could not break down here; she must be strong for these children. She stopped once again next to a very young girl. They were all so small it was difficult to guess their ages, but this one could not have been more than three or four, yet she was working as hard as all the others.

Grace knelt down beside her, no longer caring about dirtying her gown or her gloves. "Hello, darling. Can you tell me how old you are?"

Mrs. Thatcher started to speak, and Grace held up her hand to stop her. She put her finger under the little girl's chin to raise her face to her own. "Just tell me your name, little one. That will suffice for now."

"Jane," she whispered.

"Oh, there are two Janes. You must be very close friends."

The little girl then said, "Six."

Grace was very surprised. "Are you sure you are six, darling? That would be quite old," she said, smiling.

"Jane six."

"Very well, Mrs. Thatcher, explain this to me," she said, perilously near rudeness. "This little girl is no more six than I am."

The housekeeper was no longer so talkative.

"Very well, I'll go directly to Mr....Brownlow, did you say? Perhaps he does not know enough about what goes on here."

"Yes, 'e knows, my lady. I ain't takin' the blame for this. She means she's Jane number six."

This was too much. "Why is she Jane number six, Mrs. Thatcher? Do you have so many Janes then?"

"Many come 'ere not knowin' who they be, my lady. We can't think up new names for all of 'em."

Grace fought back tears again, but this time out of anger. "Little Jane, would you like to come outside and play with me?"

"They...they don't 'ave no time to play, yer ladyship, ma'am." The woman cleared her throat. "The shops keeps us supplied with jobs to keep 'em busy. These is the cobbler's shoes. The tykes learn trades, ye see."

"I will come visit you again, Jane," Grace said with her sweetest smile. Then she turned to the housekeeper, unable to hide the anger from her very soul. "I want a tour of this *hovel* from top to bottom. I want to see where these children sleep, bathe and eat. I want to see your kitchen and what they eat. And I want to meet all of the staff, if there is anyone here other than you."

Anyone who knew Grace would recognize the determination behind her demands and the trouble it meant. She certainly hoped it was conveyed to this woman, as well.

Chapter Ten

Brandon knocked on the door at three o'clock, hoping Grace would not mind that he was early. By Jove, he had missed her, and he could not remember when he had ever missed anyone! The oddest part was that they had seen each other at some point every day for the past week. But he felt as if he had to share her with the *ton.* He missed *her,* her wit, her smile when she tried not to, her conversation and those eyes that changed color with her mood and allowed him glimpses into her soul. Sometimes he would intentionally say something to provoke her just to see them flash!

The park would be much less crowded now and he was looking forward to two hours of unadulterated Grace.

Jamison slowly opened the door and allowed Lord Weston to enter. "We were not expecting you until five, my lord," he mumbled.

Brandon was beginning to like old Jamison. Grace had explained he had been with the family his whole life. They had talked to him of retirement with a pension that would allow him to live his life in relative ease, but as it had only caused a fierce tirade, and since they visited Town so seldom, he remained a fixture there.

"I know, old chap, I am very early. Dare I hope that Lady Grace is at home?"

"No she is not at home. And she is where she shouldn't be." The vehemence in the butler's voice shocked him; Brandon had never heard the retainer say so many words at one time or show such emotion.

"Her and that hunk of metal she calls Max, talking like it's an everyday thing. Then using footmen and hackneys, as if she does not have a maid and we don't have a carriage. I do not go for it, your lordship," Jamison exclaimed, completely confusing Brandon.

He did not like the sound of anything he had heard, but decided he would address the issues in order. "What has this got to do with Max?" he asked in the calmest voice he could conjure up.

"There is no use getting upset over it, your lordship, sir," Jamison mumbled, heading over to the suit of armor. He buffed a spot on Max's arm and wheezed in exhaustion. "Says *this* is her idea of the perfect man, the strong, silent type, she says. Been saying it since she was ten years old. Max just keeps his watch and listens to Lady Grace when she talks."

Brandon smiled deep inside as he pictured Grace talking to her knight in shining armor. He supposed nothing less would do for her. But what of the rest of the story?

"Jamison, what were you saying about footmen and hackneys? Is she not with Lady Lydia or her aunt?"

"No, your lordship. Miss Lydia is with that nice Lord Hendricks." The butler resumed his injured tone. "Mrs. Burstow is watching some foolish balloon. And Lady Grace takes it into her head to do her good deeds when there is no one here to accompany her. And she will not take the carriage because *Max* doesn't think it is honorable." Jamison was rambling and Brandon was getting worried.

"Are you telling me Lady Grace went somewhere alone in a hackney?"

"No, she took a footman, but she sent him back as soon as she got there. She said he was to pick her up again at four, as she had to meet you at five."

"Where did she go, man?" Brandon asked in a voice that was harsher than he meant it to be.

"To some orphanage. She ministers to everyone and no one takes care of her. She cannot stand to be idle, that one. And more people are better off because of it," he added.

Brandon nearly jumped out of his skin. "Some orphanage? What orphanage?"

Jamison almost fell over the deacon's bench at the noise reverberating around the hall.

"Jamison, most of them are mere hovels in shady back streets. If she is out there alone, she could be in danger." Blast! What had she done?

"I don't know if I caught the name. She told Max, not me," the usually stoic butler protested.

Brandon drew his hands through his hair, then grabbed the old retainer gently by the shoulders. "Can you summon the footman who accompanied her? I must know the address."

"I'm sorry, sir, he just left to go get her."

"Jamison, Max is not alive. I cannot ask him where she went. Please think, man. Think. She may be in real danger. Where did she tell you, I mean Max, that she was going?

"She shouldn't be in any danger, your lordship. She knows how to take care of herself."

Brandon was as frustrated as he had ever been in his life.

"I think she told Max someplace with a *B* in it. Brackett, mayhap?"

"Brackett, Brackett…*Baxter?* Jamison, could that have been what she said?" He gently shook the old man's shoulders to keep his attention.

"Yes, I think that may have been it."

Brandon wasted no more time. He grabbed his hat and gloves and ran back out the door, jumping into his curricle as fast as he could. What on earth was she about? Baxter Street Orphanage had the lowest reputation in London and was situated in the worst part of Town. How had she even heard about it? And what in blazes made her go there alone?

For the first time in a long time Brandon was really afraid. He gave orders to his groom to be quick.

This must be what Grace meant when she talked of being able to trust only one thing when there was no one or nothing else to trust. When you couldn't *do* anything. He had a tight grip on the reins through the busy London streets, but he was asking Grace's God to protect her.

* * *

Demanding paper and pencil, Grace had taken notes on every inch of the orphanage. She wiped back angry tears as she wrote, and berated Mrs. Thatcher. This was not an orphanage, it was a disgrace. Children were underfed and overworked. They lived in the most unsanitary conditions she had ever seen, could ever have imagined. And the filth and squalor made Grace physically and emotionally sick to her stomach. Her stables were cleaner than this house.

And those sad, vacant faces—faces she thought would haunt her dreams for the rest of her life.

God, please protect these children until I can see Your way to take care of it. Give me boldness to demand the cleanliness, nutrition and unconditional love that as Your children they deserve.

"I have seen quite enough, Mrs. Thatcher. You may tell Mr. Brownlow that I will be back next Thursday, and I will want to see the books, as well."

"We does our best, my lady, 'onest we does," cried Mrs. Thatcher into her dirty apron.

Grace could not even summon the energy to intimidate the woman. She was too brokenhearted. "You will do better from now on or you will be gone. Do you understand?" How could anyone treat other human beings this way? Her eyes filled with tears again as she turned away from the woman at the door. She must think. She must not let this overwhelm her to the point of distraction or inaction.

She would notify the authorities. She would find out who administered such places, and she would notify them. She would hound these rich Londoners to get this changed. If all the women she knew gave the price of even one of their gowns, those children would have decent food to eat for a year. If necessary, she would drag each of them here, to see the vileness only streets away from where they lived and languished. She would make every last one of them feel guilty.

But how could she possibly leave the children there now? They were so small. They were devoid of any emotion. Had they learned that from whoever put them there or had they become that way at the orphanage? Should she send for some things and stay with them until that horrid caretaker visited again?

She could get them bathed. She could cook; it would be a simple meal but it would be proper nourishment. She could take them out-of-doors. She shook her head as tears started anew. There was no fresh air anywhere near this house. Could she take a couple of them home with her now? She might be able to get the horror out of her mind if she thought she was at least helping a few. Yet how would she ever choose?

She would talk to her aunt when she got home. Aunt Aggie would know where to start with the ladies of the *ton*.

Having walked in circles outside the door, crying uncontrollably, Grace did not notice that the hackney was not waiting at the end of the walk. She looked at her watch and cried again in additional frustration. It was only three forty-five. She could *not* go into that house again when she could do nothing to make life better for those children. She took herself to the end of the walkway, now shivering from what she had seen, trying not to notice the children outside the orphanage running through the mire in the streets. On the way here, she'd thought those urchins were the most unfortunate souls she had ever seen. Now she knew the children inside deserved that title.

It wasn't until a man bumped into her, almost knocking her down, that she realized her mistake in waiting out-of-doors. "Well, what 'ave we 'ere, gents? Looks like a fish out o' water, don't it?"

There were three of them and she had to blot her tears with her handkerchief to see them. They were blocking her way back to the orphanage, but she was sure the hackney would be along any moment. *God, protect me from the evils of this place.*

They began to push her, one by one, knocking her against each other like balls on a billiard table. They smelled of liquor and spoke disgusting taunts as they toyed with her. She was more scared than she had ever been. Each time they pushed her the force was harder; as they slowly closed in, hands bruised her arms as they grabbed her again and again. She needed to do something before they completely cut off any line of escape she had. When the one who had been mocking and jeering pushed her again into the other two, she lowered her head and turned her shoulders to use the force with which they pushed her to divide them. Then she began to quickly walk away. There were many people outside who could help her once she was free of the men.

"Just leave me be," she shouted over her shoulder. "'Yea, though I walk through the valley of the shadow

of death, I will fear no evil, for Thou art with me…'"
She had to catch her breath and could not finish the verse.

The men overcame her easily.

"You jest com wif us and we'll treat you real nice. You give me that little purse you got there, we'll all go to 'arry's place and…get to know each ofer better."

Grace was too frightened to think. She lifted her skirts and began to run, knowing there was no way to handle all three of them. She screamed as she ran, calling for help from those lounging in doorways and sitting on stoops, but all they did was watch.

She knew her pursuers were gaining ground, and she tried to reach into her reticule as she ran. By not looking ahead of her, she found it quite a surprise when she collided with the body of a man, who put out his arms to steady her. She pummeled his chest, screaming, "Let me go, I am armed!"

She almost fell to her knees when she heard Brandon, *her* Brandon, say, "Go to my curricle, Grace, and take the horses' heads. My groom cannot come to me unless someone takes their reins."

"Oh, thank You, God," she cried, as she threw her arms around his middle. She heard the men stopping behind her and let go of him, but only to stand beside him.

"Well, well, a dandified gent," said the slimy man who had originally accosted her. "But I expect the gov'ner 'ere is carryin' quite a 'eavy purse 'imself. Could be our lucky day."

"I don't know about your lucky day," Brandon said, in a voice so devoid of emotion it scared even her. "But you will soon be meeting a heavy reckoning if you do not walk away. Now!"

One of the other two laughed. "'Ey, Burt, these two dainties think they can take on all free of us."

The next thing Grace knew, Brandon had grabbed the nearest ruffian's arm and bent it up behind his back, effectively turning the man to face his friends. It happened so fast, Grace was amazed.

"Perhaps," Brandon said, as he bent the attacker's arm a little higher, "you two would like to do your friend a favor and keep him from having his arm broken in several places. Turn around and walk away, and maybe, just maybe, you will come out of this without serious harm."

The man's scream as Brandon bent his arm farther startled Grace. "Do as 'e says. 'E's breakin' me arm!"

From behind his back, one of the other two men drew a knife and began to come slowly at Brandon and his captive. He kept tossing the blade back and forth between his hands as if he would strike at any moment. Grace heard Brandon's groom jump to the ground, but he could not leave the curricle knowing any noise might bolt the horses. She didn't know what to do, but she could not leave him as the man with the knife took a step closer.

"Very well," Brandon replied, "we'll do it your way."

Grace thought she actually heard the man's arm break as Brandon threw him to the side, ready now to face the knife-wielding one. She was shaking so hard and was so scared for Brandon she almost forgot her reticule. But she reached in and pulled out the small palm pistol her father had taught her to shoot, and told her always to carry. With shaking hands she aimed it at the man with the knife.

"You st-stay th-there," she said, trying to sound brave, but stuttering to get the words out. She pointed a pistol at the thug's chest. The third man took off running, as the original attacker lay moaning on the street. Grace noticed that those who had been previously oblivious to her trouble now came closer to watch the show being played out before them. Was this type of thing all the entertainment they received in their dreadful lives? Was this who those little children in the orphanage would grow up to be?

Grace returned her attention to the man with the knife. She thought she saw fear in his eyes as he watched her warily.

"Ain't no woman gonna shoot a man. And even if she did," he sneered, "she'd miss by a mile and I'd 'ave you both at me mercy." His looks belied his words. He was worried. She tried to steady her hands. "Ye know that as well as I does, guv'ner."

Brandon crossed his arms over his chest. "To be honest, I don't know how good a shot she is, but I have the feeling if you threaten someone she loves, she's going to attack. As she is betrothed to me, I believe I would qualify." He stopped, as if thinking for a minute. "And even if she did not *kill* you, she would probably hit enough of you to make it painful for you to take on the three of us. Now, what will it be?"

The knife dropped to the ground and the attacker took off, leaving his injured friend to fend for himself.

* * *

Brandon turned and reached for her. He got his first good look at her face and was immediately sorry he had let any of them go. He pried her fingers from around the gun. "Is it loaded, Grace?" At the nod of her head he cursed under his breath. She could have been terribly hurt…or worse.

"Perhaps you feel more inclined to get into the curricle now?"

Grace did not say a word. He thought she might be in shock, until he turned her to face him. She seemed to come to herself, and laid her forehead against his chest. Somehow that simple gesture touched him more than words could have.

"I thought he was going to kill you with that knife, and the fault would have been entirely mine." She shifted a little so that her cheek was resting on his coat. "What an awful day this has been." She started to cry as she grabbed his lapels. "All those poor children."

He had never seen her upset like this. She was always a pillar of strength. Her terror must have been great. But she had not mentioned that; she only spoke of worrying for him and the children. He led her, sniffling, to his curricle, just as the hackney pulled up.

The footman jumped down, greatly agitated. "Where did you get to, my lady? Why didn't you remain at the orphanage? I've been that scared. I knew I should have stayed with you."

Brandon paid off the hackney driver and sent the footman home with him. Grace sat in his curricle, tears rolling down her cheeks, silent and remote. He would take her someplace where she could recover her poise. Hyde Park was out of the question. He opted for the smaller Green Park. It was much less traveled, especially this early, and he hoped he could soothe her wounded sensibilities.

Once he did, he was going to kill her!

She had worried him out of ten years of his life on that curricle race to Baxter Street. Once she calmed, he was going to make his feelings known to her about women who wandered around the seediest parts of London unescorted.

Traffic kept him from watching her closely, but he knew she was still crying, albeit silently. When he handed her his handkerchief she apologized. "I am so sorry."

They reached the park and he asked if she felt up to walking a short distance to a bench by some trees. She nodded. He asked his groom to walk the horses until they were needed again.

When they sat down on the bench, he took her hand soothingly into his. He tried to make her look at him. "Feeling better now?"

"Yes, thank you." But her shivering told a different tale. "If one of those men had hurt you because of me, I would never have been able to live with myself."

He finally began to understand her, and his anger began to burn anew. "Are you telling me, *can* you be telling me you were worried about *me* and not yourself?"

"Me?" She looked up at him for the first time, surprised. "Of course I was not worried about myself. I worried that if I did not kill him outright he would still be able to hurt you with the knife."

"If you were not worried about yourself, why were you running when I found you?" he asked between clenched teeth.

"I had my pistol, but it was in my reticule. I had to run to get the time to pull it out. When they were surrounding me, they might have taken my purse and the gun with it, so I took off, looking for a place where I had the advantage. I prayed all the while. And God answered with you."

His expression darkened further still.

"What is it? Brandon, are you angry with *me?*"

"Am I angry with…" Shaking his head, he jumped to his feet and began to pace. "You little fool, anger does not even begin to do justice to what I feel at this moment."

"But—" She got no further.

"Say no more." He enunciated each word. "I went to your house early, hoping we might be able to go for a drive when the park was not so congested. What do I find? That lame excuse for a butler muttering about you going off alone, with only a suit of armor knowing your exact location." He was trying very hard to rein in his temper.

"If it had taken me five more minutes to get out of your butler where he *thought* you told Max you were going, you could be dead now…or worse." He sat back down, grabbed her shoulders hard and turned her toward him. "They would have robbed you, at a minimum. You are old enough to understand what else they might have done to you, Grace. You cannot think it something to take lightly."

"Of course not! I was so thankful when I heard your voice. But the man with the knife could have hurt you."

"Arghh," Brandon roared in frustration, jumping to his feet again. "I do not want your thanks! I want you to realize what almost happened to *you,* so you never do such a cork-brained thing again."

"Please sit down. I cannot think. I do not wish to think anymore."

"Blast!" was all he could say. How could he get through to her? "Grace, London is dangerous for a woman alone in the *best* part of Town. But in the place you were today, your life was not worth anything more than the contents of your purse. You risked your life for that today. Not mine, *yours.* You see, *I* could have handled all three of them, knives or not. My groom was with me. You did nothing but risk yourself, and the anguish it would have caused everyone who loves you."

His anger was spent at his final words, and surprise took over. *He* was one of those who had come to care about her; he realized that was why he was so angry.

She got up from the bench and turned away from him. He went to her, turned her around and gently pulled her to his chest, surrounding her with his arms. He could have lost her.

"Brandon, I am sorry that I put you through this. You are absolutely right. I had no guarantee I could have escaped those men." She started to cry again.

He held her tighter for a minute, surprised she did not put up more of a fight. He finally put her a little away from him, and then whistled for his groom to return with the curricle.

Once they were seated, he dismissed the groom, knowing propriety was the least of his worries. When they were alone, he began a slow walk with his horses and asked the question that had been burning in him all afternoon. "Why did you go there, Grace? How did you even know about that particular place?"

She kept looking straight ahead, too ashamed now after his harsh words to meet his eyes and see what he must think of her. She answered softly, "Since coming to London, I have sought information from the ladies I have met as to how they help the less fortunate. Most of the time I just received blank stares, but occasionally someone would say they gave to an orphanage fund, but they really had no time to help."

"I am not surprised," he muttered.

"Finally, I heard someone mention the orphanage on Baxter Street. I do not remember who. As it was the only name I received, I thought to offer my services there once a week while I remained in London." She began to cry again, sobs coming from deep inside. He had never heard such heart-wrenching torment. He pulled the curricle to the side of the path and stopped.

"Tell me about it, Grace. What happened there?"

She put her face in her hands, her head bowed over her lap. "It was so terrible. I know it will haunt me until I die." She wiped her cheeks. "I will not go there alone again, I promise. But something must be done for those children and I intend to do it."

He could barely understand her as he listened to her

recount her visit. Her usually soothing voice came out
hoarse and raspy through her tears. "The food they feed
these little children was rancid. They get no baths. Why
should they, when the housekeeper obviously has not
had one in recent memory? They did not understand
me when I asked them where they played. Oh, how God
must cry over the horror." She blew her nose, but the
tears ran down her cheeks as she sat up straight. Her
voice was barely a whisper and he knew she was seeing it all over again.

"They work all day, no matter how little they are or
what condition their health is in. One three-year-old girl
had needle imprints in her fingers from sewing the soles
of shoes. I cannot even fathom it—three years old!"

She cried quietly until he thought her heart would
break. "I asked one little girl her name and it was Jane
number six. Brandon, they have numbers. I could not
bear it. I wanted to gather them all to me and wait for
carriages to take them home to the Abbey." She tried to
staunch the tears. "Don't you see, Brandon? There but
for the grace of God go I or you, or any one of us. Why
was I born into a family that could provide for me, and
those children into a world so very dark?" She answered
her own question. "Because I can do something about it.
I can take them all to the Abbey if I cannot do something
here." She finished defiantly, "But I am going to try."

"Something *is* being done, Grace," Brandon said quietly. She turned to look at him, and reached up to touch
the tic in his jaw.

"I need to show you something," was all he said as
he guided his horses back onto the path.

They rode in silence for a while, both deep in thought. His were tumultuous. What kind of woman was she? There was no other female of his acquaintance who would have worried about charity work. Was this second nature to her? Or was this from her God? He needed to learn more. He had known from the beginning that she was different, but with each passing day his pride in her grew to new heights. And she had gathered more information about Baxter orphanage than he or Dennis ever could have!

Gads! The woman had stood by his side in the shabbiest part of Town, threatening to shoot someone who might hurt *him*. Most *men* would be shaking in their boots in that situation. And when it was all over and he had vented his spleen on her, she had apologized and appreciated his plain speaking.

He had never told anyone about the place they were going, except Dennis and Lord Langdon, but he knew he could trust her. And he knew what she needed to see if she was to get the picture of what she had witnessed out of her head.

They left the park and travelled to the business district. Vendors hawked their wares loudly. Once through the busy throng, the noise began to subside a bit and quiet storefronts lined the street. Brandon went one or two blocks beyond and pulled up to a large building with a fresh coat of paint. She looked at him with questions in her sad green eyes, but he stayed silent as he handed her down and proceeded toward the front door.

Of a sudden, a side door opened and children of all ages, shapes and sizes rushed outside and began to laugh and throw balls and chatter loudly. The front door opened as Grace turned to look at him, and a buxom woman of indeterminate years stepped back in surprise.

"Lord Weston! We weren't expectin' to see you today," she said as she smiled warmly. "The children will be a mite glad, they will."

"Mrs. Dickerson, I would like you to meet my betrothed, Lady Grace Endicott. I believe she wishes to volunteer to help, if you can use another pair of hands."

He was thankful and proud of Mrs. Dickerson's reaction. She beamed at Grace. "Come in, come in, my manners have gone abeggin', they 'ave. I can just send for tea and your lordship can look at the books and the lesson plans while we wait 'ere in the parlor."

"That will not be necessary, but I thank you," Brandon told her. "I just wanted to introduce you to Lady Grace today and then I think she would like to make arrangements, say next Tuesday—" he looked toward Grace to be sure that was acceptable to her "—to come and meet the children and perhaps set up a schedule to help you."

"Saints preserve us, your lordship, we can use as many 'ands as we can get! We got three new little ones in yesterday alone! Thank you, my lady, I will look forward to it."

"I will, t-too," Grace stuttered, as she tried to absorb all that was happening.

They took their leave, and after a few minutes, Brandon spoke. "Grace, Dennis's older brother and I committed ourselves years ago to attempt to be productive in one area of our lives. I certainly was not in any other. We both had an interest in workhouses and orphanages.

When David was killed, Dennis took his place in the venture, and this is the third orphanage we have been able to get renovated and reorganized."

She did not interject, so he kept on. "After the first one, we realized we needed more help, from higher places, shall we say. We wanted to be sure the previous owners were prosecuted, or at least put in debtors' prison until they repaid the money they basically stole from the mouths of the children." His anger was rekindled as he thought of the struggle it had been to make a judge see the wrong being perpetrated on defenseless children.

"We were approached by Lord Langdon. I believe I mentioned him to you when we were making our plans for London. He is a respected and active member of Parliament and could be our voice in legislative change, as well as in the legal arena. He agreed to assist us on the condition that we curtail our more ribald behavior.

"These children are taught trades, as well," he continued. "If they do not get adopted, then they can still be useful members of society when they are old enough. But they get good food, exercise and learn to read and write."

She still did not speak, but looked at him as if he were a total stranger. Gazing at him with admiration that he knew he did not merit.

"Grace, do not put me on some stupid pedestal," he said harshly. "It will only topple tomorrow."

Chapter Eleven

"*You* did all of this?" she asked in wonder. "You make people believe you are hard and unfeeling, and *you* did all of this." She could not stop saying it. *This* was the man she had always wished to know. This was a real-life Max who would fight wrong and change history.

"Do not get sentimental over this, Grace. It is an investment that also pays monetary dividends. The local businesses that teach the children trades pay for this service, unlike the one on Baxter Street. If they end up apprenticing a child, they pay again, because they know they will be getting a healthy, well-schooled employee."

"And where does that money go?"

He hemmed and hawed, saying that *most* of it went back into the orphanage, but that he and Lord Hendricks were compensated enough.

He could talk about financial gain all he wanted, but she knew the truth now. The label of rake had been thrown on him when he'd made that disastrous decision to help someone unworthy of his help, and subsequently had decided to live up to it for all he was worth. But he was the furthest thing imaginable from a libertine.

Since she had met him, she had seen nothing but honorable things from Brandon Roth. She would not have agreed to their venture otherwise. And now this. His dissolution was all a facade, and the truth never became known because nobody took the time to look deeper. They liked having this handsome rebel in their midst. They wanted a wicked marquess, not one who saved children. There was no food for gossip in that!

She saw him through new eyes, and realized it was more important than ever that they break their connection soon. If she found out any more about him, she would not want to let him go. She could scarcely think of it already.

But no matter what she quietly wished for herself, she knew he still did not want marriage.

She listened as he spoke about the financial rewards, struggling to make himself sound less philanthropic. "Baxter Street has been in our sights for several months," he explained. "But Brownlow is sleazier than most. You may rest easy, love, those children will be returned to healthy and happy states as soon as Dennis and I can arrange it."

She turned and smiled at him, tears of joy now filling her eyes. "Thank you so very much. Thank you for everything today. What I thought was one of the worst days of my life has now turned into one of the most special ones—all because of you." He began coming up with more excuses, so she interrupted him. "Tell me how I may help."

"Grace," he said, the firmness of his tone telling her to listen closely. "I understand your desire to help, and giving Mrs. Dickerson a hand will be a great start for now. You can do nothing at Baxter until Dennis and I have done our parts. You will need to be satisfied with that.

"No, do not rip up at me. I promise as soon as we have taken over Baxter, you may work to your heart's content. We have already begun renovation on the new building where the children will be housed. But until then, it is not safe for you there. Especially now that Brownlow knows you are looking at his operation. All he has to do is hire someone to make sure you never tell anyone…ever. And after today, I know of three angry men who would probably do the job for free." He paused for effect. "I may not always be able to save you."

He went on. "Brownlow does not know about Dennis and me, so you see, you could even jeopardize our work if you do anything else there now."

"But Brandon, I will not be in London that much longer. I wish to see those children smile."

Her heart was heavy as she thought of leaving him, while knowing it must come, and soon.

"Do not be silly. We should have something accomplished there by the end of the Season."

She did not argue with him. She would accept that he would take care of those children, as he had the others.

"Grace?"

"Hmm?"

"Grace, pay attention to me." Her mind had wandered. "I need two promises from you, and if I do not get them, I will send you packing. You'll be on your way home tomorrow."

She thought about withholding her promise. It would be so much easier to go home before she found out more things to like about him.

But she just smiled. "That is no threat to me. Only recall, home is where I wish to be."

He would not be teased. "This is not a jest, Grace. The orphanages are a private business matter. Lord Langdon and Dennis are the only others privy to what I have told you today. I will allow you to volunteer with Mrs. Dickerson, but only escorted by me or someone of my choosing. I allowed you to know about this place and my business here because I trust you. That is the only reason."

Her thoughts were too jumbled to rein in.

"Should it be discovered that Dennis and I are involved in this, it could undo all that we have accomplished. Do you understand what I am saying, Grace? You may not even tell Lydia. If Dennis has not told her, you must not, either."

"Another secret, my lord?" she asked him, quietly, with no real anger in her tone. She did not wish to upset him any more. "I will tell no one. I do want to help, however."

"Then we understand each other."

He was not finished. "However, I require one other promise." She knew what was coming. And before today, she would have put up a fight over his demands. But she felt as if she truly knew him now.

"You must also promise me that you will never again

do what you did today, going off unescorted and informing no one other than *Max* of your destination." He turned icy dark eyes on her. "I want your word on this. I will not dissemble. Do you not see that if you had come to me in the first place all of this could have been avoided? I would have taken you directly to Mrs. Dickerson, and there would have been no attempt to take your life." His frustration was palpable. "If you want to go somewhere or know something, I would be the logical person to ask, as I have been here in Town longer than most. Do you understand, Grace?"

They turned onto Berkeley Square. She felt as if she had been away from the town house for weeks. "Do not rip up at me. I will come to you if I should need help."

"No, Grace. You will not leave this curricle until I have your promise that if I cannot escort you somewhere—which you will ascertain by asking me first, and not by simply assuming I am occupied—you will always take at least one footman with you, and permit him to *stay* with you, instead of sending him home. And you will inform your household where you have gone."

She tried not to be, but she was finally irritated. "I have no wish to drag you around with me every time I go out-of-doors, and indeed, you would quite soon tire of it. You have no idea how many times I go out or how many places I go, and it would become quite irksome for both of us if you did."

She gave up the fight at last, but behaved badly in doing it. "Very well, I will either invite you or send a courier to your club, letting you know where I am going, each time I go out. You will become the laughingstock of all your friends."

"Grace," was all he said.

They were both emotionally spent, and she apologized.

"I am beginning to believe the gentlemen from Essex are not the nodcocks I originally presumed. Perhaps they simply knew themselves insufficient to the task of keeping up with you." They pulled up in front of her house. "Friends, again?" he inquired as he put his hands on her waist to lift her down.

As she straightened her gown, she muttered, "I pity the woman you actually do wed. One moment you will berate her as you would a child, and the next you will expect all to be forgotten."

He laughed and gently touched her cheek. As she started to turn to go into the house, he held her there with his hands on her waist. "You forget, my sweet, that I have several other excellent qualities besides those two."

She couldn't resist. She laughed at his words.

"Grace, look at me."

She was uncomfortable standing on the street this long with him holding her, but she obeyed.

"I am loath to bring it up, because I am quite sure you did it unconsciously, but you called me Brandon today. Several times, in fact."

A surprised flush crept up her cheeks. "I certainly did not."

Oh, my! She had! She had been thinking of him as Brandon for weeks now. She decided to ignore it, and stepped from his grasp.

As he entered his vehicle and she began to mount the steps, he called to her. "Do not think I am done with you, love. We will also need to discuss the little matter of carrying a loaded gun with you everywhere you go."

She just smiled and began to hum her favorite song as she went into the house. She stopped beside Max and stared at him. As she slowly began her ascent to her room, a sad thought came to her. *I have found my living knight in shining armor, only he will never be mine.*

The very next day Brandon sent a message to Grace asking if she would join him on a morning call. After the previous day's debacle, he'd determined it was time to introduce her to Lord Langdon. Brandon knew his lordship had been waiting for such an introduction.

When he told her where they were going, she looked at him with wide eyes. "What a horrid man you are!"

"My, my, yesterday I was a paragon. You know, we really should have kept that list we started at the Blue Swan. You might see that my good characteristics balance out the bad."

She looked up at him from under the brim of her hat. She was not smiling.

"What have I done now?"

"You could have warned me. I would have taken more care with my gown and my hair. I would have—"

"You are perfectly well aware that you look lovely, and if I did not make that plain to you when I first saw you this morning, then I *am* a horrid man. There, you got the compliment you were fishing for!" He looked over at her and winked. "Minx!"

An uncomfortable silence fell for a moment and he wondered what was going on in that pretty head of hers.

"Brandon?"

"Yes, love?"

"What is the impetus behind helping the orphaned children? You made it clear yesterday that you receive financial reward, which is the obvious answer as to how you afford your horses."

"Sarcasm, what I enjoy most in you," he mumbled.

She glared at him and went on as if he had not interrupted her. "What motivated you to take on such a task?"

His instincts suggested she was looking for more ways to compliment him on his good deeds, so he deliberately answered her provocatively. "Trying to work my way into heaven, of course."

She put her hand on his arm and turned to face him. "You are teasing me, are you not?"

"Afraid not. With my history, it will take until I am—" he pretended to calculate in his mind "—one and seventy years to break even."

She did not laugh. "Please tell me you do not really believe that."

"I may be off by a few years, but not many."

"Brandon, be serious."

"I am afraid to. You are going to try to convert me to something or another."

"Sorry," she said, as she put her hands in her lap.

"Grace, petulance is very overrated." She did not laugh at that, either. "Very well. Of course, I do not believe that. But you know of my sins. If heaven exists there is no place for one such as me."

"Have you ever heard the saying, 'Grace is getting something we do *not* deserve and mercy is not getting what we *do* deserve?'"

"No, but I expect you are about to explain it to me."

"I know I will be in heaven, you see."

"I know you will be, too."

"Why is that?

"Your whole life has been nothing but doing good. Who could doubt it?"

"We do not get to heaven based on our works. Because heaven is perfect, even one mistake keeps us out."

"Then no one would get there."

"That is the point! '…but where sin abounded, grace did much more abound.' Because of God's grace, our sins don't have to keep us from heaven. His unmerited favor provides a way for us to get there that has nothing to do with how much we do…good or bad."

"What about 'we reap what we sow'?"

"There *are* consequences to our choices made here, but it does not have to affect our standing with God."

"Grace, this is obviously very important to you, and because it is, I will gladly hear it. But I can deduce that this discussion may take more than the time we have left before we reach Lord Langdon's house. I promise I will give you another opportunity to save my soul, but may we schedule it for when we have more time?"

"Of course, Brandon." She did not pout or put on a disappointed air. He was a little surprised, but he often was when he was with her.

"Tell me what I should know about Lord Langdon before I meet him. Will I like him?"

"I think I shall let you decide for yourself whether you like him or not, but I must remind you that he believes us engaged, *as do I, my love,* and it will not do to cause him unnecessary pain by alluding to it any differently." He thought she was going to speak, but apparently she changed her mind.

"He plays the most important role in our endeavors with the orphanages. Our efforts affected little before he became our mouthpiece in Parliament." He wished to tell Grace that his lordship was much more to him than that, but that relationship was separate, too personal, and he was not yet ready to share it.

They entered Lord Langdon's morning room, where their host awaited them eagerly. He greeted Brandon with a handshake that turned into a bear hug with a slap on his back. At one time Brandon would have been embarrassed by that, but not now and not with Grace present.

"My lord, may I introduce you to my betrothed, Lady Grace Endicott." He brought her forward with a hand at her waist and Lord Langdon took her hand into both of his.

"I am delighted to make your acquaintance, my lady," he said, with an aside to Brandon, "at last."

Brandon laughed outright. "Once you hear all that she has been up to of late, you will soon understand the delay."

"My lord, I am very glad to meet you, as well. Can I convince you to call me Grace, sir? I assure you I answer more readily to it." Brandon thought her smile could charm the spots off of a leopard. "Unlike you, I have only known about you for a short period of time, but I am no less pleased."

"Tell me, young lady, have you and Brandon set a date as of yet? I own it will break the hearts of many who have had their sights set on this rake." Langdon leaned in a little closer and said, "Though I suspect we both know that it is nothing but a front. He thinks it makes him more dashing."

Grace laughed in pure pleasure. "After yesterday, my lord, I am quite at a loss as to how he keeps it up." She began to tap her chin with one finger. "I suppose one kiss of the hand or a well-turned compliment *could* keep up the pretense, and he is certainly not stingy with either. Yet there must be *something* else that makes him notorious. I suppose I must study the beast a bit more in his own habitat!" The twinkle in her green eyes made both of them laugh.

Brandon noticed she completely ignored the question about the wedding date, and he was proud of her. "Very well, you two, you have had enough pleasure at my expense," he interjected. "You both already know me, and I wish you to know each other."

"I own I am quite at a loss over the pointed remarks about the event of yesterday. Am I to be informed or shall I hazard a guess, my boy?"

Brandon noticed the surprise on Grace's face at Lord Langdon's informal address. "Sir, I believe you will be shocked to hear that Grace, completely alone and without anyone's foreknowledge, visited the orphanage on Baxter Street."

"What?" the elderly man exclaimed, one of the only times Brandon had ever heard him speak in anything but a calm manner.

"My sentiments exactly, my lord. And as you know, I had not as yet shared word of our endeavors previous to her visit."

Brandon knew his lordship's interest in Grace would now become eminently more serious. "Am I ever to be told the circumstances surrounding this astounding information, or was this recounted solely to remove several years from my life?"

Brandon began to speak. "You will not credit it, I know, but—"

Lord Langdon stopped him with a raised hand. "Son, do you mind if I hear it from the lady? Should you tell it, I would no doubt get your feelings on the matter at each detail, and I believe I can imagine *them* on my own!" He smiled to remove the sting.

Then he turned to Grace. He led her to a sofa covered in blue brocade and sat down beside her. "May I ask you first, my dear, why you sought the orphanage out?"

She hesitated and Brandon wondered why.

"My lord, God tells us to love one another, but He specifically tells us to take care of widows and orphans."

Brandon held his breath. He had forgotten to warn her about the openness she had about her faith.

"Since coming to London, I was reminded of the Season when I came out. The elegance and opulence awed me then. This time, I am wiser and a little grieved at the money we spend, no, *waste* every day on things that really do not matter, not to mention the time devoted to frivolous concerns that benefit no one. I made a vow to myself that on this visit I would give back in some way, make better use of my time and money. My sister and I started a very, *very* modest home for orphans in our county who lost fathers in the war. So it is what I knew."

Lord Langdon stared at her intensely and Brandon, though wishing she had not brought God into it, prepared himself to do battle on her behalf.

It was not necessary.

"My dear girl, God must have smiled at your actions."

Brandon was taken aback. He had never seen his friend so touched before. He reached over and grasped her hand, speaking soft words of wonder from his heart.

Brandon had seen small indications of a spiritual side to the man, but his lordship seemed so much more touched by what Grace had told him. How prevalent was this idea of living your life for an all-powerful God?

He was brought back to the conversation at hand. "No, my lord, nothing about that place brought glory to Him. Indeed, it only emphasized the degradation we can fall into if left to our own devices."

"How very true, my child. I hope Brandon was able to relieve your fears on that score."

"Oh, yes, my lord. I left there with such feelings of despair, but when he took me to Mrs. Dickerson…"

Brandon watched her as she relived her experience

of the day before. This time his anger and worry were gone and he actually *heard* her. There was such an intimate understanding between them as they talked.

She radiated graciousness and *gracefulness*. He had thought her name a little old-fashioned upon first learning it, but he now associated it with the person that she was, not what she was called.

It was the first time Brandon had simply watched her for any length of time, and he was riveted. He heard her careful retelling of the story, but he *saw* a depth to her caring that she attributed to her God. And Lord Langdon understood her completely. This visit had given him much to think about.

His thoughts changed as they shot him a sideways glance. She was now telling about their incredulous run-in with the three miscreants. Miscreants? How could she use that word for men who were nothing but thatch-gallows and would have killed them without a second thought? Ah! She was making fun of herself, and Lord Langdon appreciated her descriptiveness. When she began to make fun of *him*, the two laughed themselves almost to tears. He was again filled with pride for her.

"More fun at my expense. I would not wish to give you both set-downs."

"I say we let him try, my lady," Langdon murmured. The pair gazed at him innocently.

"Perhaps his lordship would like to hear the truth now?" Brandon looked at them with one eyebrow raised. "I noticed she did not include any details about her conversations with suits of armor or deaf butlers."

"No, indeed she did not," Langdon said with an endearing smile and gentle tone. "One day, Brandon, when I am dandling your firstborn on my knee, I shall ask you for your version of the tale."

Grace's brows furrowed for a moment and he feared she would lose her composure. But though she blushed, she smiled and said, "My lord, I believe you must ask him sooner than that or the story will have been embellished to the point where there were a dozen attackers and I not even present!"

Very soon after, they took their leave, and Brandon did not miss the message in Lord Langdon's eyes that they had much to talk about. He kissed Grace's hand and sincerely asked her to come and visit him again.

"My lord, you have been most gracious and I shall look forward to our next meeting." She shyly brought her other hand up to hold his with both of hers. "God bless you, sir, for what you are doing for those little ones." With glowing eyes, she added, "That you all give so much without the least desire for accolades speaks more highly of you than any words I can express."

As Brandon drove Grace back to her home, there was an easy silence between them. For a while she hummed the song Lydia had given him the name of. He could not remember it, but he was beginning to like it. As he lifted her down, he said, quietly, "Thank you, Grace."

"Whatever for, my lord?"

"For being who you are. I know of no other woman of my acquaintance, and very few men, I would have taken to meet Lord Langdon. You captivated him, as you captivated me on *our* first meeting!"

"I will remind you that you disliked me intensely at

our first meeting, but I liked him so very much. Truth be told, much more than I liked you at first."

She smiled at him with an ease he was glad they had reached, and he kissed her hand as he said, "Impudent minx!"

"I am very glad to know that when I am back at the Abbey, you will have such a man in your life. You deserve the respect and admiration he has for you."

She twisted away and ran up the stairs, past Jamison, before he could say anything further.

Back at the Abbey? For some reason, those words ruined what had been a wonderful day.

Chapter Twelve

The two weeks that followed were both a boon and a penance to Grace's soul. She stored in her mind each drive, each dance, each shared look and wonderful moment of laughter with Brandon, to call upon when her future seemed lonely. The time had come to end the betrothal; she had fallen in love with Brandon Roth.

She had finally met the equivalent of Max, in the flesh. The man she could actually marry. What was worse, she was betrothed to him, but could never marry him. And what seemed so strange was that should she decide she did not want to go home, he would keep his word and marry her. It was the first time she really understood what he meant each time he told her not to worry about her conscience, they *were* betrothed.

But she would not do that.

His reputation mattered not; she knew the man he was inside. She did not care that he snubbed his nose at Society, because she had come to see that they expected it of him—and she was not at all convinced that

Society truly deserved him. She had found a man she respected, trusted and loved more than she thought she could ever love any man, and she had to leave before her heart broke completely.

But each time she tried to broach the subject; he brushed it aside or told her they should hold off until after Lydia's ball. Therefore, Grace tucked away each memory for safekeeping.

They spent considerable time with Lydia and Lord Hendricks. Grace's prayers for her sister had been answered. Her suitor loved her so much and she positively glowed in response to it. Grace would not have thought it possible that Lydia could be more beautiful, but love matured her. She was not a shy chit just out of the schoolroom any longer; she was a confident young woman knowing her future promised the realization of her dreams. And though it was everything she had ever wanted for her sweet sister, sometimes it was hard to watch, because now *she* knew how it felt.

There was little time to dwell on it and for that she was thankful. The ball for Lydia was only days away and there always seemed to be something to do. Aunt Aggie could not contain her joy when Lord Hendricks requested permission to write to Lord Pennington. It would no longer just be a come-out ball; it would be a betrothal ball, for *both* her nieces! She predicted it would go down in history as the Season her girls caught two of London's most eligible bachelors. What a coup! Grace hated that she would not actually see that come to fruition.

So she accepted Brandon's request to postpone the

demise of their engagement, if only to allow Aunt Aggie joy for the nonce. But as the ball drew nearer, Grace dreaded it more and more. She was on edge, anxious and more than a little overwrought. They would officially announce *her* betrothal, as well, never knowing it was set to be dissolved very soon. And while she wanted the engagement to end, she knew it meant her time with Brandon would be over.

When the night of the ball arrived, Grace stared at herself in the mirror and wondered what Brandon would think of her. There was no getting around it; everything seemed to revolve around his opinion. She had never worried about such nonsense before, and it rankled a little. Regardless, it was important to her that on one of the last nights he would ever see her, she might one day be a sweet memory to him.

She wore a green silk gown, happy that her age permitted the color. She worried a little that even at her age *this* green might be a little beyond the pale. The waist was Empire, the accepted norm now, but there was nothing ordinary about the dress. It had long sleeves and the square cut bodice was perhaps a little lower than she was accustomed to, but nothing compared to those of others she saw every night at every event they attended.

The overdress was a sheer green gauze with sparkling emeraldlike stones haphazardly strewn, as if the modiste had let them slip through her fingers and then attached them where they landed. The effect was what had drawn Grace to the gown. Since the stones were the same color as the underdress, they were barely noticeable until she moved. Between the silk below and the gems atop, shards of green reflected the candle-light, rendering an effect that was both surprising and graceful.

That was her hope, at any rate. The gown was of a simple style and she was afraid it would not look to others as it did to her. She worried that it would not impress anyone, much less Brandon.

She tied up her hair with a green velvet ribbon and let the length fall in a cascade of curls at the back of her head. She wore only a single strand of pearls and decided she would be happy with the result. She would not begin to be taken in by this modern day Babylon. She would appreciate what she had.

As the ladies gathered in the drawing room, waiting for Brandon to arrive, Aunt Aggie's spirits were high, Lydia seemed thoughtful and Grace felt agitated. She could not shake the myriad of emotions plaguing her.

"Must we do this, Aunt?" she asked quietly.

"Yes, my dear."

"But the betrothal is so widely known, it will seem like we are seeking attention. And I do not wish to infringe on Lydia's special night."

"Oh, Grace!" Lydia cried. "*Infringe?* What a horrid word. I wish to *share* the night with you!"

"I vow no one will ever be able to top this night!" Aunt Aggie exclaimed in anticipation.

With those words, the door to the drawing room opened and Grace turned her head, expecting Lord Weston's arrival. The surprise that met her eyes, however, made her cry out in shock, "Father!"

"Father, what on earth are you doing here? We had

no idea of your coming," Lydia said, running to put her arms around his neck.

"By all that's incredible, you *should* have expected it. I may not find the same allure in London that everyone else does, but it would seem rather shabby did I not show up for my own daughters' betrothal ball." He walked farther into the room. "You could have knocked me over with a feather after receiving two requests for permission to marry my daughters. Of course I am come." He sat down next to Grace on the sofa. "Max looks pretty good still, what?"

"Well, well, well," her aunt said, stepping forward with her arms akimbo, "Robert Endicott finally doing the right thing by his daughters. Will wonders never cease?"

As the two of them started one of their time-honored battles, Grace went to sit beside Lydia. "You *do* realize I am seriously in the suds now?"

"Oh, Grace, I think it is wonderful that Father is here."

"Have you forgotten?" Grace asked, looking over her shoulder. "There are many who surmise I met Brandon through their shared interest in two-hundred-year-old artifacts. As he reminds me daily, they *are* both interested in history, but most people will assume they have met!"

"Grace, with all the excitement, might it go unnoticed?"

There was a short knock on the door, then Jamison entered and announced Lord Weston in a stately manner. The butler could also be heard muttering about certain people appearing without his knowledge, and that he didn't think he could abide two people talking to a piece of armor as if it were real.

"Excuse me, Father, Aunt Aggie," Grace almost shouted, as she rushed to keep Brandon from coming into the room. Over her shoulder she said, "I must speak with Lord Weston alone for a moment."

"It appears you have grown lax with age, Agatha," her father stated. "Betrothed or not, I think politeness requires the lad present himself first."

Grace ran headlong into Brandon's chest just outside the doors of the drawing room, and he grabbed her arms to steady her. "Now that is the kind of enthusiasm I like to see, my sweet life," he teased, and quickly kissed the tip of her nose. "I knew you would get the lay of this eventually!"

"Oh, dear, do not tease me now, Brandon. We have a serious problem." She took his arm, pulling him into the library, where there was a low fire burning and only a few candles lit.

She did not realize what the glow of those few flames did to her gown and skin, but she noticed the marked change in Brandon as he stared at her with a look she had never seen before.

"What is it, have I broken out in spots?" She put a hand to her forehead. "Come to think of it, I would not be in the least bit surprised!"

"You really don't know, do you?" he asked, his voice lowering as he came closer. He removed his greatcoat, which Jamison had forgotten to take from him in the foyer. "You have been living in the shadow of your sister for so long that you do not realize how absolutely beautiful you are. And for some reason, you do not expect me to notice, either. My sweet life," he whispered, "that dress makes your eyes so green a man could gaze into them for an eternity."

Grace blushed and looked at him shyly. He had not called her "love" for a while now. He had begun to call her his "sweet life" more often. What did that mean? Oh, dear, she remembered her father!

"Blast!" she exclaimed, and Brandon stopped in surprise.

"My compliments usually lead to a more…intimate response, but it should not surprise me that you would react differently than others." He leaned back against the mantel, noticeably perturbed.

She was instantly contrite. She had wanted just this response to her appearance from him. But she had to be practical; she always had to be practical. "My lord, an hour ago I would have given the world to hear you say those words, true or not. I was so worried about letting you down. I thank you, truly. But we have a bigger problem and I need to put you on your guard." She began to pace. "You will never guess who just arrived, not five minutes ago, and announced his intention of attending the ball."

"Hmm, I have just given a woman the most sincere compliment I have ever given to anyone, and she wants to play guessing games. Maybe rakes *do* lose their touch."

She loved him when he was like this. Despite the frustration it sometimes caused her, she thought his sense of the ridiculous one of his best features. But she could not tell whether he was being facetious or was truly hurt by her words. "I am sorry. I did not mean to take your compliment lightly. I am so pleased you think I will do tonight. You look very handsome, too, you know." She looked past him for a moment and said in a lower voice, "But then, you always do."

She shook herself. "It is just the most wretched thing. *Father* is here!"

"Ah, now I begin to understand. Have no worries, I have gotten out of tighter spots than this, and once was with you! We will come about. May we now return the subject to you and me?" he asked, ignoring her concerns. "I did not mean that you will *do* tonight." He raised her chin with his finger and whispered, "I meant that you will be the most dazzling woman in London tonight."

She became shy and lowered her eyes. "You are a dear, strange man, but you have not yet seen Lydia, my lord. I would not commit myself too early, were I you." When she raised her eyes to his with a smile, she realized she had made a serious mistake.

"Grace Endicott, listen to me." He pulled her toward him, his grip on her shoulders tight. "I grow weary of the comparison you make between you and your sister. You are too intelligent to think there is only one kind of beauty. The beauty you have is not the same as Lydia's, but it is beauty nonetheless. And that you are beautiful has little to do with the real you. One may think so at first glance, only to discover a mind, humor and those incredible eyes." He was staring at her as if he could see into her soul.

It was the most beautiful compliment she had ever received. That it came from the man she loved to distraction caused her heart to do very unusual things. Her eyes filled with tears. She had not known that words alone could cause such a sensation. Could she truly believe him or must she remember that a rake knew exactly what a woman wanted to hear?

He did not say anything further, but set her aside. He went to his greatcoat and took something out of a pocket. He came back and stood before her with a velvet box lying in his palm. "I have something for you and I believe you will complement them as no other would."

Grace watched as he opened the box, then stared in amazement at the emerald necklace and earrings she found there. They were the most astonishing stones she had ever seen, and the setting was beyond anything she could have imagined. They matched the ring perfectly. Somehow she'd thought that the family heirlooms would be ostentatious, if not downright pretentious. With no bark upon it, she had assumed the necklace would be a very large, square-cut emerald pendant, heavy enough to choke a horse.

But it was not. It was amazing!

A small square-cut emerald surrounded by diamonds was reproduced every inch or so, with smaller diamonds in between each emerald. It was not a heavy piece at all, but a choker that fit tightly around the neck.

She took the earrings and clipped them onto her

lobes. Then she turned her back to him and, lifting tendrils of her hair, asked, "Will you put it on me, please?"

She knew it would take the wind out of his sails; he would be expecting a fight. But she had lost all sense of practicality for the moment and could not wait to show the jewels to him…on her.

He took the choker out of the box, and she thought his fingers were shaking slightly as he laid the box on the table. He reached around her, his hands brushing her neck, then hooked the clasp at the back. She turned to face him. It took all her bravery to ask, "How do they look?"

He was so handsome as she gazed up at him, she wanted the engagement to be real. She pretended it was.

"For the moment, I can only admire the reflection from the most beautiful green eyes I have ever seen."

She continued to gaze at him; actually, she could not drag her eyes from his. "If the rest of London ever saw you look at me as you do now, no one would doubt our betrothal."

She was aghast! Had she shown him, revealed in her eyes, the love she felt for him? What was she doing?

He would not let her back away. She knew he was going to kiss her, and at this moment, she wanted him to. She wanted to have one real kiss to remember, along with the rest of her close-kept memories of their time together. She knew he despised marriage and love; he had said so many times. But she no longer cared. She loved him and wanted that kiss.

He leaned his face down and she swallowed nervously, staring at his mouth. Neither of them was prepared when the door to the library slammed open and her father bellowed, "What is going on here? I thought you needed to *speak* to this gentleman! Grace, you know better than this."

She closed her eyes and waited for the explosion that was about to occur. Her father might be disappointed in her, but he would be mad as a hornet at Brandon. And she had lost her kiss. It stunned her a little that she did not think she could make it through this night without it.

"Lord Pennington, sir." Brandon went forward with his hand outstretched. "Good to see you again. I am sorry we took so long, I am solely to blame. You see, I have wanted this age to give the family emeralds to Grace, and only today got them back from the jeweler. I wished to give them to her privately—I am sure you understand. And she looks most beautiful, does she not? I know you cannot fault a man for wanting to be alone with the woman he loves, on such an occasion."

He sounded so convincing she could pretend it was all true.

"But we are ready to be on our way, and delighted you have come to preside over the festivities," Brandon added. "Grace looks up to you tremendously, sir, and I am glad she will have you here to share this evening."

After shaking her father's hand, he came back to Grace, putting her hand on his arm and grabbing his coat. "Come, my sweet…sweetheart, we must get your wrap. And I know you wish to say good-night to Max." He winked at her father, as if they were the best of friends. "But keep it short. My sisters will be fit to be tied if we are late."

Her father seemed dumbstruck and Grace took advantage of it. She ran from the room, gathered Lydia, Aunt Aggie and their wraps, and they all climbed into Brandon's carriage. The ladies raved over the emeralds and greeted Brandon with warmth and joy. Grace kept up much of the conversation, but knew her father would not be quiet for long.

"Great guns, Grace, what has happened to you since coming to London? I've never heard you prattle on so. I feared I would have to spend the ball updating you on each and every yearling on the estate. I never knew you to care so much about gowns and gloves." He sounded disappointed, and Grace was a little embarrassed. He was right.

"Do not worry, sir," Brandon drawled in defense of her. "She has not changed at all. She is a bit nervous tonight, which is also unlike her, but we must let our betrothal announcement account for it. She rakes me down regularly for not sharing more information on how my crops are rotated."

She would have been able to see the mischief in his eyes if not for the darkened carriage.

"And you will be happy to know that very recently, the pistol in her reticule came in quite handy."

"Ha!" her father exclaimed. "Told you, girl, did I not? Can't wait to hear the story!"

She would have been angry that Brandon had thrown her to the lions, but it caused such a stir between the ladies that with the ensuing questions, they reached the ball without further incident.

She hoped they would be able to handle the debacle that would inevitably come.

Chapter Thirteen

The night seemed interminable to Grace, and they were only halfway through dinner before the ball. As she pushed a lobster patty around her plate, all she could think of was how even a quarter of the price of the excessive food here could have bought a month's worth of healthy, nourishing supplies for all the Janes at the orphanage on Baxter Street. Brandon gently nudged her knee with his, an action that would have shocked her only two months ago. But she recognized it as a signal to let her know he was thinking the same. "Soon, my sweet life," he said quietly. She was so preoccupied that it never occurred to her to wonder that they could be so in tune to each other's thoughts.

Brandon's sisters were delighted to welcome Lord Pennington, and Lydia was delighted that the privilege of the first dance would go to her father. Grace thought that her sister's happiness was complete with their father there, and she no longer begrudged it to her. Perhaps his presence would be the catalyst to end all the subterfuge. Perhaps it was God's plan all along.

But she forgot all that when Brandon claimed her for the first dance. The minute the musicians began a waltz, Grace knew it was of Brandon's doing; however, she did not care. Permission to dance the waltz had come weeks before, yet during the entire Season, she had never once danced a waltz with him. Sometimes she'd bit her lip in vexation as someone else asked, seconds before him, and other times she'd thought he purposely avoided it. But when he took her into his arms this night, all other thoughts flew from her head. She relaxed in his embrace and all the nervousness surrounding the ball drifted away in the music.

"Grace?"

"Yes, Brandon."

"We are back to Brandon. I thank you."

They circled lazily, sometimes avoiding another couple by mere inches, but she followed where he led, and smiled as she realized that a rake *must* be an exceptional dancer. He led her so easily that her body responded naturally, moving in whichever direction he chose. And he smelled *so* good.

"I believe I could get used to holding you in my arms." He pulled her toward him just a fraction. "You dance as gracefully as you do everything in your life. Shall we dance toward those open doors and finish the song out on a moonlit balcony?"

She smiled up at him in pure pleasure, and could see admiration in his eyes. "I think not." How she wished she could say yes. "As we are being watched by a thousand eyes, it would only cause a dust up, and I am quite happy where I am."

"Then we shall remain here."

He pulled her close enough to clasp one of her hands against his chest. She could have laid her head against his shoulder and remained there all night. She knew at last why chaperones and dowagers thought the waltz was scandalous. But as his betrothed, she was allowed this small intimacy.

"Shall I dance every dance with you tonight, my sweet life? I believe I have found the way to keep you from scolding me at every turn."

She dropped her eyes and spoke to his cravat, choosing to tease him, though the answer was very important to her. "You have stopped calling me 'love' tonight. Have I done something wrong, to be so lowered in your esteem?"

"My sweet life, have you heard me call others 'love' from time to time?"

"Of course! I assumed it was a high honor to be called so by a rake."

"It is, it is. But have you ever heard me call someone else 'my sweet life'?"

"No, I have not." She slowly raised her eyes and smiled up at him, and was taken aback at the intensity in his gaze. She lowered them again. "Brandon, I am happy to have this time with you." She did not tell him it was more than she could ever have hoped for in the way of a loving memory. "But very soon the tenor of the evening will change, the announcements will be made and we will still be in the same entanglement we have been in all along. I need not tell you that I fear the ramifications of this evening."

"Then do not," he said, sounding a little angry.

She looked at him again with a question in her eyes.

"If we may not have this dance without talking of ending the engagement, or the appearance of your father, or deluding my sisters, or whatever seems to prey upon your mind at all times, then just dance," he muttered.

"I am sorry, Brandon."

"I know you are. As am I."

That could have meant a thousand things, but she knew it was frustration. She ruined many things because of her practical nature. And it was ruining this memory. So, ever so lightly, she leaned her cheek against his shoulder, and heard the buzz go up around the room. It might be the only benefit of dancing with a rake, and she would take it. But when she felt his cheek rest against the top of her head, she closed her eyes and she did as he asked—she just danced.

He returned her to where her father and Lydia awaited them. Brandon and Grace did not speak to each other, but he bowed and said he would get the ladies each a glass of lemonade.

Lydia kissed her father's cheek, telling him how much she would miss him once she and Lord Hendricks were married. She blushed and looked up at her future husband as she said it.

"No need to be downcast, daughter. With the roads so improved, traveling is more easily accomplished, and we will all be able to visit and spend holidays together." He pinched her cheek. "The Abbey, however, will not be the same without the two of you. I have put too much of my responsibility for the estate on Grace. I will jump back into the thick of it and will only be a little sad about her leaving me for this marquess." He smiled at her, as well, as he added, "Though I'll be hanged if I can remember where I met him before."

Grace blushed at both statements. "Father, do you think I can give up the Abbey? I will still spend time there. You know I love it too much to completely remove myself."

"I do not think that husband of yours will fancy that."

"He knows my feelings, Father."

"Well, my beautiful girls, I see your next partners drawing near, and I believe I will seek out acquaintances in the card room until the big announcement." He kissed their cheeks before he left them.

Grace felt a tear leave her eye and could not pinpoint for which sadness it fell.

Lydia put an arm around her waist for the few seconds they had left. "Do not worry, Grace. I know you feel you must, but why not let God take your cares for this evening? I love you."

Too quickly, the time came to make known the purpose for the ball. Brandon's sisters had the musicians pause, and introduced their special guests, Mrs. Agatha Burstow and Lord Pennington. Then they stepped aside to allow them to take center stage.

Grace began to shiver. Her moment of relaxation in

Brandon's arm was gone and all her reservations returned, making her want to jump out of her skin. The whispers of the excited crowd heightened as her father escorted her aunt to the front of the room, but they quieted when he cleared his throat.

Aunt Aggie drew Lydia forward. "As you all know, this ball is for the coming out of my lovely niece, Lady Lydia Endicott." The crowd applauded politely and expected the party to continue.

"However," her father said in a louder voice, "our Lydia has made an attachment. Her aunt and I would like to announce the engagement of Lady Lydia to Dennis Henderson, Lord Hendricks!"

Dennis joined Lydia, and the applause this time was louder and the congratulations true and well meant. Grace knew a moment's peace in her heart at her sister's happiness.

That disappeared in an instant.

"Before you get back to the festivities," her father continued, "we would like your indulgence for a few moments more." He came to Grace's side of the room, took her hand and placed it in the crook of his arm, leading her forward as he signaled to Brandon to join them. "Since this is the first time I have been with you all, I would also like to congratulate Brandon, Lord Weston, who had the good sense to offer for my other daughter, Lady Grace." He paused at the general laughter. "His sisters and Grace's aunt and I are happy to celebrate their betrothal, as well."

Brandon moved close to Grace, taking her hand in his, intertwining their fingers. She would have loved the gesture had it been in private, but she assumed the only reason he did it was to be sure to keep her by his side, when he knew she did not wish to be there. He lifted their intertwined hands to kiss hers.

It was her own fault. She had allowed herself to give in to her heart when she'd rested her head on Brandon's shoulder during their dance. Her boldness then had given him license for this gesture now.

People began to look at each other, to gauge the approval of this rather intimate display. But when the applause started, slight at first, but thundering around the room very soon after, she realized it was what was expected of a rake, and he aimed to please. She heard them begin to chant, "Speech, speech," and she prayed Brandon would not appease them.

Her prayer was not answered. He let go of her hand to put an arm lightly around her waist, making her step forward with him. He had a decided twinkle in his eyes. "As many of you know, I never thought to find myself in this position, so you cannot be surprised to learn that I have no speech prepared."

The guffaws of the gentlemen and the titters of the ladies showed their appreciation for his charm.

He went on in a more serious manner. "All I can say to you is that tonight I am the luckiest man in the kingdom."

Grace looked up at him, surprised at his words, and when he glanced down at her she knew he saw her fear and nervousness. But she was completely unprepared for him to lean down and kiss her lightly on the lips.

As the crowd gasped in surprise, applause took over,

and everyone began to gather around them with congratulations.

It seemed to Grace that she stood there for hours,
smiling and saying goodness knew what to a thousand
people. Brandon never took his arm from her waist,
making her feel even more self-conscious in front of
them.

When the musicians finally resumed playing, she and
Brandon found themselves alone for a moment. Her sensibilities were at the breaking point. She lashed out quietly, but fiercely. "My lord, I believe the little displays
of affection went a bit too far tonight. You shocked half
the guests in the ballroom. More importantly, we are
supposed to be on the verge of ending our engagement.
I think it might have been a little easier for people to di-
gest if they had seen a couple a little more…restrained."

She felt him tense up, and realized she had said the
wrong thing at the wrong time. Again. She wished he
could understand how all the playacting, when she was
not playacting, was affecting her.

His hand left her waist, but grabbed her arm as he
began pulling her toward the double doors that led to
the veranda. "You are quite right. It is time we had a
little talk, my lady."

If the guests were not shocked before, they would be
now, and he cared not a jot!

When they reached the veranda, she tugged at her
arm so he would stop, but he held on fast, dragging
her by the hand. He went down the steps, then farther
down the path, until he came to a tall tree with leaves

that shaded the area in quiet darkness. There he finally let go of her hand, and she stood staring at him, trying to catch her breath. He had taken appalling liberties in his anger and was not surprised when she lashed out at him. "What on earth are you doing? If you wished to speak to me, we could have talked on the veranda."

"My little displays of affection are bothering you, are they, Grace?" His jaw was clenched and he ground his teeth. "Just what do you think those small displays cost *me,* my lady?" He remained silent for a moment, trying to control his anger. She was an innocent and he…was not.

She did not shrink from him. He feared his question, uttered with such vehemence, might scare her, but she stood her ground. "I can see I have made you angry, my lord, but I am not sure how. I do not understand your question."

"Of course you do not, *my lady.* The reason you do not understand it is because you *are* a lady," he said between gritted teeth. "You are a naive, green girl from Essex who apparently has not ever known a real man. A green girl who has neither the nerve nor the backbone to show her true emotions."

She gaped but said nothing.

He forcibly tried to calm down. He paced back and forth in front of her, running his hands through his hair. When his anger died down somewhat, he turned his back to her to stare down a pathway that overlooked a lake. "How many times would you say we have kissed, Grace?" he finally asked, seriously and quietly. He did not need to see her to know she had never expected such a question. She did not speak for a moment. "I assume that is what you meant when you alluded to our displays of affection, is it not?"

She was a smart woman. She shed no tears at his ranting. "Yes, I suppose the public kissing, hand holding and the proprietary use of your arm around my waist would be the gist of it." She spoke clearly and softly. "I do not see others doing such things and it makes me feel…awkward, for want of a better word."

He could feel her frustration that she could not put into words what she wanted to say to him. But her frustration did not begin to match his own, so he said nothing.

"Even in private you tease me that way." He heard *her* begin to pace.

"My lord, as I said, we are on the brink of ending this. We should appear less affectionate, not more so. I do not understand the purpose of your actions."

"Grace, I told you, all the way back from the Blue Swan Inn, that if we were to pretend to be in love, people would expect a rake to flout convention. I now see the foolishness of my past. Believe me when I tell you that I am daily reminded…" He shook his head and stopped. He had not meant to tell her that. "I told you from the beginning, did I not?"

"Yes, my lord, you did. I suppose I did not understand you then. I did not understand what it would look like." The rest came out in almost a whisper. "Or how hard it would be."

His laughter was harsh and it startled her. "*You* did not realize what it meant or how hard it would be? What do you suppose that little scene during our waltz cost me? *That* was not of my doing!" He turned to face her and saw her acceptance of that rebuke. She closed her eyes. "Please just answer my original question, Grace. How many times have we kissed?"

"I do not remember exactly. I suppose three or four," she said after some thought. "Why?"

"Because if you had asked me how many times we have kissed, I would have said none."

He watched her tilt her head to the side, perplexed. She was so trusting, so calm. He no longer wanted to be angry at her.

"How could you say none, when you just kissed me in the middle of a ballroom?"

He leaned back against the tree. He stretched out his hand and she automatically put hers in it. He pulled her toward him and said softly, "Because *this,* Grace, is a kiss."

He had leaned back against the tree, and when he pulled her to him, the distance between them disappeared. With one hand on the back of her waist, he slowly touched his lips to hers, and she involuntarily closed her eyes.

It was nothing like she had ever felt before. It seemed as if her stomach became filled with butterflies. As he increased the pressure, she decided to stop trying to find something to compare this to. He deepened the kiss with a hand on the back of her head, but when she sighed, quite unintentionally, he moved it to join the other at her waist. It felt completely natural to put her arms around his neck.

The kiss felt more comfortable as it went on, and she never wanted it to stop.

She knew it must feel this way for *her* because she loved him so much. But what was it like for *him?* He was not in love with her. Why did he wish to continue?

He finally stopped the kiss ever so slowly. "You see, my lovely green-eyed enchantress, *that* is a kiss. And for a man like me, it is only the beginning." He looked at her with such intensity that she tried to understand. "The chaste kisses we have shared up to now and the childish hand holding are torture for me."

She lowered her head and pulled away from him, staring unseeing at the lake so he would not witness her tears. When women fell into his arms they did not grumble at his kisses, or go stiff. They gave him whatever he wanted because they, too, never wanted the kiss to stop. Of course, he did not know what to do with someone who actually stopped them!

She did not want them, because they were not real. But, oh, how she wanted them to be. She could not tell him that her actions when they danced were directed totally by her heart. It had nothing to do with fooling Society.

Now it was clear. She no longer dreaded ending their engagement. God was showing her that Brandon would never be the man for her. It was not because of his past; he was assured of God's grace and forgiveness when the time came that he wanted it. It was because they were too different. He would never be satisfied with a green girl from Essex who wanted his love, and she would never be satisfied with a man who did not love her.

She wiped her tears quickly and turned back to him.

"Do not worry, Grace. I would never go further with you, because I respect you too much to take advantage of this betrothal."

What was he saying? He was still trying to explain why her kisses only frustrated him.

He took her hand and put it in the crook of his arm as he began to walk back to the ballroom. They were silent until he apologized. "I am sorry, Grace. I have insulted you and I never meant to. You do not deserve such treatment. Perhaps my nerves were nearer the surface than I supposed."

Yes, he was under the same public scrutiny she was, only certain things were expected of him.

"Please say something, Grace."

"I am sorry, Brandon. I am afraid I have made a mull of this, as I knew I would. I should never have agreed to this betrothal. Regardless, I did not realize how difficult it would be for you, either."

They reached the house and both stopped. "Will you be able to remain for the rest of the evening with me?" he asked.

She nodded, and they continued into the house as if they had been out for a moonlit stroll on the veranda. But Grace knew nothing would ever be the same again, and despite her nod to his question, it was time to end it.

They left the ball about 3:30 a.m., most of them tired and happy. Brandon was just glad it was over. The others had fallen asleep by the time they reached Berkeley Square, but he knew that Grace had not. He wished he could read her mind.

He had gone too far with her tonight. Though she was six and twenty, she was an innocent, and she did not need to be chastised for it. But he had wanted to truly kiss her for some time. It began as a desire to show her what it could be like, but ever since the day at the orphanage, he'd wanted to be closer to her. He didn't understand the feelings; he had liked her from the start, but lately it had been more of a *need* to share things with her.

All she wanted to talk about, however, was how soon they could break their betrothal and how they should go about it. He was running out of excuses for more time. For now, he did not want her to leave. What he had to determine was whether this was a fleeting feeling because she was so different than anyone else he had ever met, or whether it was more.

But the problem did not lie with him alone. She must not feel the same, if she could welcome their parting so easily. He knew it was not distaste for him personally that had her seeking an end to the engagement— in truth, he was sure that she was as good a friend as he had ever had. The *ton* would never understand that. Great guns! He would never have understood it if he was not experiencing it. But friendship was not the same as love, and he knew that she would never marry a man she did not cherish with all her heart. And that could never be him, especially not after tonight. If everything about him went against all she believed in, he had nailed the coffin shut this evening.

The carriage pulled up to the door and he handed them all out, lastly shaking hands with her father. Brandon wanted just one moment alone with Grace, but with the handing off of cloaks and calling for servants, he could only kiss her hand and hope she could see in his eyes that more had happened that night than just a physical connection.

It *was* more for him. But how much more?

Grace did not go upstairs with the others. Though they were more than likely going straight to bed, she did not want to risk that Lydia might wish to talk over the excitement of the evening. So she picked up a book she had brought downstairs earlier, and told everyone she would follow momentarily after she returned the book to the library. She dismissed the servants and promised to be sure all the candles were out.

When she was finally alone, she sat on the bottom step in the foyer and put her chin in her hands. She should be ready to fall into bed and sleep for a week, but she knew she would not. She was so confused. She spied Max out of the corner of her eye, standing steadfast, never changing, and guarding their home without faltering.

"Max, he is right about me. I *am* stupid and naive when it comes to men. He is like you, Max, and I have loved you for ages. He is hard and cold on the outside, but on the inside, I know there is a warm, caring, funny knight. He would laugh to hear me say that, probably just as you would if you could. But I do not know how to make him believe me.

"I had no idea that love was so complicated. I must stop hoping he will one day tell me that he is not pretending anymore." And in her heart she knew that even if he said it, she could not marry him. He did not believe in God. He would soon tire of a wife who did, while she could never be truly happy in a marriage that lacked a foundation in faith.

She took her bed candle and went to stand before the regal suit of armor. "It is all dreams, Max, like the ones I always had of you." One lone tear ran down her cheek as she turned from him and began the ascent to her room. She would talk to Brandon on the morrow about her plan, and then put this part of her life behind her.

Chapter Fourteen

At first light, after she had tossed and turned to the limit of her patience, Grace rose, dressed quickly and decided a ride in the park might clear her head of the dreams and nightmares from the night before. She tiptoed down the stairs, apologized to Max for bothering him last night, and went to saddle her horse. She found herself virtually alone in the park except for a few vendors setting up their wares.

After a wonderful gallop, she walked her horse to cool him down. One good thing to come out of her tossing and turning was that she had hit upon the plan to break with Brandon. It would more than likely be a week before they could actually part, but they could argue immediately and continue to pretend animosity for a specified number of days.

She was so lost in her thoughts that she did not notice the man in the black coat until he had hold of the bridle of her horse. She jerked the reins in surprise. "What you are doing? Let go of my horse." She tried to speak calmly, sure there was some mistake, but she was uncomfortably aware that she was alone. And Brandon had warned her.

"Unfortunately, I cannot do that, Lady Grace. If you would slowly dismount and begin to walk beside me, I will do my best not to hurt you." He was not very tall, but his voice was menacing enough to make her compliant. That and the fact that she had left her reticule, with her gun in it, at home. She chastised herself for the oversight.

She dismounted, but held tightly to the reins. She wondered if she could somehow use her mount to dislodge the man, even if only for a moment. Should her horse arrive home without her, her groom would soon send up a cry. But the cloaked man seemed prepared for that eventuality and spoke ominously.

"Lady Grace, I would advise you not to do anything that will make me hurt you or your horse. I can arrange things to make it look like you had a terrible accident while out riding alone." The realization that this was a life-threatening matter caused her to forget any plans for escape, and listen to what he would say. Brandon had predicted that she might have angered the caretaker of the Baxter orphanage. Was this man Mr. Brownlow, or perhaps his emissary?

"Now we will have a friendly chat, my lady. If you give any other indication in outward appearance, you will be sorry. Do you understand?"

She looked at him and nodded. She knew she should be doing something to help herself, but she was so scared she couldn't seem to think. *Remember what he looks like, Grace,* she thought, trying to get a look at his face. But he was well covered in a black greatcoat and a hat pulled low over his features.

"What do you want from me?" she asked. She kept trying to think rationally. If he truly wanted to hurt her, he had had ample opportunity in the previous hour, when she was alone.

Dear Lord, protect me. I do not see my way out of this by myself.

"It is very simple. I want the Weston emeralds."

No! The orphanage caretaker was trying to get his revenge on Brandon through her. He would punish them both at the same time. "They are not mine to give you." She did not know how far to push him, but he needed to know he could not get them through her.

"I don't care. You are in possession of them, so you will give them to me."

Think, Grace, think. Buy some time. "They belong to Lord Weston and are under his protection." She chose her words carefully. "He merely loaned them to me last night for our ball." She prayed that she sounded convincing.

"My lady, the sooner you stop taking me for a fool, the better off you will be. I have sources who have reported that Lord Weston *gave* you those emeralds last night as your betrothal gift. I am quite sure the safe in Berkeley Square would provide enough security that you might keep them on the premises."

She was truly afraid now, but he would be the last person to know it. "I am certainly not carrying the emeralds on my person at this time, and I refuse to go fetch them for you." She was preparing herself for the worst.

He must have some means of making her turn them over to him or he would not have accosted her so brazenly.

"Do you think to outsmart us?" He laughed. "Here is what you will do."

His use of the word *us* surprised her. Was he connected to the three men who had tried to hurt her and Brandon? No, this man's voice was more cultured. She must now find a way to keep the emeralds safe and to prove Mr. Brownlow was the force behind this plan. *How do I do this alone?*

"What makes you think I would hand the jewels over to you? I am not afraid for my life and would give it up before the marquess's heirlooms."

"Yes, my lady, your reputation precedes you. You were ready to kill for him once before, were you not?" So this man *was* from the orphanage! "You must stop thinking I know nothing about you." He drew the horse to a halt, but kept staring straight ahead. "I know your betrothal is a fraud." She involuntarily swung her head toward him and he laughed. "You may have hoaxed the *ton,* but you have not hoaxed us."

How could Mr. Brownlow know such a thing? Only Lydia knew the truth about their betrothal and she would never tell anyone. Had this man and his cohorts been watching Grace since her visit to the orphanage? Her actions were the cause of this and she must find a way out. She must think.

"If you know the betrothal to be false, I am surprised you would approach me at all. Why would Lord Weston leave his prized family heirlooms with me? He let me wear them to keep up the pretense."

Her assailant hissed in her ear. "I am not a fool, and curb your tongue. You begin to wear on me. I do not care whether you have the emeralds or not. All I care about is that you get them. I will give you one week. You will tell no one and you have a week."

What could she do? She wanted to cry. She wanted someone to rescue her from this nightmare. She had promised she would go to Brandon with everything. Could she do that with them watching her?

"You will meet me at the Whitefriars Stairs just below the Black Lion Inn one week from tonight at nine of the clock," the man ordered her. "I want the entire set and you will bring them alone. I will have you watched, and if you bring reinforcements, I will not answer for their safety."

"You said you have already had me watched." As she said it out loud, she felt spine-tingling fear at just exactly what that might mean.

"Yes, my lady. That is how I will keep you from telling anyone else. I think you will not put someone you know at risk. You have been warned."

So, she could not tell Brandon. She would never put him in harm's way no matter what she'd promised him.

"And if I refuse?" she asked, trying to show a brave face.

He spoke as if addressing a child. "I do not think the *ton* would be too happy to hear of the game you and Lord Weston are playing."

Did things like this really happen? She had asked herself that when she went to the orphanage. She could not credit so much evil. "I do not care what the *ton* thinks. I will go to my home and be perfectly content if I am shunned by Society. And you must be aware that Lord Weston's reputation would survive anything."

"You might not particularly care about the ostracism awaiting you. However, your sister, recently betrothed to a young viscount, might. You will not ruin their reputations so easily."

His mention of Lydia and Lord Hendricks raised the hair on the back of her neck. She could never keep them all safe by herself. *Get more information, Grace. Get as much as you can.*

"My sister and her affianced plan to live at his country estate, and both would understand and accept a choice I made to save Lord Weston's emeralds."

"You are *not* paying attention!" the man in black said, anger making him louder. "You will tell no one of this meeting or what I ask of you, and as you have learned, I will know if you do." He paused for effect. "You may offer to give up your own life, but if you do not do as I say, then Lord Weston will lose his. Engaged or not, I think you would not wish to be responsible for his death."

If this was about the orphanage, then likely they wanted Brandon dead regardless, and her choice now would make no difference. But she could not take the risk with Brandon's life on the line. She could no longer even be sure they would not kill them both, anyway. She was defeated; she must do as he said. But she would keep trying to find out who was behind this. She had to keep Brandon safe.

She forcibly pulled the bit from the man's hands and said, "You will have your emeralds," then mounted her horse.

"I thought you might change your mind," he said, and turned to walk back the way they had come.

Grace paced back and forth in her bedroom. It was too much; she could never do this by herself. As she thought it, she knew who she should turn to, and got down on her knees next to her bed.

Father God, I do not even know what to ask of You. My loved ones are in danger and I cannot be in two or three places at one time. Only You can. Please show me how to play my part in Your plan to keep them safe, and give me Your strength and grace to get through it.

She wrote notes canceling all her appointments for that day, even her drive with Brandon. He would not like it, but she had no choice. She claimed a severe headache, which was certainly the truth, and asked that she be left alone.

At one point during the morning, she received a bouquet of yellow roses from Brandon, with a note expressing his hope that she would feel better soon, and that nothing he had said or done the previous evening had caused her to cancel their drive. As she read it, tears welled in her eyes and her mind went back to his tender kiss. He thought she was angry at him, but it was actually a treasured experience she would always remember.

For a moment, she thought about going to Lord Langdon with the entire truth. He loved Brandon as a son. But no sooner did she think about it than she ruled it out. She was being watched and could not put another person at risk. She had gotten herself into this by barging into that orphanage, so she must bear the consequences. There was no Max to come to her rescue.

By noon she had decided what she must do to protect the emeralds, but it would have to be implemented soon and in secret. She would take them to a jeweler and have them replaced with paste copies. She knew women of the *ton* did it often when they needed more pin money or when they outran their quarterly allowances. She did not know exactly how it would work or how long it took to make a copy; she could only pray it wouldn't be too difficult. If the replicas could not be made in time, she did not know what she would do.

She also tried to determine what was best to do about Mr. Brownlow. Brandon had warned her that she could interfere with everything they had already accomplished at the orphanage if he knew she had visited there. How could she make sure that didn't happen, as well? She shivered at the thought of going back to that place alone. And even if she did, that would not protect Brandon's life. No, she must get the fakes to the man in black as promised, and pray she could convince him that it was enough payment to leave her loved ones alone.

Knowing she was being watched was the hardest part. If she went to a jeweler, these spies might realize what she was doing. Without knowing how long it would take to make the copies, she decided it must be the first thing she did. Everything depended on being able to accomplish it, and she knew she could not do it alone; she would be followed for certain.

She called on her maid, Betsy, to help her. Grace told her that she needed to do something for Lord Weston but did not want anyone to know. Betsy, a hopeless romantic, saw an opportunity to help her lady with affairs of the heart, and agreed to her plan.

At noon that day, when Lydia and her aunt were out making morning calls, the maid, dressed in one of Grace's gowns and wearing her pelisse and hat, walked out the front door and directly into a hackney, heading in the direction of Richmond Park. If the man spying on her followed the hackney, it would free hours for Grace to accomplish her mission. She watched through the front window, trying to catch a glimpse of her stalker, but realized he could have been hiding anywhere. She would just have to assume he was following Betsy.

Half an hour later, Grace left by way of the servants' door wearing Betsy's cap, hat and cloak. She walked several blocks from their house to catch a hackney to the jewelers. She could do nothing but pray for the success of this endeavor. It was all she knew to do.

By one o'clock she was in front of a small, lesser known jeweler off Bond Street. She asked the hackney driver to wait, and entered the shop. She looked around, feeling very self-conscious, and asked to speak to the owner.

When the short bald man appeared, Grace played the part of a maid on an errand for her mistress. She explained her need, and offered to pay handsomely for the copies and originals to be returned to her within three days. She even thought to warn him that her ladyship would have another jeweler inspect them both to be sure she received the real pieces.

The shop owner looked up in surprise after he opened the velvet box.

Grace could see from his expression that he recognized the jewels, and knew she needed to come up with a plausible reason for the needed copies even if he charged her a fortune to do it.

"Yes, they are Lord Weston's emeralds. My lady is affianced to his lordship," she said, and curtsied. At the nod of the shopkeeper's head, she continued. "She's that scared she might lose them or, glory be, they should be stolen. She's convinced she ought to have copies made. She'll feel better wearing the real ones on special occasions, like." Grace's accent got worse the more she tried to sound like Betsy, and she was afraid the man would think she had stolen them herself.

Dear God, I am in waters too deep for me.

"His lordship told her she was being silly, but my lady is still afraid."

"I will do my best, miss. But three days, that is not poss—"

"My lady says three days or no payment."

It was at that moment that Brandon, walking down the street with a friend, stopped suddenly. He looked into the window of a small jewelry broker and thought he saw Grace's face. When she turned away, he realized it was a lady's maid, but his instincts told him to wait and watch. "You go along, Frederick. I spotted something I would like to purchase for Lady Grace, and I may be a while. I will meet you at the club shortly."

Brandon watched from the side of the window while the woman talked with the jeweler. Something was out of place. Then she turned to sign something and there was no question it was Grace. She was alone again and dressed as a maid! What was she up to?

He disappeared back into the alley as she left the shop and stepped into the waiting hackney by the curb. Clearly, she was perfectly capable of getting herself into trouble again, but he would not let her get away with it this time!

He entered the store as the man was about to go back to his office. When Brandon interrupted with an "Excuse me," the jeweler turned back, looking over his shoulder. His face drained of all color.

"My lord!" the store owner said, as he jumped in surprise. "T-to what do I owe this honor?"

"Cut line, man. If I had not suspected something before this, your face just now would have given it away. Why don't you tell me what happened here," he said calmly.

The bald man began to sweat profusely and became agitated. "I was going to tell you, my lord, believe me. I was just getting ready to send you a note, asking what you would have me do. I would hope you could count on me, sir, my lord, sir."

"What in blazes are you talking about?" Brandon asked, now concerned.

"That maid just gave me the Weston emeralds and asked me to make paste copies of them in three days. I was not going to do it, I swear, your lordship," he practically whimpered. "I was going to give them to you directly."

What was she up to now? Brandon's first reaction was surprise. Had she planned this all along, even as far back as the inn? No, he would bet his life she'd had no idea who he was the day they'd met. That alone would preclude her from knowing about the emeralds. And she had fought him at every turn when discussing their betrothal; she would not tell a single lie. She had even tried to refuse the emeralds when he'd first offered them.

No, he trusted her implicitly.

But why would she have copies made of the jewels? The little minx was up to something, and he could not believe that the dressing down he'd given her after her last adventure had not quit her of recklessness. But if she thought she was going to exclude him again after her promise, she was far off the mark.

"Do as she asked," he said, and turned to leave the store.

Did she not trust him?

The next day Brandon entered Grace's home, to find her waiting next to Max as she pulled on her gloves. He nodded in Max's direction and smiled at her. "Should I challenge him to a duel?" he asked as he kissed her hand.

She smiled back at him, but he noticed it did not reach her eyes. "No," she said, much too serious for his liking. "I would not want to see either of you hurt."

"Still a little unwell, my sweet life, or still angry with me for my actions at the ball?" He became concerned when she remained quiet for some time. She was not nervous as much as pensive, and he wondered what was going on in that beautiful head of hers.

"No, Brandon, neither of those things. I am not unwell and I know, after thinking about it, that I deserved the lesson you gave me at the ball. I am afraid I am not as worldly-wise as I thought."

"Why so melancholy, then?" Would she tell him why she was having the emeralds copied?

"I suppose it is the result of lying abed all day yesterday." She sighed.

But she had not been in bed all day yesterday. He had seen her at the jewelers.

Then she pretended to cheer up, and apologized. "I am sorry to be such bad company. I do have some things to talk to you about."

She did trust him! And it pleased him excessively.

"Do you remember my telling you about a little boy named Nicky, at the orphanage, who never participates or speaks? I was there the other day with Mrs. Dickerson. I spent quite a bit of time with him and he actually played with me." She sighed again. "I will miss him so. I will miss them all."

He scowled, not wanting to talk about the orphanage, but held his tongue, knowing he needed to give her time. When they were in his curricle, the streets were busy and he was sure she was waiting until they reached the park and he could concentrate fully on what she was telling him. "Why will you miss them?" he asked, not yet grasping her meaning. His thoughts were on the emeralds.

"I have decided upon a plan for ending our betrothal. As soon as we do it, I must go home. I have been away from the estate too long as it is, and now that Father is here, there will be much to do. I know you must be wishing me long gone."

"Grace, what is this all about? If I wished you gone, I would have told you so." She was beginning to scare him. "Lydia's wedding is less than a month away. Why would you leave and then come back?"

He reverted to humor. With a rakish smile he quipped, "Never say you are tired of my charms. It will appear to the *ton* as if I have lost my touch! I was certain I would have you swooning over me."

She smiled at his antics and said, "Oh, no, my lord, not swooning. That would ruin *my* reputation."

He laughed. She had been trying to tell him from the day they'd met about her shockingly staid character, but he did not believe it, and he loved that she could make him laugh guilelessly. But the curtain lowered again almost immediately and the sparkle disappeared from her eyes.

He spoke before she could. "Enjoy London while you may. Soon we will have the orphanage on Baxter Street for you to work with."

"No!" Her vehemence shocked him. More softly, she said, "We cannot keep putting this off. I have seen enough of London to last a lifetime. My plan will allow me to be home by the end of the week. Tomorrow we will go for ices after our drive and have an audible argument. I thought we could disagree about the time I still wanted to spend at Pennington Abbey. It seems to be the type of thing that would make a real rake, who loves the city, angry. But if you can think of something better, it does not really matter."

She never looked at him during the entire speech, and he thought he heard a trembling in her voice. It did not take a genius to know there was more to this than she let on. Did the emeralds have anything to do with it?

She gathered herself and continued nonchalantly. "We would, of course, show considerable tension at the Torringtons' ball tomorrow night. I will go home a few days later with Father and you can send the announcement to the papers that our engagement is at an end. When asked, I will say we did not suit."

"My, you have thought this out." He could see she would not be moved. And she had not spoken of the emeralds at all. A jolt pierced his heart. He was not ready for it to end. He needed more time to…to what?

"Lydia is taken care of, the purpose for our betrothal is no longer valid and I need to get home." She seemed to be trying to be lighthearted. "And you have been fighting off marriageable daughters for many years. It was a mere convenient advantage, our being betrothed. You will be fine." She smiled, but still stared straight ahead.

He did not know how to tell her how much he wanted her to stay. He could promise her nothing. He had made it clear from the beginning that he was not interested in marriage. But she *did* bring out sentiments in him that he had never experienced before.

"Grace, we can—"

She interrupted him. "We are agreed, then?"

"I…suppose so. You have managed it all quite neatly." He drove on, thinking she must have been more offended the night of the ball than she had let on. And it hurt to know she still did not trust him enough to tell him about the emeralds.

He felt her slipping away from him. And in spite of their agreement, he was not at all willing to let her go.

Chapter Fifteen

After leaving Grace, Brandon was restless, confused and in need of counsel. That in itself was out of the norm. He had learned early to take care of himself. If he relied on no one, he could not be hurt.

But tonight, before going to his club for dinner, he sent a message to Lord Langdon, asking him to be his guest. He received a missive in return stating that he already had plans for dinner, but if Brandon wished to join him later at his home, he would look forward to it.

Brandon was welcomed with opened arms and a hearty bear hug. It was interesting that he felt comfort in such a show of affection from this man, when he would disdain it from almost anyone else. He always felt peace when he was in this house. There was no judgment of his past, only high expectations that Brandon hoped to one day live up to.

Lord Langdon sent him ahead to the library while he gave instructions to his butler that they weren't to be disturbed. Brandon walked over to the fireplace, where he leaned against the mantel. He kicked a lone piece of coal farther into the flames as his mind ran amok. Perhaps this was not such a good idea, after all.

He wanted to ask someone what it felt like to care about…to love…another person enough to want to marry her, to spend the rest of his life with her. He wondered what it would be like to wake up next to the same woman every day, breakfasting, dining and living with her for the rest of his life. He had always shuddered at the thought. But when that face belonged to Grace, it was not so hard to imagine. Indeed, every day had been a new experience with her.

He remembered once telling her he abhorred dull women. He smiled at the recollection of her tirade on the subject of trying to hold a conversation with a madman.

But he could not ask Lord Langdon those things; he was already supposed to *know* them. His mentor believed him to be happily invested in a loving engagement, with every plan to devote his life to his new bride-to-be. And his deep inner fear was that he already knew the answer to the questions and that love was planning on leaving him at the end of the week.

Brandon stood straighter when Lord Langdon entered the library. "I was glad to get your note today. You have been in my thoughts much of late. Is all well with you?"

"Perfectly," he said tonelessly. "I had no taste for dancing this evening and hoped you might wish to continue our chess game."

"Why don't we sit and enjoy the fire first?"

When they were seated, his lordship remained silent, prompting Brandon to begin the conversation. That was not what he wanted. He wished to become involved with thoughts not his own tonight. "My lord," he finally started, "do you know a song called 'Amazing Grace'?"

Langdon smiled at him and said, "Of course, why do you ask?"

"Of course?" Did everyone know it but him?

"It might not come your way often, Brandon. It is a hymn, mostly sung during church services."

"I see. What self-respecting rake would be singing in church?"

"One who was a self-respecting gentleman."

"Well, that certainly leaves me out. Shall we play chess?"

"The board is still set up. If you will bring the table here between us we may relax while we play."

Brandon did so and for a quarter of an hour the two men moved pieces in relative silence. But he could not turn off his thoughts and made bad moves. When Lord Langdon quietly said, "Checkmate," Brandon was not the least bit surprised.

His lordship still seemed to be perfectly content not saying a word, so Brandon tried nonchalantly to begin a conversation that might alleviate some of his disquiet.

"Sir, may I ask you a hypothetical question?"

"Certainly."

"I am curious as to why a woman might have paste copies made of her jewelry."

"The obvious answer would be for money."

"I have thought of the obvious and it does not fit

my—" he shook his head "—this situation. I wish to go beyond the obvious."

He felt Lord Langdon's eyes scrutinizing his face, but did not look into them. "The need for money is not always dishonorable. Many women do it when they have run through allowances. They receive the needed cash, yet can still wear the jewels, so a husband might never know."

"What if money was not an issue?"

"I know my dear Gwyneth used to often say she lived in fear she would lose some of her more valuable pieces, and she would suggest we have paste copies made of them all." Langdon smiled. "Indeed, she once told me to only buy her paste jewels from then on." He stared at Brandon. "Is safety the issue?"

"I suppose it could be. I had not thought it so, but perhaps."

"Why not tell me what the issue *is,* to save time? You know you may talk to me about anything, son."

"What if, hypothetically, she thought she might have to give the real ones back?"

He saw the surprise on Lord Langdon's face. "That adds a rather shadowy side to this hypothetical situation. I suppose she might opt to keep the real jewels and return the copies to the original owner."

"Yes, that is a conclusion I reached, too."

Lord Langdon rose and placed a hand on Brandon's shoulder. "My boy, it is time to empty your budget. Why don't you tell me all, from the beginning, and perhaps the truth this time?"

"I have made a mull of it, my lord, and you will not be proud of what you hear."

Lord Langdon reseated himself. "Son, you once again mistake me for your father." He put up a hand to stop Brandon's denial. "It was not a condescending statement, my boy. You have a lifetime of habits to break. I merely need to remind you every so often."

Brandon smiled, but kept his eyes on the fire and said nothing.

"Being proud of you does not come and go. We all have our moments where we fall short of what we wish to be, make no mistake, but it does not break the bond. You may talk to me of anything. I am not so caper-witted as to have missed the undercurrents between you and Lady Grace during your visit. I accepted that it was not the proper time to discuss it."

"I would never call you caper-witted, I assure you." Brandon smiled again. "But I have tried to curb my more outrageous behavior to show you that you can, indeed, keep your stamp of approval on the work that Dennis and I do. The bumblebroth I have created might make you change your mind."

"I pray one day, Brandon, you will understand the nature of real friendship. I know, I know, you do not presume to think yourself my friend—you have placed me on a pedestal and look to me as a mentor at most." He leaned back in his chair. "But I will have you know that I liked Lady Grace immensely, and if I can help you in any way in your relationship with her, I would be honored." There was a pregnant pause. "Am I correct in assuming this hypothetical woman is Lady Grace? I find it amusing. I cannot picture the lady in any one of the scenarios we discussed."

"Nor I, but there has to be some explanation for it. She *has* commissioned copies to be made of the emeralds."

"Start from the beginning, Brandon."

He struggled with his thoughts for a moment. They had promised each other not to tell anyone else the truth about what started at the Blue Swan Inn, not even Grace's father or aunt. But Grace was getting ready to fall into trouble over his family jewels—he could feel it—and then she planned to leave him. He had never had this kind of a relationship before, either with Grace *or* Langdon, but he needed it now. So he shared the truth with him, watching for signs of disgust and disapproval, and waiting for remonstrance that never came.

"There you have it, my lord, the whole with no bark upon it."

"It would certainly appear at first glance to be a deuce of a coil. But I must take a second and third glance." Lord Langdon sat with his fingers steepled together. "Let me say from the beginning that I am proud of you for doing the honorable thing for Lady Grace, though it seems very unlike you to trust someone so implicitly, as you have trusted her. What made that so easy with this woman?"

"I have asked myself that many times. She is so very adamant concerning the things she feels strongly about. She was inordinately sorry for getting us into this position. She was not interested in marriage—she made that very clear. She also had the most uncompromising stand about telling a lie. I supposed if that were true in all our dealings I would have no fear as we went along." He ran his hands through his hair as he said, "It is really inexplicable."

"Yet you just explained it, and it makes perfect sense. And you still trust her without hesitation since you have discovered she was making paste copies of the emeralds?"

"Yes."

"Then why the hypothetical questions now? What about it do you distrust?"

He spoke normally again. "First and foremost, I distrust her self-reliance. She could be in a miserable coil and not telling me." He continued more softly. "Which leads to the real problem—I need to know that she trusts me, as well." He got up and began to pace. "Why hasn't she told me her reason? I could only think of bad answers to that question, and I will not believe that of her. I hoped you might have different answers that would explain it all."

"Perhaps the time has not been right for her to give that explanation."

"I believed that, too, until today, when she told me that she thinks it time to break the engagement. She plans to leave me—" he coughed to cover his last word "—and go home by the end of the week." He sat down again and put his elbows on his knees to cradle his chin in his hands. "And she does not trust me enough to tell me about the gems."

"Is not the termination of the engagement what you had planned from the outset?"

"Yes, of course, but I—we have been enjoying the Season together. I thought we could wait a little longer."

"Brandon, my boy, look at me." When he did so, Lord Langdon continued. "Have you fallen in love with Lady Grace?"

He jumped up, no longer able to sit still. "What would I know of love? My one attempt at it ended rather badly, if you will recall."

"Did you feel the same for your runaway bride as you do for Lady Grace?"

"No, nothing like!"

"Then you cannot compare them as your basis for understanding love."

"It matters not. She would not love a rake. Her God would not let her. But if she did, I would not be worthy of her."

"Do you think she would say that?"

"I cannot but think that she should."

"Brandon, why did you ask me if I knew 'Amazing Grace'?"

He laughed out loud. "You never fail to surprise me, sir. I have bared my soul to you and all you can think to ask me is that? I am indeed blessed in my benefactor!"

"Why, then?"

"It is silly, actually. Grace hums it often, and if we are with her sister or aunt, they chime in together. I asked Dennis once if he knew it and was surprised to find out that he did. I wondered if I was the only one ignorant of it. By your earlier answer, it would appear so."

"How did you get Lady Grace to go along with a mock betrothal if, as you say, she would not lie?"

"She would not agree to it until I assured her that she had been compromised and that she was good and engaged whether she wanted it or not. If she did not choose to end the betrothal as we had discussed, we would have to be married."

"But you had no fear she would *not* end it?"

"No, none."

"Why did she refuse to lie, my boy?"

"I have thoroughly lost the train of thought in this conversation. Each question you ask has little to do with my concern."

"Try me. I am not in my dotage yet."

Brandon laughed outright. "Far from it, my lord!" He sat back down again. "In the event you did not notice, she is of a religious bent. Her God demands a high moral code. It quite amazed me, actually. She knows immediately whether something is right or wrong."

"Did you not wonder why *I* knew the song?"

"No. My lord?"

"I am of the same 'religious' bent, Brandon, and I have some serious explaining to do to God if you have never noticed that about me."

"I have never doubted your word, your goodness or your fairness, my lord. That made you different than any other man in my life."

"But you did not wonder why I trusted you enough to work with you on the orphanage projects, knowing your reputation."

"On the contrary, I often wondered at it."

Langdon sat on the edge of his chair so he could look into Brandon's eyes. "It is because I believed if someone trusted you enough in the good deeds you wished to accomplish, perhaps you would stop believing that everything you did was contemptible. If someone set the standard high enough for you to live up to, you would no longer live down at the lower standard.

"My boy, Lady Grace had to put the same trust in you as you put in her. Her only knowledge of a rake would have been, at the very least, bad. You could have made her and her sister the laughingstock of London for entrusting her reputation to you. You would have given the *ton* a nine-days wonder and Society would have loved you the more for it.

"I shall not begin proselytizing, Brandon, but you must never say you are unworthy of love, hers or any others'. We have been given the gift of grace from God. Not her God, not my God, but *the* God of all. He knows we cannot be flawlessly good of ourselves, but He loves us in spite of it. She and I know all about it because we have accepted that grace. We cannot be unworthy because we do not get what we deserve. That is why she trusts you, despite your past."

"I do not precisely understand, sir," Brandon said, rubbing his eyes. He wasn't sure he wanted to understand.

"No, I did not expect you to at this moment. All I want you to understand now is that Lady Grace may not love you. I, for one, have not yet reached a conclusion in either direction on that score. But if she did, she would never consider you unworthy."

Brandon just stared into the fire.

"We have discussed many important things, Brandon. Things I probably should have discussed with you long ago. But I cannot stop the uneasiness you feel about the emeralds. I cannot give you the reason she is choosing this moment to end the betrothal. All I need to know for now is—do you love her?"

After a long pause Brandon looked into the eyes of his…friend. "I do not know. I suppose it is why I must try and make her stay, why I want her to stay. I just do not know."

But he wanted to.

A week later, Grace and her father were waiting in the drawing room for Lydia. They were attending a ball at the home of Lord and Lady Dorchester.

Grace's thoughts were in chaos and her nerves were raw. She had told Brandon days ago that they must argue publicly, that she needed to go home tomorrow when her father went. But Brandon had thwarted her. He had canceled each outing they had planned, every drive in the park, and had backed away even from accompanying her to the orphanage, giving her no outlet for the quarrel she'd intended to stage. She did not understand. Terminating the betrothal had been planned from the beginning, so why was he being so stubborn?

In theory, she could set it all in motion without him. They had not been seen together for days; the whole town must be wondering at it. That would certainly pass as a public display of the change in their relationship. She could send the notice to the *Gazette* herself and still leave tomorrow. But she would not do that to him, despite his dismissal of her.

She could not worry about that tonight, however. She would be meeting the blackmailer with the paste emeralds. And she was scared. She knew she was being followed everywhere. What if they mistook some simple action on her part as suspicious behavior? It could endanger Lydia or Brandon. She wished so much that she could share this burden with him, but she could not risk it. So she would go alone.

She had been unable to find out anything about who was behind the blackmail. The man who had threatened her early in the week had not contacted her again. She only knew they watched her. But if she could be brave enough, she hoped to get more information out of him once he was in happy possession of the emeralds. If Mr. Brownlow was the one behind the scheme, she could go to Brandon about the blackmail and they should be able to imprison him right away.

She had tried to keep her courage up all week, but it was quickly waning. She left a letter for Lydia and one for Brandon in the event something happened to her.

Father, please replace my fear with Your strength. Protect and deliver me and those I love from harm this night.

She could not think about it anymore.

Lord Pennington was reading the newspaper and she had to call his name twice to get his attention. "Papa, you *will* be back for Lydia's wedding, right? You will not hide in your library and forget?" She knew he would do no such thing, and even if he did, she would be home by then and able to drag him away.

"No, no. Believe it or not, it has been good to be in

London a little this Season. I may have avoided it for too long," he said, turning a page.

"What's this?" Grace asked with a painted-on smile. "Perhaps you have come to appreciate the advantages of being an eligible earl in Town. Have you been fawned over and petted?"

His face turned red and he sputtered, "Do not be impertinent, my girl. Everyone has been everything that is polite, but I am too set in my ways to be thinking of marriage again."

She kissed him on the cheek and said softly, "I only tease you, dear."

He became thoughtful and carelessly tapped his chin. "There is one woman, now that I think on it, who seems to latch on to me each time we meet although we have absolutely nothing in common. Beauty, though, I will say that." And he began reading his paper again.

"I do not think having anything in common is a requirement these days, Father. If one wants to be an earl's wife, beauty alone can sometimes make that happen."

"The strange thing is," he said, putting down his paper once again, "all she wishes to do is talk about you and Lord Weston."

Grace almost dropped her fan. Were the blackmailers letting her know just how close they could get to her family? "That *is* quite odd. Did you get her name?"

"Grace, you know how I am with names. I think it begins with a *W,* like Winthrop or Windsor? Something like that, but I am not sure at all."

Oh, dear! This could make things so much worse.

"Could it be Winslow, Father? Lady Patrice Winslow?" she asked.

"My dear, I think that is it! Do you know her?"

"I believe she had some hope of bringing Brandon up to scratch. She is no friend to me."

"By Jove, that explains it, then. She wanted to hear the details of how you met and how quickly the match developed. She even asked when the boy came to ask for your hand. I thought it just the normal gossip some women take to, but if it is out of jealousy then that explains it."

She tried to speak calmly. "What did you tell her, Father?"

"What could I tell her? I don't remember it myself. I told her to ask you. But I understand now why she did not want to do that! Perhaps you will see her at the ball tonight."

Chapter Sixteen

As Grace rode in the hackney, heading to the White-friars Stairs, fear overrode every other feeling. She did not think she could take much more. All she could do was rely on God.

She could no longer think straight. Was Mr. Brownlow the one behind the blackmail, after all? Or was someone else involved? She supposed she could mention different names to see if the blackmailer would reveal any indication that she could use as proof.

She couldn't think about it anymore. She had to be prepared to survive whoever was trying to hurt her and her loved ones.

The hackney stopped and the driver jumped down to open the door. "You catchin' a boat, lady?"

"No, I have to meet with someone. Will you wait, please? It should only take a moment and I will pay you for your time." Grace was pleading with him. It seemed safer, somehow, knowing there was someone close by, even if just to whisk her away from this scene.

"Sorry, lady, this ain't no place to be loiterin' after

dark. Might be you ought to think twice about gettin' out of this 'ere cab."

"No, I must go," she said, her voice sounding small, even to herself. "Will I be able to get another to take me home?"

"Lady," he said, frustrated, "there ain't no 'ackneys jest sittin' 'ere waitin' for fares. It's too dangerous, I tell you." She looked at him with pleading eyes. "I'll wait 'ere 'alf an 'our—no more. If there's trouble, it'll be less than that. You'd be smart to send a note to your 'ome now and have 'em pick you up 'ere straight away."

"No, if you will wait, that won't be necessary." She thanked him profusely and gave him a one-pound note. "Please wait if you can. I will pay you double that when I return." She turned and walked into the darkness. She would be brave from here on. No more shaking with fear. She had given it to God and she would trust Him.

She suspected her foe already knew she was here, but wanted her far enough away from the hackney before he approached. She heard ribald laughter as she walked by the Black Lion Inn, and tried to imagine Max at her side to ward off any evils. But he looked uncommonly like Brandon.

She was getting closer to the river; she could smell the foul garbage and wet wood. The sound of the lapping water against the wall sounded like a death knell to her. She had no idea how far she would have to walk; then, suddenly, he was behind her. He grabbed her arm and pulled her toward the stairs, at the bottom of which barges rocked in the water.

"Very good, my lady, right on time and alone as instructed," he hissed in her ear. "Do not rely on the hackney driver you had waiting. He has gone."

"Let me go," she said quietly, and wrenched her arm from his grasp. "Did Mr. Brownlow promise you a share in the jewels? I am sure it will be paltry compared to the total worth."

"What are you talking about? Shut up," he said, louder than he meant to. He softened his voice. "Just give me the emeralds."

"You might want to know that the law has already been apprised of Mr. Brownlow's nefarious schemes. You will never see your share if you must wait for him to find a buyer. He hasn't enough time."

"Woman, you are becoming tedious. I don't know who you speak of, but my share will be paid by..." She was surprised; he had almost let slip who would be paying him. "Give me the emeralds. Now." He said each word very slowly. She had never heard anything so sinister.

"I have them here." She tried to be brave, but knew her voice trembled. As she reached into her reticule, she wanted to be sure she had a grip on the pistol she had *not* forgotten this time.

She had to find out if he knew anything of Lady Winslow. The woman was clearly up to something, otherwise she would not have nagged Grace's father for information. She could not let Brandon be hurt by that lady's idle gossip.

"Hurry up," the blackmailer demanded.

"And what of Lady Winslow? What do you intend to do about her?"

His head shot up and he grasped her arm. The blackmailer *did* know Lady Winslow!

He began to stammer, realizing he had implicated

the lady. "I d-don't know these p-people you keep talking about, and I am weary of it." He ripped the reticule off her wrist and dug into it for the gems. She hid her hand, and the pistol that was in it, in the folds of her skirt. It gave her courage to keep trying for answers.

His response seemed to indicate he knew nothing of Mr. Brownlow. Not if his reaction to Lady Winslow's name was any indication…

Her mind began to race. Oh, how could she have been so stupid?

She had tried and tried to determine how Mr. Brownlow could know about their fake betrothal. It never made any sense, but suddenly, everything became clear. Mr. Brownlow had no known associates within the world of the *ton*. It was much more likely that Lady Winslow might have learned about it, not Mr. Brownlow! Grace had heard from her father only hours ago that the woman had been asking questions of him about their betrothal.

Could she be the one behind this? Was she in dire financial straits? Or…she could not be so malicious to do all this to discredit Grace with Brandon, *could* she? It was easier to believe it had come from the underworld of Mr. Brownlow. But if it was true, Lady Winslow would never have harmed Brandon. Grace had wasted so much precious time thinking it was the orphanage caretaker. Now, she had to be sure. God had given her the courage she'd prayed for!

"Lady Winslow will not be able to give you a portion of the money…ever." Grace hurried on. "She knows that the Weston emeralds are too widely known for her to try and sell them. And if she asked you to do that, as well, the outcome would be no different. None of *your* intimates would be able to pay you even half of what they are worth. She duped you!"

"You lie! You have no idea what you are talking about." He raised his arm, pointed his gun at Grace and cocked it. The sound was deafening.

She cocked her own much more quietly.

Brandon had arrived shortly behind the blackmailer and was shocked at what he heard.

She was being blackmailed for the emeralds! Brandon crouched behind a large cargo of barrels, listening to her quietly goading the man with the gun. This was no game. She was only making a dangerous man angry at her. Did she never know fear?

Brandon had had her followed since the day she had made the copies of the emeralds. It was the only way he could keep her safe. He realized she was going to give the man the paste copies, and for a moment understood the lengths she had gone to for him. But understanding gave way to anger at the risks she had taken. Why would she do this alone? She could have kept her promise to him and not entered into something like this again, without him. He could not think about it now, about how much it hurt that she did not trust him to help her.

Brandon would make himself known the minute she might be harmed, but for now he listened as she tried to make the man admit he had an accomplice. If she were a man, he would think her pluck to the backbone, be proud of her. But she was his Grace and she was putting herself in danger for a set of fake gems.

He had been concerned when she did not put in an appearance at the ball. It was then he received word from his under groom that she had hired a hackney, and Brandon followed her to Whitefriars. His heart lurched at the thought that someone was doing this to her for *his* property. Did she actually think he would rate the emeralds higher than her life? He did not know, because she had taken it upon herself to deal with this man.

His attention was jolted back to the present.

"Hurry up!" the blackmailer declared. Then the man pulled her reticule from her wrist.

Brandon had his own gun ready to intervene when Grace spoke again. She was playing fast and loose with her life each moment she lingered, and he could not wait any longer.

But he stopped abruptly at her next words.

"And what of Lady Winslow? What do you intend to do about her?" Brandon heard the man's gasp. What on earth...?

"You never would have killed Lord Weston. She would not harm him. Yet that was the threat you held over my head."

Brandon rose from where he crouched and began to walk toward them, outside their peripheral vision. He might have to shoot quickly.

As the blackmailer started backing away from her, Brandon knew the man was buying time, trying to get into the darkness before he resorted to shooting her. He would have to disappear quickly.

Grace looked confused at the sound of a second gun cocking, and then saw Brandon come up behind the blackmailer and put his gun against the man's head.

Brandon thought he saw her sway on her feet, and he willed her not to faint. "Grace," he said, trying to keep her focus on him.

"Brandon," she said breathlessly.

"Are you hurt?" At the shake of her head, his voice became ominous. "You will excuse me if I take care of this little matter before I escort you home." He spoke through gritted teeth, anger emanating from his entire body. The gun the man was holding dropped to the ground as Brandon twisted his wrist to the breaking point. He then moved his arm up and around the black-mailer's throat, the gun still pressed against his temple.

"Lady Grace gave you more credit than you deserve, little man. I do not believe you *were* planning on see-ing Lady Winslow again. She would make you give her the emeralds. No, I believe you were going to hop one of those barges and ferry to the first ship leaving Lon-don." Brandon growled low as he squeezed the man's neck tighter. "You will be leaving, but not on the ship that you hoped for."

Brandon asked again if Grace was safe, and at her nod, relaxed inside just a bit. Only God would know how scared he had been at the thought of losing her. "Would you please stay over by those casks for a mo-ment? I realize I cannot count on you to remain there very long, but I hope to have my business done swiftly." He had the luxury of being fully and unremittingly angry with her, now that he knew she was safe.

He dragged the cloaked man several yards to a moor-ing that was attached to a large freight boat at the bot-tom of the steps. Brandon thought he recognized the man in a beard leaning up against it.

"Evenin', me lord. I thought that was you, but you ain't been round these parts of late."

"Good to see you again, Captain. You are just the man I need. Still doing your runs to the colonies? Perhaps you are interested in those who would bring a good price as indentured servants?"

The blackmailer began to shake and tried to break away from him. When Brandon tightened his grip on the man's collar, it was all he could do not to choke the life out of him. "Little man, if you struggle too much, you will take a fall that will end badly for you. Whether you die here with a broken neck or from scurvy in the hull of a ship is of little importance to me."

"No, let me go. I will not hurt you or your lady, I promise. I will just disappear. Please let me go." The man pleaded like a child.

"As you were going to let my lady go?" Brandon asked, so angry his teeth were clenched and his jaw muscle twitched. "You *are* about to disappear, my friend, where no one dear to me will ever be threatened by you again." He threw the captain a bag of coins and the sailor snapped his fingers. Four dirty seamen appeared out of the darkness and dragged the crying man down the stairs to the Thames and the barge waiting there. Something was stuffed inside the man's mouth to stifle his cries.

The captain tossed the bag of coins up and down in his hands a few times and said, "Always a pleasure doin' business with ye, my lord." And he, too, disappeared.

Brandon walked to the casks, but did not say a word to Grace. He took her by the hand, only to realize she once again had a gun in it. He removed it and pulled her down several side alleys to where his carriage waited.

He was a little surprised she did not utter a sound, but perhaps she understood his mood.

When they entered the carriage and it started to move, she began to speak quietly. "Brandon, I can explain everything. They were not your emeralds. I never would have given them the real emeralds."

"Grace," he said, in just as menacing a tone as he had used with the blackmailer, "do not say a word. Not one word. I could hear your conversation, so there is no need for your explanation."

"But you could not have known from that conversation that the emeralds were copies."

"I *should* have known from you telling me yourself, long before this. You promised me, Grace."

"I had to break my promise. I had to go alone. They threatened—"

"Stop! You promised me never to do this again. You have known my overall impression of women as a whole as untrustworthy and false, but I thought you were different."

He heard her crying yet he was too hurt to feel for her. He could not think about Patrice and the havoc she had played with their lives. There would be time to address that; right now all he could see was red. "You all resort to tears, thinking we dread the sight of them and will want to make you feel better. Well, I do not."

"Can I at least explain…?"

"No." His voice was dangerously quiet. "You lost my trust tonight, Grace."

He wanted to get one last thing off his chest, then he would be finished. "Where was all your talk about not being able to tell a lie, Grace? Does your God not frown upon using His rules indiscriminately? Or is it just me you lie to? I trusted you, because I saw all of your actions match your words. I will not trust you again, you can be sure of that."

"No, Brandon, please do not say that, please..."

"Blast! Grace, in the event you are not aware, I am angrier than I have ever been. If you do not stay quiet, I cannot answer for what I might say. Just *do not talk.*"

And they did not, for several days.

Once again he did not call for their daily ride. He did not offer to escort her to the Midforths' soiree. He had not spoken to her or tried to contact her in days.

Grace was brokenhearted. She wanted the chance to explain. She wanted to tell him everything. She needed to share the whole experience with him, her own fears, the fears for his life and her family's. She wished she could tell him how safe she'd felt the minute she had heard his voice there. It was unusual for her to want— no, *need*—to share her thoughts and feelings with someone else, and he would not listen. She had braved it all for him, and he was angry that she had gone out once again alone.

It was definite. She loved him with all her heart. It was the complete trust in another person, an overwhelming feeling of safety and coming home. Putting someone else's welfare over your own even if it meant your life. But she could not tell him that, and he would not permit her to even explain the rest. It was not the way they had planned it. She had promised she would not fall in love with him. It was what the entire relationship was predicated upon. And it was clear that even Brandon was ready for the end of their idyll. She would keep her promise to him at the cost of her heart.

Brandon could not remember ever being so angry at anyone. It had hit him between the eyes—he was so angry because he loved her so much. She had promised she would never put herself in such danger again and she had broken her word. He'd waited and waited patiently for her to tell him beforehand. So many times he'd wanted to tell her that he'd seen her in the jewelers, but he wanted her to trust him enough to tell him on her own. How could he have ever imagined such a scheme was afoot? He wanted her to trust him, to need him as much as he did her. He wanted her to love him as he loved her, to distraction.

How had he ever thought himself in love before? When he wasn't with her, he wondered what she was doing. When caught in the middle of a humorous situation, all they had to do was make eye contact and she understood. If she was not with him, he could not wait to tell her. His life revolved around her.

He had grown used to life revolving around *his* desires. His work with the orphanages was a priority, but everything else was by his choice—what to do, where to go, who he wished to be with. Now there was no question; he wanted to be with Grace. But he wanted her to trust him. He had been a fool to believe that this time what he wanted might actually be within his grasp. After all, it never had been before.

He had promised she could walk out of the betrothal. But he had expected it all to end with an open quarrel— as agreed upon and planned. He had never expected Grace to go behind his back, to lie to him for any reason. And he already knew she could never love him. Lord Langdon had tried to make Brandon believe he could be worthy of her love, *was* worthy of her love. But Grace had to feel that way, as well, and he knew she did not.

When he took her home that night, he'd let her down from his carriage stoically. After he led her to her front door, he had turned and left without a word. He was afraid of what he might say if he tarried. She could have been killed, probably would have been killed if he had not followed her there. She was so reckless. It was not to be borne. And even then he did not speak, because he was afraid he would crush her in his arms, telling her, and her God, how grateful he was for her safety.

So he took his anger out on the blackmailer. He headed straight back to Whitefriars and went immediately to the barge. The captain led him to the corner where the man was cringing in fear. Brandon spent over an hour getting every detail out of the miserable cur. He knew the blackmailer hoped he had forgotten about the emeralds in his hurry to see Grace safe. Brandon had purposely let the sniveling excuse for a man believe he would be able to either buy himself off the captain's ship or sell the jewels to live as a rich man when they reached the Americas. It had been a pleasure to tell him the emeralds were paste.

Great as his amusement was in that moment, the time

preceding it had been more soberly spent as he learned all he could of Patrice Winslow's involvement in the scheme. Would she truly go to such lengths? Could she have threatened Grace's life as well as his own in a plot to get him back? He did not want to believe she was capable of it. But he got enough information from the man to confirm it, and all it did was fan the flame of his anger.

There were details he had to look into before confronting Patrice, and he decided he needed to do that before he saw Grace again. It might lessen the feelings that had wrought such fear in him at the thought of her there alone.

It was the night of Lord and Lady Hilliard's ball and Brandon was supposed to escort her. She did not feel like attending such a gathering in her state of mind, but Aunt Aggie was a little under the weather and Lydia needed a chaperone. Would she see Brandon there? She did not know—nor did she know how she might respond to the sight of him, or him to the sight of her. She had been ready to end the connection, but now that she knew the night at the dock was the last time she would see him, she wished she had not pressed for it. Yet the matter was out of her hands now. He was done with her.

Lord Hendricks greeted them as soon as they were through the receiving line. He graciously kissed Grace's hand, then turned adoring eyes to his betrothed.

"Lydia, love, you look rather fetching tonight," he said, and winked at her. He was the perfect man for her. Lydia's beauty was not the reason for his love. "May

I have the pleasure of this dance, darling girl?" Lydia put her hand into his, but they did not move on. "Grace, may I take you to your first partner? I have not seen Brandon yet."

"No, do go on. I was not sure I would attend, so have the luxury to greet friends."

They left her and Grace caught snatches of the sweet endearments they whispered to each other as they walked away. Tears welled up in her eyes. Brandon would never say those things to her; well, never say them and mean them. She missed him so much. How would she cope back at the Abbey, where there was not the smallest hope of seeing him, even catching a glimpse of him?

It was as if God heard the question as a prayer, as she saw him across the room. He must have come in after her as she'd wandered aimlessly about. Her first thought was to go to him. She started his way, then stopped. He likely had no desire to see her or talk to her. Would he cut her publicly?

A group of young people who had been waiting for the next set moved toward the dance floor, and her view of him was no longer obstructed. There he stood, with his head bowed low, listening to the whispers of *Lady Winslow!*

It broke her heart into a million pieces. She knew he was angry at her, but he'd been there that night. He knew the truth about what Lady Winslow had done. Yet he was still tantalized by the woman who had threatened to kill him *and* her! The pair stood there, close as inkle weavers, when he had gone without so much as a word to Grace in days. She watched as he put out his hand to lead Lady Winslow through the French doors next to them.

Grace began to inch her way around the crowd of dancers, hoping to follow them outside. It sunk her beyond reproach in her own eyes, but she had to know what they were doing, what they were saying to each other.

"Brandon," Patrice said huskily, "to what do I owe this honor? Do not tell me there is trouble in paradise?" She smiled seductively. "Has your country maiden bored you so soon?"

She pouted and pressed closer to him. "I know I should not forgive you so quickly. Indeed, I ought to make you beg, but I cannot. I knew you would come back to me, so I will not waste the time." She gazed up into his eyes and he put her arm in the crook of his and led her outside.

Once there, he let go of her and leaned back against the balustrade on the veranda, with one leg bent at the knee. He crossed his arms over his chest and stared at the garden to the left. He wanted her to squirm, to worry about his actions. "It occurs to me, my dear..." he uttered in a low voice, then turned to look at her. "You seem to know quite a bit about my engagement, do you not?"

"I know she was too provincial for a man like you, Brandon. You need a more sophisticated woman who can, shall we say, keep your interest," Lady Winslow drawled. "And you were coming to the conclusion that the woman you needed was me, before you left for your house party. When you came back engaged, I admit I was angry, but then I realized it was just a matter of time until you induced her to cry off."

"But, Patrice," he said, with no indication of his inner mood, "you know I fell head over heels in love with Lady Grace. Why would I want her to cry off?"

"You know you did not—" she said quickly, then retraced her steps. "I mean, you barely knew her, by all accounts I heard. I was sure it could not be serious."

"I believe you started to say something entirely different, Patrice. You started to say I 'did not' what?" His eyes bored into hers and he didn't know how long he could play this part without strangling her. "You started to say that I met Grace at an inn, and not at her father's home. You started to say I had never even been to her home."

"I do not know what you are talking about, Brandon. I just knew you could not want *her!*" She started to walk down the steps, but he stopped her with his voice.

"But you do know what I am talking about, my dear. You see, I know everything. I know about the blackmail attempt. You must not mistake me, I said *attempt.* I believe you will find my perspicacity quite astounds you. Let me see, yes, I know that you have been interrogating Lady Grace's father." It was getting harder with every word to remain calm. "And I know you threatened my betrothed with my death if she did not turn over the Weston emeralds to your lackey."

His companion had not moved and he said, with his finger tapping his chin, "The only thing I do not know,

Patrice, is how you planned to use the emeralds. You certainly could never wear them. I am the only person who could put them around your neck without raising the law against you. So, was it for money, then?" He continued, more at ease now that they were getting to her part in the crime. "No, I think it could not have been for that. They are too recognizable to sell, and I've investigated your finances. Seems old Winslow left you pretty well set up. No, the trouble of trying to sell something so easily identifiable would not be worth the risk simply for money you do not need."

He stood up straight now, with his arms still crossed over his chest. "Therefore, I can see only one reason for the whole sordid attempt. You were trying to discredit Grace. Apparently, you were not *so* sure I would tire of her, after all."

She turned back toward the house, whipping the train of her gown down the steps behind her. She tried to walk past him, saying, "I do not know what you are talking about. Your country mouse has your emeralds, not me."

He grabbed her arm tightly and turned her to face him. "Did you never wonder why your minion did not bring them to you? Or perhaps you did not even care if he ran off with them, because you still could have brought to light that Lady Grace had lost my family heirlooms."

He gripped her arm tighter. "Had the *emeralds* fallen into your hands, you *would* have been able to make a case against her."

"Let go of me, Brandon, you are hurting me!"

"Yes, my dear, but Grace still has my gems. And do you know why? Not because your man failed, but because my provincial lady was smart enough to have copies made first." He felt her flinch. "You would have come to me with the story that she had lost the set, and you would have handed me these." He reached into his pocket and pulled out the paste jewels. "And she would have produced the real ones."

He smiled menacingly. "But when your little cohort did not show up with the emeralds, you had no evidence. Were you planning to accuse her of selling the gems, Patrice? Once again, she could produce the real ones. Either way you would have been caught."

She tugged at his arm, but he had no intention of letting her go yet. "No harm has come to the emeralds—they remain in the proper hands. The true problem, though, is that you could have gotten my affianced hurt or killed. I am afraid I cannot let that go unpunished." He seethed in anger. "And if I find out that Lady Grace heard about Baxter Orphanage from you, and you sent ruffians there to hurt her, I will wring your neck with my bare hands."

He had never wanted someone to suffer more than he did at this instant. And in this totally inappropriate moment, a picture of Grace appeared in his mind, telling him never to hate, that it would only hurt him. She would remind him again that "there but for the grace of God go I."

Lady Winslow began to tremble, and he tried to loosen his hold on her so he would not hurt her, but not enough that she could run away.

"Brandon, darling, someone has been making up lies about me. I tell you, I know nothing of this. Your betrothed must be more jealous of me than I thought to have concocted this wild tale."

His anger burned and he pulled the woman's face closer to his. "No, Patrice, I have done my research. Your sleazy little friend did not trust *you* any more than you trusted him. He left written notes all over London in the event you didn't come through with his payment. I have also talked to Lord Pennington about your questions to him. And I was there that night at Whitefriars. I heard your man incriminate you. You have accomplished nothing but your banishment from England. That is, of course, *if* I let you off so easily." And with Grace's face in his mind, he knew that was the worst he would do.

But Lady Winslow tried a different tack and turned fully toward him, putting them very close together. She brought her free arm up around his neck. With crocodile tears filling her eyes, she whispered, "No, Brandon, don't you see? I love you so much. I would never have harmed you or her. I just wanted you to be mad enough at her to come back to me. I have missed you, Brandon. I love you." Then she pulled his head to hers and kissed him.

He tugged the arm from around his neck and pushed her away with both hands. Languidly, he said, "You never had me, Patrice. Now listen to me. Your slimy cohort has been shipped off to a life I would not wish on my worst enemy. But not before he testified against you. I will give *you* a choice. But only because I would not put Grace through a public trial unless I have to."

She gasped at the word *trial*. "You would not! Please, Brandon…"

"Either you will leave England of your own volition within forty-eight hours or I make you a solemn vow I will press charges. Do you understand?"

"Brandon, you cannot mean it. Leave England? Where would I go?"

"To be honest, I could not care less what becomes of you. But you had better make your plans in a hurry."

She must have decided her innocent act was useless, and began to speak in a shrill voice. "You would not press charges against me. Think of what the *ton* would say. Think what that will do to your own name."

He laughed out loud. "I do not give a hang about my reputation in London. In fact, as you well know, it just might enhance it."

His humor was only a facade. His anger made him hard. "If you do not leave of your own accord, you will either be transported or you will be so shunned by Society that you may as well be gone. I will not be understanding or forgiving about this. I want you gone from England. If I see your face again, I will have Bow Street on your heels." He pushed her aside and strode down the veranda steps toward the stables to order his coach.

Once again, his thoughts turned to Grace. Would she approve of his punishment for Patrice? Even when she spoke of God's grace, wouldn't there still be consequences? Patrice was certainly not getting what she deserved. He could not wait to ask Grace about it.

* * *

Grace finally made it through the crowded ballroom to where she had seen Brandon and Lady Winslow walk outside. When she rested her hand on the doorjamb she saw them on the steps. They were standing face-to-face, mere inches apart, with Brandon holding tightly to one of her arms. Grace saw their mouths moving. How she wished she could hear what they were saying! Why would he even spend a moment with her after all he knew?

Then Lady Winslow put her other arm up around Brandon's neck, brought his head down to hers for a kiss. Grace's heart broke. She turned away from the window, tears blinding her eyes.

She picked up her skirt and hurried around the outer circle of the ballroom. She was making a scene, but she did not care. The longed-for public disagreement was happening, even now, and no one would ever suspect she was pretending. She found Lydia and Lord Hendricks and told them she had to leave. Dennis offered to escort her home, but Grace only wanted him to make sure that Lydia got home safely.

"Grace, what is it? You are as white as a sheet. Dennis, would you get our wraps and meet us at the door?"

"No," Grace ground out, and then apologized. "No, darling, you stay. I am only in a hurry to get back to Berkeley Square. I am leaving at first light to return to the Abbey, due to a sudden emergency. I have much packing to do in a short period of time." She kissed her sister's cheek and whispered in her ear, "I will see you soon." She left without another word.

In the carriage ride home, sobs engulfed her. She felt as if she had done nothing but cry since she'd met Brandon. Her thoughts ran unchecked in every direction. It was as if he had slapped her in the face, she hurt so badly. She told herself she must think about it outside of the fact that she loved him. He was free, to a degree, and had been from the outset. She had no grounds on which to accuse him of anything. If she had let herself love him, that was her problem, not his.

But, no, even if *she* had no hold on him, why would he be with *her?* Was he really the rake he said he was? Had they plotted the blackmail together? Oh, she could not think that. But Brandon knew Lady Winslow had forced her hand under the threat of harming him. Was she telling him all the details he did not learn at the dock? Was it a good joke between them? Grace felt sick to her stomach and had to catch her breath. The sobs became silent tears rolling down her cheeks.

It was not his fault that she had fallen in love with him. But it was his fault that he could not even wait until the engagement was officially broken before he resumed his relationship with Lady Winslow. Anyone else could have looked through that doorway at exactly the same time she had. Their excuse could no longer be that they did not suit. All of London would smirk and wonder how she could have expected him to be faithful to her.

She swiped at the tears on her face. But this green girl would not be here to see Society's response. She had been naive enough to believe he had only been acting the rake so no one suspected the altruism behind the facade. She believed it no more. He had never stopped being the rake. She remembered their betrothal ball and how angry he had been with her because she would not kiss him properly. Oh, she had seen everything through the eyes of a fool.

But the silent tears began again at the hurt, and the memories she had collected and stowed away in her heart, with the intent of cherishing them in the days to come, were now tainted.

Brandon was alone in his library, emotionally spent. He wished now that he had returned to the ballroom to see Grace. He had missed her, though the divide was self-imposed. And it was the fear of losing Grace that had angered him to the point of staying away from her for a few days. He knew he could trust her. He had known it all along. But he wanted her to trust him, to *need* him, too. Once he learned the blackmailer had threatened his life if she went to him, he knew her reasons. He would have done the same thing.

But when he thought about what could have happened to her that night, even before she met up with the blackmailer, he cringed. He knew now he could not live without her. She was everything he wanted in a woman. Little wonder he loved her.

And she was planning their parting of the ways. He could not let it happen. He had to think of some way to convince her to remain in London. He could make her love him. He would make no more mistakes with her. He wanted to be the man she needed; he would change, but he would need her help.

He had to make this betrothal real.

Chapter Seventeen

Brandon received the package from his butler on a
silver salver at breakfast the next morning. Recognizing Grace's handwriting, he broke the seal and began
to read the missive without waiting for his servant to
leave the room.

He was eager to meet with Grace today. He felt almost dirty from his scene with Patrice, and Grace was
goodness, and laughter and…grace. He would apologize for his silence and anger the other night in the
carriage. He would begin his attack on her heart. More
than anything, he wanted this woman to love and trust
him. He would explain it all to her and ask *her* to show
him grace and mercy! He would ask her how he should
handle their disagreements in the future. If only she
would agree to a future with him…

Therefore, he eagerly opened her missive.

Brandon,
I believe our plan for a public disagreement has
now become unnecessary by our actions of the

past two days. This is as good an opportunity as any, so I sent a notice to the *Gazette* this morning (from you) announcing the end of our engagement. Thank you for all of the help you and your family have been to Lydia. We owe you a debt of gratitude.

Your servant,

Grace Endicott

P.S. This messenger also returns your emeralds.

His shocked shout informed the servants that the missive had not been a pleasant one. "Have my stallion saddled and brought around immediately," he growled. He was going to see her and he was going to see her now. What kind of note was that? *Gratitude?* He did not want her gratitude!

When he arrived in Berkeley Square, he knocked loud enough to wake the dead, and almost pushed Jamison over in his hurry to get to Grace. "Sorry, old man, I'm in rather a hurry. Don't worry, I will announce myself. Where is she?"

"I am sorry, my lord," the butler informed him, pulling on his cuffs and brushing himself off. "Lady Grace is not at home."

Did she think he could be pawned off with that sad excuse? "You may tell her she is at home to me!" If she was hiding somewhere in the house, he wanted her to hear him.

Lydia appeared in the doorway of the drawing room, with Dennis right behind her. "My lord, what is amiss? Why are you shouting the house down?"

"Lydia, will you please tell your sister that I wish to see her, *will* see her. I will sit in this foyer with Max and old Jamison until I speak to her."

Lydia spoke quietly to Dennis, who retreated into the drawing room. She pulled the door closed behind him. "Will you come with me to the blue room, my lord? It is not often used, as it is in the back of the house. We may speak freely there."

He followed her. "Lydia, we do not need to speak freely anywhere. I just wish to talk to Grace."

"Lord Weston," she said, looking at him in confusion. "Grace is not here. She left for home early this morning." She lowered her voice so no one could hear. "I assumed it was all part of the plan and that you knew."

He sat down on a divan and gestured for her to sit next to him. "Tell me from the beginning, my dear. When did she decide to go to Pennington Abbey?"

"I do not really know, sir," Lydia explained. "Last night at the Hilliards' ball, about halfway through the evening, she sought out Dennis and me to let us know she was going home. I thought she meant here, but there were tears in her eyes, and when we offered to accompany her, she told us that something had come up and she needed to go to the Abbey. She was leaving to pack."

Lydia began to fidget. "I thought you'd had your argument. You have been avoiding each other for days. I had hoped that it would turn out different... Well, no matter. There were real tears in her eyes, my lord. If it was not you who made her cry, then who did?" She began to wring her hands. "It was apparent to those around us that she was distressed. I was sure you had ended your engagement."

He gently laid his hand over hers for a moment, then removed it to run it through his hair.

"So this was not planned?" she asked, now growing agitated. "Then something must have occurred to upset her. I am so stupid. Obviously, she could not have received word in the middle of a ball regarding the Abbey. Excuse me, my lord, but I must pack," she said, adamantly. "I must have a courier get a note to her that I am returning home."

"No, I will go," he said quietly. He feared his foolish behavior of keeping his distance had sent her running home. His only chance of happiness went with her. "We had planned a way to sever the connection, but it was not for now, and not in this way. Yet today I received this note." He handed it to her as he spoke. "I need to get to the bottom of this. I will go to see her at the Abbey."

"I do not know what happened, Lord Weston, but whatever it was, it appears she used it to bring your betrothal to an end." She looked up at him through blue pools of water in her eyes. "I think things must not have happened the way she thought they would. You know her, my lord. She usually manages things for the best."

"For whose best?"

"For all of us, to be sure, but probably still putting herself last." Lydia twisted her hands again. "My lord, I do not think you have realized how hard this was for Grace. Indeed, she has been so different these last two weeks I hardly know her." She teared up again. "I know you both did this to prevent any stains on your reputations, but do not think I am unaware that the most important part of the arrangement was to give me a chance to secure the happiness I have found with Dennis."

"Lydia…"

"No, you must listen. I know for you the engagement was beneficial, amusing even, but Grace was often distraught. If someone or something hurt her or angered her last night, she would not normally run away. She would have stayed to face it. Perhaps it is just that she wanted to be home again."

He did not want to listen. He could feel himself deflating more as each moment passed.

"I will write her to be sure she is well," Lydia said. "She does not usually tell me things that upset her, because she does not wish to upset *me*. She probably won't let me come, but I might at least assure myself that she is all right. Whatever the trouble is, she is using it to dissolve your betrothal. I would not wish for you to cut up her peace. I will tell her you would like to come and see her, and if it is agreeable to her, I will send you word. May we please do it that way?"

"Is that what you think I wish to do, cut up her peace? I lov— I look for the opportunity to get my own assurances."

"My lord," Lydia said to him, making him gaze at her as she handed him back the note, "is this not what you wanted? Whether it was exactly the way you planned or not, it has come to the same end. Why *must* you go after her?"

When had this child grown up? When had she become the protective one? And why did she show such bravery now? He did not know what to say except, "It is not what I want." He ran his hands through his hair once again. "But I will respect your wishes for now. And only on the condition that you send me word as soon as possible, whether she wants to see me or not."

She nodded, almost as if this conversation had taken everything out of her. In the midst of the turmoil in his heart, he was proud of her. "Before I go, I would like to beg a favor of you, and ask that you not question me about it."

"Of course," she said, though when she heard his request, her eyes opened wide.

"I do not know, sir. I do not know if she would want him moved. Never mind. Of course you may do it."

Why did he still feel as if his heart was breaking?

Grace sat thoughtfully as her father calculated his next move on the chessboard. She had been back at the Abbey for three days, but her thoughts were never far from London or Brandon.

She had received Lydia's note. She smiled as she realized Lydia was now worried for her. In her letter she had asked if she and Lord Weston could come to see her. Grace had sent a gentle refusal aimed at them both. She was happy to be home and back to normal. Tearing Lydia away from her adored Lord Hendricks was unnecessary, and as far as seeing Brandon... No, that was not to be considered.

Her father nudged her back to the present with his words. "Grace, it is your move, though why I should tell you, I know not. You will capture my king with three more." He looked at her strangely, and she knew her cheeks turned a rosy red. "I could have moved several pieces around to my advantage, and you would not have noticed. Are you not in the mood for chess?"

They sat in the drawing room in front of a warm

fire. "No, no, of course I wish to play." She looked at the board and made the first of the moves that would make her the winner.

When Grace appeared at the Abbey, she had told her father that she and Brandon had decided they would not suit, but she'd claimed her tears were the result of being so happy to be home. He did not question her decision, but it was soon apparent that he was afraid she had ended the engagement for his sake. He was upset that she had taken it too much to heart when he'd told her he didn't know what he would do without her taking care of the estate.

She had sat in the crook in his arm and told him through her tears that he was being exceedingly chuckleheaded. She gave him truthful answers: she did not fit in Brandon's world and life in London was so shallow and purposeless. But she did not tell him the real reason she had come home. Afterward, she unpacked her things, began her normal routine, and they had not spoken of it since.

"Grace, it is your move again."

"I am sorry, Father."

"What is on your mind, girl?"

"It is not any one thing. I have much to do before we begin to get ready to go back to London for Lydia's wedding." She smiled at him. "I keep making lists in my head and am very poor company. Would you mind if I went to bed and read myself to sleep?"

"Not at all, dear, not at all."

She kissed the top of his head. "Good night, Father." But she got little sleep that night. She could not get

Brandon off her mind. Each night her heart and her head betrayed her with thoughts of him. She must forget him. He had moved on; so must she.

Instead of lying in bed, she got up early, determined to banish him from her thoughts. She had many duties that needed her attention this day, and she would go about them in her old manner, with pleasure and practicality.

But when she reached the foyer at the bottom of the stairs, Stone was ushering in several men trying to fit a *huge* crate through the front door. It was over eight feet tall, and several servants stopped to stare at it.

"Stone, what on earth…?"

"I cannot tell you, my lady."

"Who sent it?"

"There is no indication of its origin, and the men who delivered it knew nothing about it."

"Well, get something to pry it open," she said, awed by the sheer size of the box.

"I just sent a footman, my lady."

Between the four of them, they finally pried the front cover loose, and Stone made her stand back as he unhinged the huge lid and moved it to the side.

Grace's hands flew to her mouth and her eyes opened wide. Inside the crate stood Max. With a greatcoat wrapped around his shoulders and a top hat balanced precariously on the headpiece of the armor, he looked ridiculous and…marvelous. She walked up to him, not knowing what to think. Who would go to all the trouble to send Max here?

She noticed Max's left hand was propped up and had

a velvet box tied to it. She lifted the box and started shaking, knowing what was inside. She opened it and found the emeralds. Brandon had certainly thought of the most creative way she could have ever imagined to give them back to her; it was one of the many things she loved about her rake. But she knew he did not truly want *her* back. She had seen him with Lady Winslow.

As she started to turn away and give Stone directions where to place Max, she noticed a piece of paper stuck on the point of the lance he always had in his right hand. She reached up and lifted it off. She could see it was one of Brandon's calling cards, but when she turned it over, she saw the writing on the back.

Grace,
I have sent Max to his new home at the Abbey. I await you in town, where I might be your knight in shining armor and the hero of your heart. Can Max take second place?
Yours always,
Brandon

Grace covered her face with her hands. Why was he doing this to her? He had taken up with Lady Winslow again, had he not? *He cannot be Your will for me, can he, Father? Please show me what to do.*

Suddenly, the most preposterous thought popped into her mind. Could she do it? She would have to try.

In the two weeks since Grace had been gone, all of London had been abuzz at the news of their broken betrothal. The *Gazette*'s notice had shocked everyone, including Brandon's sisters and Lord Hendricks.

All of them had appeared on his doorstep within hours of the notice, and all had been told it was none of their business. He was old enough to know how to handle his own affairs.

Lady Wright was unsympathetic. "Brandon, must you constantly bring scandal down upon this family? What did you do to the girl?"

He ignored her remarks and sent her packing, but it was harder to be dismissive when Maggie came to him. She held both his hands and looked deeply into his eyes, and he only hoped he successfully hid his pain.

"Brandon, do not let this kind of love slip away. I cannot explain it, I do not think it is anything you *can* explain, but you must know that marriage to the one you truly love is unlike anything else. It is communication on a deeper and more intimate level than you have ever known. It is sharing things you never thought you could share, the good and the bad, with so much joy over the good and no condemnation over the bad."

He started to turn away, but she kept hold of his hands. "I know you truly love Grace. And *you* have been different. I do not know if I can say happier, because you always play your tricks and I never know when you are completely serious. But you seemed more content, especially when Grace was at your side. She *changed* you. And I know she loves you. I could see it often in her eyes as she watched you."

He squeezed her hands and smiled his true smile down at her, though it did not banish the sadness he felt. "I fear we could not love each other as much as you think, Maggie, because we have not been able to solve our problem. Do not worry over me. You go home to that Irish husband of yours and enjoy your own love."

He did not add that he knew he didn't deserve Grace. God would not condone her marriage to a rake...even an ex-rake. He never knew if it was God that made her different than any other woman he had known or if her managing, stubborn, self-reliant personality was to blame. But he loved her just the same, and realized she would laugh with him if she knew his thoughts.

Lord Hendricks was a little more forthright when he came. "What happened, Brandon? I have never seen you so happy as when you were with Lady Grace."

For a quick moment Brandon thought about the promise Lydia had made to tell no one of their secret, and he was impressed that she had been able to keep that difficult promise for them, especially from her intended.

"Dennis," Brandon began, attempting to rein in his temper, "it is a long story." He was trying to remember that Dennis was truly his friend and only asking out of worry for him. "Our differences *seem* irreconcilable to us. I just don't have answers now."

Lord Langdon never mentioned the broken engagement at all. Perhaps he knew that the others hounded Brandon, and he wanted to give him some space. But Brandon could certainly have used his advice.

And Grace? She had never even acknowledged his message sent by way of Max. But she had not returned the emeralds, either. He wanted to believe she was waiting until she came back to London for Lydia's wedding, that she would tell him he *could* be her Max, but it was too hard to anticipate a reconciliation.

The rest of London had watched him closely and had been speculating about the pair. Most thought he would return to Lady Winslow. They knew he was never without female companionship for long. But she had left Town, so they watched, wondering who would be next. And Brandon did not disappoint. He threw himself into the Season with abandon. He made an appearance at most social events and flirted with some, danced with others, all without ever singling out one particular lady.

It had become the only way he thought he could get Grace off his mind. It failed miserably.

After a week of his old way of life he realized that Maggie had been right. Grace *had* changed him. He got no pleasure from his idle, wastrel activities of the past. As soon as Dennis's wedding was over, he would throw himself into getting Brownlow sent to Newgate, and the orphanage habitable. Or he would go to Westmoreland and rusticate for a few months; he would meet with his estate manager. He would be the man he should have been long ago.

But he had to remain in Town another week, and the anticipation was building. He was Dennis's best man and Grace was Lydia's attendant. He knew Grace had offered to withdraw from the honor, as had he. This wedding needed to be all about Lydia and Dennis. But neither Lord Hendricks nor Lady Lydia would allow it. So he waited for the wedding day and the disruption he and Grace would cause.

Chapter Eighteen

When Max had been firmly established at the bottom of the staircase at the Abbey, Grace had written a letter to Lydia asking if she was completely sure she still wanted her to come to the wedding. Grace *wanted* to be there, *needed* to be there, and she had been seeking God's will to determine what she must do regarding Brandon. But she would not have Lydia's wedding become a circus to the shallow, gossiping *ton*. Not at any cost.

So she waited to hear from her sister before she made any plans. Grace had received Lydia's letter with misgiving.

Dearest Grace,
It matters not one whit to me that the *ton* may cause a scene or pay more attention to you and Lord Weston than to Dennis and me. You know the only reason we are even having the wedding in London is because Father and Dennis are both

peers. It seems silly to me, but have no fear. I
will have eyes only for him, so nothing that happens around me can change that. But I cannot do
it without my beloved sister and best of friends
with me.
All my love,
Lydia

So two weeks later, Grace returned to London. She
hated missing the preparations and planning with Aunt
Aggie and Lydia during those weeks, but thought it
best not to be in Town while gossip was rampant. She
worked hours on end at the estate, trying to keep her
mind off of Brandon, and went to bed each night and
tried not to dream of him. But she could not stop thinking about her scheme to get some real answers from
him. It would be the most outlandish thing she had ever
done, even more so than pretending to be betrothed to
him!

She came back to London with a new resolve and
a new prayer.

Brandon's actions with Max had spoken volumes to
her; perhaps it *was* the answer to those prayers. But she
had seen him kissing Lady Winslow that night. The note
that came with Max intimated that he wanted to pursue
their relationship. But he had often flirted with her thus.
If Lady Winslow was out of the picture, he could have
easily moved on to another by now. She was confused,
but she would wait for God's indication of finality before she gave up all hope.

She feared her plan might make matters worse rather

than grant the hope that still remained, but she would not let this chance of real love, at least on her part, slip away.

She and Lydia were happy to be reunited. Aunt Aggie got right to the point. "Well, young lady," she said to Grace when they were all settled in the drawing room, "you have created the *on dit* of the Season, and I did not expect it of you!" She did not even stop for air. "You are looking quite pale, my dear. Have you been overdoing it in the country?"

She knew she was not looking her best. It was hard to do so with little sleep. "I *am* sorry, Aunt Aggie, for all of the trouble I've caused. I know I should have told you of my plans before I left. But the trip home was the only solution I could see at the time. I am sure you would have been very uncomfortable as Brandon and I tried to avoid each other. I really needed that time to pray and think, and now I would prefer discussing Lydia and the wedding."

Lydia was only too happy to change the subject. She was even more beautiful, if that were possible. "Grace, I am so happy. We are having the wedding breakfast here afterward, then Dennis and I will leave for Greece for a month! I will be so happy to be alone with him, but I am a little afraid." She grabbed Grace's hands. "You must tell me everything you know about Greece so he will not think me the biggest goose."

"Lydia, that all sounds so wonderful. Do not worry about Greece. You will love the beauty of it and you will learn about it while you are there." She felt it might be better to turn her sister's thoughts to other things. "May we go up and see your dress? I did not get to attend the final fitting."

The rest of the afternoon was spent in packing what Lydia would need on her honeymoon and last-minute arrangements. The lowest point came when they were going in for dinner and Aunt Aggie commented offhandedly, "I will never get used to that silly suit of armor being gone. It was intimidating to visitors, and I truly thought it rather hideous, but now I miss it! Why did you want it at the Abbey after all these years?"

Grace was shaken and Lydia was ready to change the subject, but her father was the first to respond. "Max looks wonderful down at the Abbey. I for one think it was a splendid idea!"

"Thank you, Father," was all Grace said. She was quite sure he knew it was not she who had arranged for Max to be brought to Essex, but she did not wish to discuss it.

Later, before they went to bed, Grace lightly knocked on her sister's bedroom door. At the call to come in, she entered, and Lydia smiled. "Oh, Grace, I hoped it was you. I wanted a chance to talk to you alone before the wedding."

"Lydia, I wanted to give this to you," Grace said, pulling a small wrapped box from behind her back.

"A present? What is it? I did not expect one, you know. It is enough having you here, knowing how hard it must be. You will never know how much I appreciate it." Then she giggled. "But, if you *insist* on giving me a present…"

Grace sat on the side of the bed and watched as Lydia opened the small velvet box. She gasped, seeing the gold locket inside, then looked at Grace with questioning eyes.

"It was Mother's," Grace said softly. "I know you do not remember her very well, but when she died, Father gave it to me. I knew even then that *you* were the one to have it. You are very much like her and I know she would have been very happy for you to wear it on your wedding day."

Tears welled up in Lydia's eyes. She leaned forward and hugged Grace with all her might. They wept together, though for different things. "I will treasure it, Grace, and I will be honored to wear it tomorrow."

There was a comfortable silence between them as they gazed at the locket. Lydia said what they were both thinking. "Our lives have changed so drastically in such a short period of time, haven't they, Grace?"

She nodded, feeling as though her heart was breaking.

"I know you probably do not wish to speak about Lord Weston, but is there no way to reconcile? I want you to have this happiness that I have discovered. I know he sent Max to you. Will you tell me what happened?"

"I cannot talk about it now. It is still a little too fresh, do you understand?" At Lydia's nod, Grace continued. "But he *is* another reason I wanted to see you tonight." She turned slightly and stared into the fire. "Though I suppose whatever his feelings were, they are more than likely gone now. I have decided that this matter is too important to be practical about. I need to do something drastic if there is even the tiniest chance for us."

She turned back to Lydia and took her hands. "I have planned something that is *very* unlike me." She smiled as Lydia laughed. "But it would happen during your wedding. When you sent the letter telling me that you did not care what the *ton* thinks, I began contemplating this, and had an idea to get his attention, maybe give us one more opportunity to talk this out. It may cause a distraction, however, and I am loath to do that on the special day you and Lord Hendricks will remember all of your life."

"Grace, I do not mind at all," she said, so grown-up now. "I will do anything to help you have another chance with Lord Weston." She squeezed Grace's hands. "I know he is the man for you, Grace. All of the things you always said you wanted in a man that I never understood, I do now. He makes you laugh. That was always on the top of your list. He trusts you and cares about your opinions. You love him and I am very sure that he is in love with you. You did not see him the day after you left. He was so downcast.

"And it was I who asked him not to rush to the Abbey, knowing you and how unhappy you were when you left the ball. I was afraid it was too soon and that you would quarrel beyond repair."

"He wanted to come?" she whispered, searching Lydia's face.

"Of course he did. Oh, Grace, do not tell me I made a mistake in keeping him here."

"You did not make a mistake, love. You were absolutely right. If he had come to the Abbey when I was still so hurt, I might have said things that I could never take back. But it is nice to know that he wanted to come."

"Will you tell me what you have planned to get his attention?" she asked, as if waiting for a treat.

"If you do not mind, I would keep it to myself for now," Grace said, looking down. "I may yet decide to be my practical self and not provoke him. I will continue to wait on God's lead regarding it."

She stood up, and as she used to do when Lydia was a little girl, she removed the box with the locket from her hand, gently pushed her down onto her pillows and tucked her in, with a kiss on her forehead. "I suppose that is the last time I will get to do that," she said, the affection evident in her voice. "Now, you must go to sleep." She fluffed Lydia's pillows a little. "I love you, darling, and I am truly so very happy for you. Dennis is a very lucky man." She turned then and hurried from the room.

The next morning dawned sunny and delightful. Lydia was a little anxious at breakfast, but it soon became a merry affair as they all tried to keep her mind off her nerves. They separated soon after to attend to their personal toilettes.

When they met again, they were all filled with praise for one another. Aunt Aggie looked regal enough to be a queen, in her signature purple gown, with an amazing diamond tiara on her head.

Grace wore a gown they had picked out weeks ago. Lydia had fallen in love with it and Grace was happy to be wearing whatever her sister wanted for her wedding. It was simple, no bows, no furbelows; but it was elegant

because of that. It was a verdant green, and when she
put it on, her eyes changed to match it, just as Brandon
had always told her. It had short chiffon sleeves that bil-
lowed when she walked, with a rounded bodice and an
Empire waist that showed off her figure to perfection.
There was an overdress of the same green chiffon as
the sleeves, and both the chiffon and the silk beneath
it flowed beautifully. The skirt was straight and long
and emphasized her regal height. She wore long white
gloves and two white roses in her hair.

Grace could not stop the welling of tears in her eyes
when she saw Lydia. Her sister outshone anyone she
had ever seen, in her bridal gown embellished with tiny
seed pearls. She wore a ring of white rosebuds in her
blond curls, with her veil hanging down behind. When
Grace saw the locket, she remembered the times their
mother had worn it, and she liked to think that their
mother was watching and crying with happiness herself. "I have no new way to tell you how beautiful you
are, Lydia!" Grace told her proudly.

Their father, waiting at the bottom of the steps,
looked handsome in his finery. Grace could tell that
he, too, was affected by the sight of the locket, and he
choked back several coughs behind his hand.

They left for the church, and the crowds of onlookers
gathered around the cathedral gasped at the elegance
of the wedding party. The family waited in the back of
the church until Aunt Aggie was led to her seat, to let
the guests know the bride had arrived. Grace and Lydia
could see their two lords standing at a distance, up at
the altar, and Lydia radiated happiness.

Grace walked to a small vestibule door to one side. "Lydia, excuse me for one moment. I will be right back." She made the split-second decision to go through with her plan, and was gone only a moment. When Lydia saw her return, her eyes opened to twice their size and she smiled from ear to ear. "Grace, you clever thing. You have been hiding a very devious streak."

"I hope it will do the trick, if it does not get me killed," she said, her nervousness obvious. "Right now, however, we need to get you married."

The music began and several children proceeded down the aisle, casting flower petals for the bride to walk on. When they reached the front, Grace kissed Lydia on the cheek and moved into the doorway to begin her own long walk to the front of the church. She was completely unaware of the quickly indrawn breaths and various mutterings as she stared straight into the eyes of Brandon Roth.

His eyes met hers the minute she started from the back of the church, and stayed locked there until she reached the altar and turned away from him. Her eyes were so green, an intense green. He heard the gasps; she was *beautiful*. No, she was striking, and he wondered how anyone had ever considered Lydia the more beautiful of the two. He expected the guests to titter as he and Grace reunited at the wedding after weeks of speculation. But now he could only attribute the buzz to her beauty.

He was drawn back to the present as everyone stood and Lydia began her walk down the aisle on her father's arm. Lydia was an ethereal beauty who glowed and blushed as she walked toward Dennis. She embodied every bride's dream. Though Brandon still did not think her the equal of his Grace, he knew Lord Hendricks was indeed a lucky man!

As the bride and groom came together in front of the archbishop, Brandon and Grace turned toward one another, closing in on either side.

It was then that his eyes widened in shock. Now he understood the indrawn breaths as she'd walked the aisle.

Grace was wearing the Weston emeralds!

Now that they faced each other, he could see the necklace and earrings glittering in the light streaming through the stained glass, shining as they never had before. But he wanted to see her left hand. Was she wearing the ring? Confound it! He would never be able to tell through the flowers she was holding. Gloves! Of course she would be wearing gloves. His frustration almost made him growl out loud.

He sent up a prayer to God to help him understand. He had let her words and those of Lord Langdon sink in, and had begun to believe that their God, *the* God, could erase his past through grace. She had said it over and over, "for by grace are ye saved," then something else, "…and not of yourselves; it is the gift of God." As long as she believed it, and could accept Brandon despite his flaws, he would begin to live his life in the knowledge of having received that grace, too.

He returned to the present, feeling her eyes on him. She stared at him boldly. When he returned her intent look he expected her to turn away. But she surprised him. She always did.

He had come to realize that her independent practicality was a natural extension of her intelligent and caring nature. But she had also been daring when she needed to be, as in her actions at the orphanage. But those times had been in private, just between them. Today she was in a public church with the entire *ton* watching, and she boldly wore the jewels as a message to him. He wished he knew what that message was, but he decided he very much liked this new side to her. Their life together would be a great adventure, *if* they had a life together.

He realized he was not paying attention to the pomp and circumstance going on around him. He was glad Dennis and Lydia only had eyes for each other. The ceremony finally ended and the guests near the front gathered round the couple in congratulations, effectively cutting off any avenue for him to reach Grace on the other side.

Still standing on the altar, he noticed her move to the back of the church with her aunt. They were more than likely to hurrying back to Berkeley Square to finalize preparations for the wedding breakfast. He knew he would not get to her through the crowd before her departure, so he would wait on tenterhooks, knowing that at the house he could get the answers to his questions. He relaxed. Was this the peace he had prayed for? Could it happen so quickly?

He felt a tugging of his left arm and turned to find Lady and Charlotte Marchmont at his side. "It seems, my lord, you and Lady Grace have not been able to make up your minds since the night at the Blue Swan Inn," she said, in a falsely demure manner, yet loudly enough to catch the notice of those around them. "We thought the engagement was over, but the lady was certainly be-decked with the Weston emeralds. What can it mean?"

He lifted her hand from his arm, knowing many heads and ears were turned his way. He lightly kissed the hand before he dropped it. "Must I be blamed, Lady Charlotte, if gossip cannot keep up? I believe I have the power to give anyone of my choosing the right to wear the emeralds."

He turned and walked away, and prayed to God that Grace's wearing of the emeralds was a good sign. But at least the last part of his comment would go a long way in explaining to the crowd at large why she wore them, if it was not to take him back.

Please, God, he prayed, *let Max have worked his influence on her one more time.*

Grace waited for Lydia in the drawing room back at Berkeley Square. When she and Lord Hendricks arrived, they embraced with feelings of joy. Lydia looked happier than any bride Grace had ever seen and Lord Hendricks positively preened with pride and love.

"Well, my lady," Grace teased as she winked at her sister, "how does it feel to be well and truly married?"

Lydia smiled broadly and turned red. "It feels wonderful so far!"

Grace walked over to Lord Hendricks and rose on her toes to kiss his cheek. "You will take good care of her, won't you, my lord?" Grace whispered into his ear through tears of joy.

"We are brother and sister now, Grace. No more lords and ladies, remember?" He took both her hands and kissed them, whispering, "I will protect her with my life. I will cherish her gentle and quiet spirit, and I will love her forever. Is that enough?"

"It is enough," Grace answered as the tears that had pooled in her eyes began running down her cheeks.

"Then, my darling husband," Lydia broke in, "do you mind if I have a few words with my sister before she is lost to me in a crowd of guests?"

"I do not mind. Indeed I expect your sister wishes the same. So I will go, but not for long!" He went to the door, but before he opened it, he turned back to them. "The emeralds look smashing, Grace, and I hope they mean what I think they mean. He truly does deserve your love, though he may think he does not." With that he left the room.

Grace fought her blushing countenance by remonstrating with her sister. "Lydia, you go right back out there, grab him by the arm and enjoy your wedding day! We had such a lovely coze last night."

"No, Grace. I did not say everything I wanted to say." It was her turn to blush. "*And* I did not know then what you planned to do today!" She pulled Grace down on the sofa with her and dropped her head, speaking in a serious tone of voice. "I need to apologize to you, Grace. All of my life I have been so jealous of you."

Grace stared in astonishment. "*You* have been jealous of *me?*"

"Yes. You are so smart and practical, as well as lovely. Everyone looks up to you, and I hoped that when

I came to London I might outshine you a little." Her eyes filled with tears. "I am the most horrible of sisters."

Grace pulled her into an embrace and held on tightly. "Lydia, darling, do you think I have never been envious of you? Our faces were not of our choosing. I never envied your beauty, but you are so gentle and kind. You love everyone you meet and they love you." She sat back again and wiped the tears from her cheeks. "I am so happy that everything has turned out as it has for you. Dennis is just the man for you and you are just the woman for him. God has answered our prayers in the loveliest way."

"But Grace, now I see how stupid jealousy and pride are. You gave up your pride today to do the right thing for you and Lord Weston. I want you to have an answer to *our* prayers about him. I want us to share our lives fully from now on."

Grace was quiet for a moment, then said seriously, "Lydia, I am afraid my managing tendencies took over when Mother passed away, and I have not let you shine in any other way aside from your beauty. However, it seems marriage has helped you grow so far past those outward things."

She sat up straighter. "And whether Brandon and I can make a future together has no bearing on how we conduct our lives as sisters. I love you and I am sharing your happiness in marriage fully. Indeed, I think it has brought us closer." They hugged once again and Grace told her it was time to get out to her wedding breakfast.

"There is one more thing I need to ask of you, Grace. May I tell Dennis the truth about you and Lord Weston while we are away? I do not think I want to keep secrets from him. You know he will not tell anyone." Lydia seemed to be pleading. Had Grace been so domineering?

"Oh, Lydia, of course you may. Dennis is my brother now and I would not want you to keep secrets from him, either. Indeed, I insist you tell him so he knows you trust him with all your heart."

Grace was pierced to her core. She trusted Brandon with all her heart, but did he know it? Perhaps all his anger at the orphanage and the dock was not because he feared for her safety but because he thought she did not trust him? She had made such a muddle of things from the start. Had he not told her to trust him with their charade in London? Yet she had given up on him that very first week, only seeing her own fears.

"Grace?"

"I am sorry, I remembered something I must be sure and tell Brandon if I get the chance."

"Do you think the emeralds worked? Do you think Lord Weston noticed?"

"I suppose time will tell. But that is nothing to you. I can hear your guests arriving and you must be standing beside Dennis to greet them." They walked out of the room with their arms around each other's waist, and Grace whispered, "You will write to me while you are gone and tell me all about Greece, will you not? And come down to the Abbey as soon as you get back? I shall miss you terribly."

Lydia did not have time to answer before she was whisked away by friends, but she nodded over her shoulder and smiled her brightest.

Suddenly Grace felt completely alone. She knew she

had several hours of mingling to do, but was almost too paralyzed to move for fear of seeing Brandon, for fear of seeing anyone who would ask the same question of her—was she reconciled to him?

She was sure Brandon had noticed the emeralds, but whether the gesture meant anything to him or not, she did not know. Truth be told, she was afraid he might be angry rather than pleased or curious. Suppose he was still with Lady Winslow; or worse, what if he had already moved on to someone else, and she did him harm by wearing them? Why had she done something so outrageous?

The sound of Lady Charlotte's voice caused Grace real fright. She would rather have run into Brandon than the woman who had caused the problem from the beginning. She knew Lady Charlotte would delight in bringing her down a peg or two.

"Why, Lady Grace, you must tell me, as we are all agog." Her voice carried as she intended, and heads began to turn their way. "Did Lord Weston lend you his emeralds for the wedding or is the betrothal on once again?"

Grace wanted to run and hide. Instead, she turned her thoughts in another direction. "Lady Charlotte, what a pleasure to see you. Today is my sister's day. My comings and goings are of no consequence."

The lady rapped Grace's arm with her fan. "Oh, we will not be fobbed off so easily. Where is dear Weston, anyway? Never say he is not coming to the breakfast!"

"Oh, she would never say that," drawled Brandon from behind them, making them both jump.

Chapter Nineteen

"Grace, Lydia asked me to escort you to the table to join the others." He held out his arm and she placed her hand through it, instead of resting it atop his. To Charlotte he said, "Excuse us, my lady, I believe you and your mother are to be seated in the smaller dining room. Quite an honor."

As nervous as she was, Grace could not help but laugh at his set-down. She whispered, "Lord Weston, you know very well everyone is seated in the same room!"

He did not look at her. "We are back to Lord Weston again, are we?"

She blushed. "My father always used my most formal name whenever I had done something wrong. It was just habit."

"He obviously did not use it enough."

She choked on a gurgle of laughter. "Thank you for rescuing me, by the by. I do not think even Max could have done it better." That slipped out before she thought, and she turned bright red and stumbled.

"That does it, Grace," he whispered. "Forget the breakfast. You and I are going to the library. We have much to say."

She hoped it was not to give her a final snub as he had Lady Charlotte. But she knew now was not the time. "You know I cannot leave in the middle of my sister's wedding breakfast, especially with you. This is her day and I want her to be the center of attention." She tried to pull her arm away.

"You should have thought of that *before* you wore the emeralds." He kept her hand in the crook of his arm and nodded at the people headed in the opposite direction. When they reached the library, he opened the door, let her step in before him and then closed it, leaning back against it with his arms crossed over his chest.

No escape that way, she thought. Did she want to escape?

He stared at her until she could not look at him anymore. She knew she should speak first; after all, she had worn the emeralds. But suddenly she had no idea where to start.

"You look beautiful today," he said casually. "Quite put Lydia to the pale."

She smiled. How like him to be so calm when she was so nervous.

"Grace, it is time," he said, not moving from the door. "You wore those jewels for a purpose today and I would like to know why. I *need* to know why." His eyes were steely.

The last words scared her. Was his need to know necessary for him to determine how to get them back? "There are several reasons I wore them, Brandon," she said, looking down at her hands and speaking in a low tone. "But first and foremost, as an apology."

"An apology?"

"Several apologies, in fact." How would she get all her feelings through to him?

"When we rode home in the carriage after the blackmail attempt, you were so angry you would not let me explain. I felt helpless. Helpless to reach you, helpless to warn you, just helpless. Then I realized that by not letting *you* explain, and leaving for the Abbey without giving you that chance, I must have made you feel the same way, and I wanted you to know how sorry I am for that." She was on the verge of breaking down and would become a watering pot if he did not say something soon.

"I tried to write it to you," she lamented, "several times. But the words never came out right. Not that they are now, of course, but I hoped the emeralds would make you at least talk to me so I could apologize."

He still looked at her intently, but finally he spoke. "Certainly, that is the least they have done. Understatement has always been your forte."

She smiled at the many times he had accused her of that in their short time together.

"What is it, my sweet life, that you did not let me explain? It seems I am a perfect blockhead."

My sweet life. She'd thought never to hear those words again. But she must not give them more weight than he meant.

"I saw you with Lady Winslow," she said, with a new calmness.

"You saw me with... What... When?"

"At the Hilliards' ball. You had stopped speaking to me after the night at the dock. I know I made you very angry, and you would not let me explain."

"Grace, I was angry because I was afraid you did not…that I would say something I regretted."

It was the opening she had been waiting for. "Before we go any further, I want to tell you something I believe I learned today. Why did you get so angry at me for going to the orphanage and for not telling you about the blackmail?"

"I thought *you* learned something you were going to tell *me*."

She smiled at him. "I did, I have—I *think*." Botheration, he was not going to make anything easy today. "*I* believed, prior to today, that the reason you got so angry was because I kept putting myself in danger and you felt responsible for me while I was in London."

"That is *one* of the reasons I was angry, and hurt, by the by. But not *the* reason."

She heaved a sigh of relief. She *had* misunderstood all along. Yet she was not on sure footing yet. "I realized today, and I should have known it all along, I suppose, that you believed I did not trust you, because I acted alone rather than relying on your assistance."

She had to go on before anything else was said. No matter the final outcome of this interview, she wanted him to know the truth. "I have always trusted you. As far back to the day we met, actually. Do you think I would have considered such an option as we chose with someone I did not trust? And then at the orphanage, and again at the docks, I could have jumped for joy when I heard your voice because I knew I was safe with you. I am so sorry if I made you feel like I did not trust you. You are the most trustworthy man I have ever met."

"How did you make this discovery, Grace?"

"I told Lydia I wanted her to tell Dennis about us, recount our story from the beginning. I told her she must always be honest with him so he would know she trusted him with all of her heart."

She bowed her head. "I do not think I ever once said that to you, and I am so very sorry."

"Grace," he said, and then started toward her.

She held up her hand to stop him. "No, Brandon, you must let me finish." She walked to a window. "That night when we rode home from the dock in silence, I did not know it was a trust issue. I only knew you were angry at me for breaking my promise, and you would not let me explain."

She turned back to face him. "But two days later I saw you kissing Lady Winslow. You knew that she was the one who... She... Oh, it matters not. I left the ball and went home."

He was beginning to scowl. She remembered how fierce she'd thought him the first time she had seen it at the Blue Swan. He was no less intimidating now. "I assumed you had set her up as one of your flirts, and I ran away. I am sorry."

"One of my flirts?" he shouted.

"Shh! Do you want all the wedding guests upon us?"

"Grace..." He drawled out her name very slowly. "Are you telling me this entire fiasco is because you saw Patrice Winslow kiss me?"

"Of course not." He could see the wheels in her

mind turning, and could not wait for her explanation. If he wasn't so frustrated from the prior two weeks, he might actually be enjoying this. "It *was* quite a shock! But…but we had planned to end the engagement in any event."

"Grace, you can misconstrue situations more easily than anyone I ever met." Suddenly, he started to laugh. "We stand here today because, while listening through walls, you thought I needed rescuing."

"Are you going to throw that in my face again?" she asked, and her pout was priceless to him.

He took one step toward her. "Grace," he said very low and very seriously, "I *did* need rescuing."

Her eyes grew large, and he could not show her how he felt until he knew her feelings.

She stood still as a statue and he asked, "Are you now offering me a chance to explain my actions that night at the Hilliards'? So you may decide whether I am redeemable or not?"

"No!" she responded vehemently. "Never say that to me! Past redemption? You know what I believe and what I have been telling you. We are all under God's grace for our past, should we choose to accept it." More quietly she said, "Brandon, you owe me no explanation about Lady Winslow. I only wish to apologize for not allowing you to explain *what I saw.* If my departure hurt you as much as the kiss hurt me that night, I am very sorry."

She never ceased to amaze him! He truly believed she would let him off without an explanation; she had seen him kissing a woman who had threatened her life! Was it because of the trust she'd talked about earlier? Did she trust that he would never hurt her in such a way? Or was she just letting him off the hook because their relationship was at an end?

"Though you say I do not need to explain, it is imperative to me that I do so." He stared at her intensely. "I spent days verifying the crimes she committed against you and me. I got the full details from the little weasel who tortured you. I got information from your father about precise discussions they had. Did he not tell you I had spoken to him?"

At the shake of her head he ran his hands through his hair. "That night, at the Hilliards' ball, I confronted her. She swore she had no knowledge of what had happened until I explained that I knew her plan down to the smallest detail. Once cornered, she changed tactics and said she did it out of love for me. I was perfectly disgusted. She threw her arms around my neck and kissed me before I knew what was happening. Had you remained watching, you would have seen me push her away an instant later. I promise you, Grace, we will never be seeing her again."

She listened to his explanation, staring at him with her hands folded in front of her. He completely lost all train of thought as he realized she carried no flowers and wore no gloves. He looked at her third finger with hope in his heart.

The ring was not there.

He went to the fireplace and leaned back against it. Was this truly only to have an audience alone with him one last time?

God, I want to be worthy of her. I want the grace she says abounds from You. Help me to keep her and learn more about You from her.

"Does that clear up your uncertainty?"

"It was never necessary, Brandon."

"You said there were several reasons why you wore the emeralds. May I ask the others?"

"Yes. I also wanted to say thank-you." She came closer to him, to stand face-to-face, seeming to implore him with her beautiful jade eyes to understand. "I tried to write this, too, but there were so many things to thank you for, it all sounded jumbled."

"Do you think that is what I want, your thanks?"

"Perhaps not, but it is what you need." Her answer startled him. "I forced my way into your affairs without cause, and *you* rescued *me* without complaint. You had to be someone else to your family and friends, and you were tied to me instead of your normal pursuits." Her eyes welled up and he wanted to hold her so badly. "You put your own life in danger for mine, not once, but twice, all the while saving lonely, hungry children all over London." She blinked and tears rolled silently down both cheeks. She was driving him mad. Did she care about him? Why couldn't one of the things she wanted to say be "I love you?"

"Then you sent Max to me. No, it was more than that—it was that you understood about Max. You know I have always been practical and managing. People count on me to take care of things. When I was little, I used to wish someone like Max would come along, see me as his lady and whisk me off, to take care of *me*. Of course, I grew out of childhood fancies, and I have come to the conclusion that I do like being practical. But Max has always had a special place in my heart, the potential of what I have always hoped for, and you recognized that." She swiped the tears from her cheeks and smiled. "I am not sure how, but you did. And he is in a very special place in the Abbey. I should have taken him there years ago."

She shook her head as if to let go of those thoughts. "For all these things I need to thank you. So much could have gone horribly wrong since that first day, but because of you, we are celebrating a wedding today. Thank you, Brandon."

He left the fireplace and walked to her until he stood directly in front of her. She lowered her eyes, and when he put his finger under her chin to lift them back up, they were filled with fresh tears. Why did she cry?

He looked into her searching eyes, put his hands on her shoulders and slowly ran them down her arms to take her hands. "You said there were several reasons you wore the emeralds today. Are there any more, Grace?" he asked softly.

"Do you not think those enough, my lord?" she whispered, still staring into his eyes.

"No, my sweet life, there is much more I would like to hear."

He pulled her hands into fists up against his chest. "I am glad to hear you say that you trust me with all your heart. No one else ever has." He was moved as she brought up their entwined hands so she could caress his cheek. She stared at him in sorrow and…something else.

"Brandon, you told me that night that you would never trust me again." It seemed she could not look him in the eyes, for she lowered her head. He raised it again.

"Grace, I want you to understand this. The things I

said in the carriage that night seem to be the impetus for all our troubles. Do you think that we can forget the words we said? I would trust you with my life and more. Please believe me."

She nodded, tears pooled in her searching eyes.

"But I do not make light of that night in the carriage. I was angry and it was at the thought of losing you."

She nodded again in understanding.

"I also want to hear that I did not need to explain," he continued, "not because I do not owe you an explanation, but because you cannot possibly believe that after you, there could ever be anything between me and Patrice Winslow."

He could still see the question in her eyes. With each sentence, with each emotion she felt, their color changed. They searched his own intently. Did that penetrating look mean she was waiting to hear him declare himself, or was she afraid that he might?

"I would also like to hear that Max's *message* meant as much to you as Max himself. You want your imaginary hero to ride up and save the day, but when it comes right down to it, you do not believe that he will. So you take matters into your own hands. Max was not only a surprise, he was a statement." He pulled her a little closer. "Grace, there *is* a man who will be your Max if you will only let him."

She closed her eyes and sighed as the tears that had been pooled slid out of the corners of her eyelids.

He prayed they were tears of joy. He finished by leaning close to her ear and whispering, "And I want the reason that you wore the emeralds to mean that you want our betrothal to be as real to you as it has become to me."

He stopped when she opened her eyes and smiled at him intimately, with a look he hoped she saved forever just for him...until he thought about what he was doing. He let go of her then and walked away from her. "I want all of that, my sweet life, even knowing all the while that it will not do."

She did not follow him, but he knew what color her eyes had turned without even seeing them when she asked, "Brandon?"

"Grace, you have been sequestered and wrapped in cotton your entire life. You know only a third of my scandals. God would not take lightly your ruin by association with me." He turned back to her and said quietly, "And neither would I."

She ran across the room and threw her arms around his neck. He would not let her go now for all the wealth or fame in the world. And she did not seem to care. She whispered in his ear, "*Our* God has enough grace to blot out all of your dastardly deeds, my love."

He held her even tighter when she called him her love, and then put her a little away from him.

"My darling, Grace, will you..." He stopped, let her go, then walked to the door and locked it.

He came slowly back to her, drew her into his arms and kissed her. He kissed her as he had at their betrothal ball, and she was breathless when he stopped.

He led her to the sofa in front of the fireplace and sat down with her, keeping his arm wrapped tightly around her shoulders. They were almost nose to nose, intently waiting for what the other would say. He whispered, "Finally, Grace, I want you to tell me you love me even half as much as I have come to love you. Will you marry me?"

"Oh, Brandon," she cried. She pulled away a little so she could put her hand on his face. "I have loved you for weeks, but I promised I would not tie you to the betrothal. I misunderstood when I saw you kissing Lady Winslow..."

"She was kissing *me,* my dear." His mischievous dimple appeared. "You will have to get used to it. Happens all the time," he declared, while kissing her nose. "You are marrying an ex-rake, you know."

"Brandon," she said, furrowing her brows, "when I saw it, I thought we had gone on too long for you." She moved her hand and rubbed his beautiful dimple. "When you sent Max, I dared to hope. But I did not know where to start. Knowing that you would be waiting for your emeralds to be returned to you, and knowing the lengths I went to to protect them, I hoped that wearing them today would get your attention."

"Ah, we are back to understatement!" He kissed her again. "My sweet life, you always had my attention. And you have not yet answered my question."

He stood and pulled her up gently with him. He put his hands on her waist and she rested her palms on his arms. There was nothing between them but honesty. "You told me that God could save me by His grace. Your life has been a testimony to me—not just now, but as far back as my first meeting with Lord Langdon, after meeting you. I was not able to lie to him because of you. Your scruples touched me."

She smiled. "I have always known you had scruples,

Brandon, from the moment you told me of your elopement. *I* had no need to know that for our connection, but you felt I needed to. I have trusted you implicitly and I promise you that you may trust me from now on." She looked up at him with an impish grin. "I do not care how many people threaten to kill you."

"Minx!" He tugged her into his arms and held her as if he would never let her go. "I want that grace you told me about, my sweet life. I want a marriage blessed by God, to be worthy of the blessing He has given me through you." In her ear, he whispered, *"Will* you marry me, Grace?"

She pulled out of his arms, though he protested. She reached up into the spray of roses in her hair and pulled something out of it. In the center of her palm was the emerald engagement ring, which she handed to him a little shyly. "Yes, Brandon, I will marry you, with all my heart, forever." And she buried her face in his chest.

He pushed her away gently. "You understand I do not intend to wait three weeks for the banns to be read and wedding gowns to be made and—"

"As soon as a special license can be obtained, my lord."

"And I will be a reformed rake, so no more of these public displays of affection, my lady."

"Lord Weston, you are perilously close to having your ears boxed."

He laughed out loud. He took her hand and placed the ring on her finger. "I missed doing that the first time. I will not miss out on those things again, I promise you." He put her hand through the crook of his arm, placed his free one on top and slowly started toward the library door. "You must not be troubled, when we announce our reengagement, if there are a number of women more than a little upset."

"You may be a rake, but now you are *my* rake. And I do not share very well!" She stopped their pace and looked up at him lovingly. It took his breath away. "Never truly believing the emeralds were mine, I don't think I ever properly thanked you for them. I hope you know that I really do love them and will cherish them always."

He turned to her fully and cupped her face in his hands, then leaned down and kissed her tenderly. He kept his hands on her face and just stared a moment into her wondrous eyes. "My one and only life, the emeralds are family jewels. They will pass onto our children, then to our grandchildren. However, my darling, that will never be of concern to me."

Grace looked at him with a puzzled expression, not understanding what he was trying to say.

"When we marry, my love, I know that every time I gaze into your beautiful green eyes, I will be looking at the *real* Weston emeralds.

"Remind me, what is that verse you told me about? 'Without grace it is impossible to please Him…'"

"No, Brandon, it is without *faith*."

"No, my sweet life, it is without *Grace*."

* * * * *

Dear Reader,

I have been so happy to share Brandon and Grace's journey with you. If you have read my other books, you know that the Regency Period comes to life for me! And I aspire to using that history to tell a story with a sincere, Godly message embedded in a wonderful love story.

It is here that I need to make an "author's note." An author's note is where we get to explain our foibles. As you have read the story, you have never heard Grace or Brandon call each other fiancé(e). That is because the term did not become practice until the mid 1830s, almost twenty years after the date of this story. However, in order to reach a broader scope of readers, Love Inspired wished to use something more approachable in the title. It is common practice when writing historical fiction, but I wanted my avid Regency readers to understand how the word came to be used in the title of the book. I appreciate your forbearance.

With *Accidental Fiancée* I have been able to introduce you to my first rake, Lord Weston. The wonderful sense of humor that emerged from him because he *was* a rake was especially fun for me. And because he could never fall in love with someone who did not share that trait, Grace was sure to give him as good as she got! I grew up with a fun-loving family and my husband has a wonderful sense of humor. I hope you got a glimmer of how important that trait is to me through Brandon and Grace.

Though Brandon saw Grace's belief in God from the

beginning, he also recognized the good she tried to do for others, which poured out from that belief. And even though her faith was something foreign to him, he did not ridicule it or ignore it. He watched her, studied her and ultimately realized she walked her talk. Therefore, he did not dampen her desire to tell him about God, but learned to embrace her spirituality as she did.

It was important for me to convey in the story Grace's question as to whether rakes were men who were rogues by nature, or turned into them by circumstances in their lives. Every day, we come into contact with others with not-so-nice labels on them, and we have the chance to touch them for God, to tell them about His grace. If we portray our belief in every aspect of our lives and to everyone we meet, He will put people in our paths. What a blessing for us!

It has been a while since my last book, so I am especially thankful you hung in there with me! I am privileged and blessed to be able to share what I love doing with you. God gets every bit of the glory for any way you were touched, because He is with me and behind me in each chapter and word. I pray the message of His grace will help you where you are today.

I love to hear from readers. Please let me know what you thought by visiting my website at marymooreauthor.com or by emailing me at mmooreauthor@swva.net. I am also available on Facebook at facebook.com/mmooreauthor and on Twitter at twitter.com/sugarbean1020. I look forward to hearing from you!
God bless you,
    Mary Moore

Questions for Discussion

1. A key theme throughout *Accidental Fiancée* was God's grace. List and discuss other themes or messages that resonated with you.

2. Did any one character strike a chord with you? Why or why not?

3. Comment on how God used very unusual circumstances to bring two people to love each other. Does it relate to any of your relationships?

4. Grace had good intentions when she decided to rescue Lord Weston. Have you ever tried to help someone and ended up making the original problem worse? Has someone ever gotten mad at you for trying to help him or her?

5. Why do you think it was so hard for Brandon to believe that his past could simply be washed away by God's grace? Did Grace's reminders give you any peace about it in your own life?

6. What does Ephesians 2:8 mean to you? How does it manifest itself in your daily walk? Do you believe that God's grace is sufficient for you? Why?

7. At one point, Grace asked herself if the ends justified the means in their decision to portray themselves as betrothed while in London. Have you ever struggled with that question and how did you resolve it?

8. Regency England had strict codes of conduct that seem silly to us today (i.e., having to marry someone because you were caught kissing her hand!). Has the moral code of today moved too far away from that time? Why or why not? Is there a middle ground? Explain.

9. Grace and Brandon go through two serious misunderstandings that are compounded by the actions they take immediately after. Do you handle misunderstandings any better than they did? How should they be handled?

10. Brandon was fortunate enough to gain Lord Langdon as a mentor. Has there been someone in your life you looked up to as a mentor? How did this person's counsel help you?

11. Grace thought no one in London would believe Brandon would marry her, because of her relationship with God. Have you ever been in a situation where you were looked down upon for your beliefs or felt as though you must hide them in certain situations?

12. Discuss one thing you really liked about the story.

13. Grace tried to live her life as God would want, so could not reconcile lying to the world about their engagement. What are some of the ways you refuse to compromise your beliefs?

14. Does Grace and Lord Weston's passion for helping the orphans of their day challenge you to want to help the orphans of our day?

COMING NEXT MONTH FROM
Love Inspired® Historical

Available February 3, 2015

BIG SKY HOMECOMING
Montana Marriages
by Linda Ford

Rancher Duke Caldwell is the son of her family's enemy—and everyone knows a Caldwell cannot be trusted. But when a snowstorm strands them together, Rose Bell starts to fall for the disarmingly handsome thorn in her side.

THE ENGAGEMENT BARGAIN
Prairie Courtships
by Sherri Shackelford

Caleb McCoy can't deny the entrancing Anna Bishop the protection she requires. A pretend betrothal seems like the best option to hide her identity. Until they both wonder whether it could be a permanent solution...

SHELTERED BY THE WARRIOR
by Barbara Phinney

After townspeople destroy Rowena's home, Baron Stephen de Bretonne offers a safe haven for her and her baby. Still, Rowena wonders what the baron stands to gain—and why she finds him so captivating.

A DAUGHTER'S RETURN
Boardinghouse Betrothals
by Janet Lee Barton

Benjamin Roth is immediately drawn to the newest Heaton House boarder. Rebecca Dickerson and her daughter appear to be a lovely family, but will he still think so after he discovers her secret?

LIHCNM0115

REQUEST YOUR FREE BOOKS!

2 FREE INSPIRATIONAL NOVELS
PLUS 2
FREE
MYSTERY GIFTS

Love Inspired.
HISTORICAL
INSPIRATIONAL HISTORICAL ROMANCE

YES! Please send me 2 FREE Love Inspired® Historical novels and my 2 FREE mystery gifts (gifts are worth about $10). After receiving them, if I don't wish to receive any more books, I can return the shipping statement marked "cancel." If I don't cancel, I will receive 4 brand-new novels every month and be billed just $4.74 per book in the U.S. or $5.24 per book in Canada. That's a saving of at least 21% off the cover price. It's quite a bargain! Shipping and handling is just 50¢ per book in the U.S. and 75¢ per book in Canada.* I understand that accepting the 2 free books and gifts places me under no obligation to buy anything. I can always return a shipment and cancel at any time. Even if I never buy another book, the two free books and gifts are mine to keep forever.

102/302 IDN F5CN

Name _____ (PLEASE PRINT)

Address _____ Apt. #

City _____ State/Prov. _____ Zip/Postal Code

Signature (if under 18, a parent or guardian must sign)

Mail to the Harlequin® Reader Service:
IN U.S.A.: P.O. Box 1867, Buffalo, NY 14240-1867
IN CANADA: P.O. Box 609, Fort Erie, Ontario L2A 5X3

Want to try two free books from another series?
Call 1-800-873-8635 or visit www.ReaderService.com.

* Terms and prices subject to change without notice. Prices do not include applicable taxes. Sales tax applicable in N.Y. Canadian residents will be charged applicable taxes. Offer not valid in Quebec. This offer is limited to one order per household. Not valid for current subscribers to Love Inspired Historical books. All orders subject to credit approval. Credit or debit balances in a customer's account(s) may be offset by any other outstanding balance owed by or to the customer. Please allow 4 to 6 weeks for delivery. Offer available while quantities last.

Your Privacy—The Harlequin® Reader Service is committed to protecting your privacy. Our Privacy Policy is available online at www.ReaderService.com or upon request from the Harlequin Reader Service.

We make a portion of our mailing list available to reputable third parties that offer products we believe may interest you. If you prefer that we not exchange your name with third parties, or if you wish to clarify or modify your communication preferences, please visit us at www.ReaderService.com/consumerschoice or write to us at Harlequin Reader Service Preference Service, P.O. Box 9062, Buffalo, NY 14269. Include your complete name and address.

LIH13R

SPECIAL EXCERPT FROM

Love Inspired HISTORICAL

Newly returned Duke Caldwell is the son of her family's enemy—and everyone knows a Caldwell can't be trusted. But when Duke is thrown from his horse, Rose Bell must put her misgivings aside to help care for the handsome rancher.

Read on for a sneak peek of
BIG SKY HOMECOMING
by Linda Ford

"You must find it hard to do this."

"Do what?" His voice settled her wandering mind.

"Coddle me."

"Am I doing that?" Her words came out soft and sweet, from a place within her she normally saved for family. "Seems to me all I'm doing is helping a neighbor in need."

"It's nice we can now be friendly neighbors."

This was not the time to point out that friendly neighbors did not open gates and let animals out.

Duke lowered his gaze, freeing her from its silent hold. He sipped the tea. "You're right. This is just what I needed. I'm feeling better already." He indicated he wanted to put the cup and saucer on the stool at his knees. "I haven't thanked you for rescuing me. Thank you." He smiled.

She noticed his eyes looked clearer. He was feeling better. The tea had been a good idea.

"You're welcome." She could barely pull away from his gaze. Why did he have this power over her? It had to be the brightness of those blue eyes…

What was she doing? She had to stop this. She resolved to not be trapped by his look.

Who was he? Truly? A manipulator who said the feud was over when it obviously wasn't? A hero who'd almost drowned rescuing someone weaker than him in every way?

He was a curious mixture of strength and vulnerability. Could he be both at the same time? What was she to believe?

Was he a feuding neighbor, the arrogant son of the rich rancher?

Or a kind, noble man?

She tried to dismiss the questions. What difference did it make to her? She had only come because he'd been injured and Ma had taught all the girls to never refuse to help a sick or injured person.

Apart from that, she was Rose Bell and he, Duke Caldwell. That was all she needed to know about him.

But her fierce admonitions did not stop the churning of her thoughts.

Pick up BIG SKY HOMECOMING
by Linda Ford,
available February 2015 wherever
Love Inspired® Historical books and ebooks are sold.

JUST CAN'T GET ENOUGH OF INSPIRATIONAL ROMANCE?

Join our social communities
and talk to us online!
You will have access to the latest
news on upcoming titles and special
promotions, but most important,
you can talk to other fans about your
favorite Love Inspired® reads.

 www.Facebook.com/LoveInspiredBooks

 www.Twitter.com/LoveInspiredBks

Harlequin.com/Community

LISOCIAL